[illegible]

By: Jeanette Hewitt

ISBN: 978-1-927220-30-6

Bluewood Publishing Ltd
Christchurch, 8441, New Zealand
www.bluewoodpublishing.com

For news of, or to purchase this or other books please visit

www.bluewoodpublishing.com

Worlds Apart

by

Jeanette Hewitt

Foreword

Survival International is a real life organisation working for the rights of tribal peoples worldwide and helping to protect their lives, lands and human rights. They oppose the racist attitudes which underpin the way tribal peoples are viewed, and seek to stop the illegal and unjust way they are treated.

Their vision is for a world where tribal peoples are recognised and respected; an end to the unjust treatment tribal peoples are subjected to; and a world where tribal peoples are free to live on their own lands, safe from violence, oppression and exploitation.

For more information go to: www.survivalinternational.org

Dedication

This book is dedicated to the memory of Kate Wasyluk. Thank you for leaving your fingerprints on our lives. Because of you we appreciate every day that we have, and everyone that we choose to spend it with.

Special thanks as always to my parents; Janet and Keith, for their unwavering love and support. Love and thanks to Darren – fiancé, friend and rock, who never fails to be there for me not only with love, but also with practical, promotional and technical care and support!

My appreciation also to Paulette, for helping me to make this book the best that it could possibly be, and to Kate Holberton and her team for allowing me to use the wonderful charity Survival International in my novel.

I would like to express my gratitude to Ffyona Campbell, for it was through her that I first discovered Survival International, in her own books which I still read every couple of years and which never fail to inspire me. Ffyona has been my inspiration for many years, and through her I learned that life doesn't come full circle, it veers off into a spiral of exciting and challenging adventures through which we can learn to become better people and give back what we take from our world. Ffyona leads by example and her work can be viewed at www.wildfoodwalks.co.uk

Lastly, thank you to all who buy this book.

Happy reading!

Prologue

Standing on the steps of the courtroom, the flashes from the paparazzo's cameras almost blinded her.

"Kate!" They shouted out her name, all jostling for the best position.

In her former life, Kate Bryant would have soaked up the attention like a sponge but, after being incarcerated for so long, the crowd frightened her.

A flame-haired woman, with out-of-style tortoiseshell glasses, elbowed her way to the front of the crowd, and thrust a microphone in Kate's face.

"Kate, are you really innocent, or has your father used his considerable wealth to buy your freedom?"

Kate looked at her lawyer, Thomas, and he leaned in to her. "Don't answer. They'll twist whatever you say, so best not to say anything."

She nodded.

As Thomas moved away to try to placate the Press, she stood alone on the steps, feeling suddenly vulnerable, easy pickings in front of all those vultures.

Looking for her father and Linda, she scanned the crowd. Then she saw him—Joe, standing next to Bruce Levinstein, and she felt like she had been hit straight in the heart with a hard and heavy fist. The crowd of people no longer mattered as she tried to read his expression. His deep blue eyes spoke to her. They seemed to be filled with…with what? Love? Loathing? From that distance she couldn't tell, and she didn't have time to ponder further as the crowd parted and a tall, striking blonde lady made her way through the sea of people. Quiet descended, row by row, until the blonde passed the flame-haired woman who had thrust her microphone in Kate's face. That microphone fell to the ground as the reporter caught sight of the gun in the woman's hand.

Kate recognised the woman—Ester Martinez, friend of Janine Finch, the young lady with whose murder Kate had been charged.

As Ester came closer, and the arm holding the gun moved upwards, Kate's eyes darted from side to side, desperately seeking some form of escape.

She anticipated a loud noise, but the gun simply popped. It was only the wisp of smoke that curled from the barrel, and the burning pain in her stomach, that told Kate she had been shot.

She staggered back and slumped down in the doorway of the courtroom as the silence was replaced by screams. Kate, lying on her back, gripped the concrete wall of the building, feeling it searing hot in the French Riviera sunshine.

She heard pounding feet and, though her vision was blurred with tears, she saw both Joe and Thomas kneeling in front of her. She tried to find the strength to tell them both how much she loved them, and how sorry she was, but as the blood filled her mouth instead, she closed her eyes and slipped into another world where the pain wasn't quite so bad.

Chapter One

Six Months Prior to the Shooting

As the plane came into land at Cannes Airport, Kate Bryant pushed her hands through her long blonde hair and heaved a not-so-subtle sigh of relief that the attentions of the businessman beside her would cease. For the fourteen hours from Singapore he had not been easily deterred. Since her solitary travels through Africa she had gotten into the habit of wearing a wedding ring as a deterrent, but even the deliberate flash of the gold band had not put him off. Seeing his time was almost up, he made a last ditch attempt to invite her for dinner that evening. She declined and, as the plane taxied to a stop, she squeezed past him and strode purposefully down the aisle and out into the heat.

She paused for a moment on the tarmac, offering up her thanks that her father had decided his new business venture was to be in the South of France as, after spending the last year in Australia, and Africa before that, she didn't think she could go back to the chill of her native England.

The thought of her father sent nervous tremors through her, and she couldn't believe she was going to see him again for the first time in ten years. He had sounded welcoming on the telephone when she had called him from Queensland, indeed he had even cried. Tears of joy, he had claimed. But deep inside she knew she had hurt him badly by staying away for so long.

She saw him as she entered the terminal building and she paused, looking at the man who, other than a smattering of grey through his dark hair, had not changed at all in the last decade. Suddenly she was running, pushing through people, startled by the unexpected surge of love that she felt for him.

Jermain Bryant saw his daughter sprinting towards him and, as she crashed into his arms, he started to laugh although it caught in his throat and turned into tears. He pulled away, holding her at arms' length and drinking in the view of her face. She looked well after travelling and living like a nomad for nearly ten years, and he had half expected to be greeted by a skinny, pale girl who had been drinking all day and partying all night. Instead she was tanned, lean and muscled, and her hair was lighter than he'd ever seen it, having been bleached naturally by the sun.

After a moment of staring at each other, they laughed uncomfortably, and he picked up her bag.

"We'll get your suitcase, and then go back to the hotel, okay?"

"Yes, I can't wait to see the hotel, but I have no case. That's all I had," she replied, gesturing to the bag he held.

"Ten years you've been gone and all your possessions fit in one bag?" His face was disbelieving.

She smiled. "You don't need much stuff living out there, Dad."

He nodded as, together, they walked out of the building and back into the heat.

"I hope you don't miss it too much," he said.

She caught the real meaning in his words: 'will you miss your former life so much that you return to it and leave me again?' She couldn't make him any promises, but she didn't want to hurt him anymore either.

"I'll give it a go out here. I've done living in the bush. I'll try some luxury for a while."

He pulled her close again and held her there until they reached his car and climbed in.

The drive to the hotel and casino he owned was quiet. She guessed he would have a hundred questions to ask her about the last ten years of her life, but she was lost in the landscape and remained quiet, soaking up the panoramic views, hoping she would instantly love his new home. She made a silent promise to herself that she would answer all of his questions later.

Before arriving in Cannes, Kate had done thorough research on the history of the city, and had been surprised at her findings.

It was not just a sleepy little holiday place for the well-off and the famous. During, and after, the First World War, Cannes had been turned into a giant hospital. The wounded came off the seas, dragging the dead, and recuperated there. After a while, the English and the Germans returned home, but the Americans stayed, attracted by the dazzling sights and the luxury that Cannes managed to exude, even in war times. In 1946, after the Second World War, the city council realised it needed something big to reinstate its place within the Southern France community. It came up with the idea of creating the International Film Festival, and every year since, producers, actors and writers gathered in the Casino Municipal each summer. In 1950 the festival was moved to the Palais des Festivals, until it was destroyed in 1979, when it moved back to the Municipal.

As they drove along the coastal road, Kate felt she could really consider settling there, and when they pulled up at the hotel that overlooked the harbour, she stood before the building and looked at it in amazement. Cannes Central, the hotel, was even more stunning than she had imagined—a white, Mediterranean style stucco-finished building, quiet and uncomplicated in design, with its simplicity punctuated by the flourishing gardens and streams.

"It's beautiful," she said. "I can't believe you own this place."

Jermain handed her a key. "Penthouse suite, it's all yours for tonight, sweetheart. Go get ready. Tonight the casino is all ours. Enjoy it."

Kate was thrilled. Making her way up to the penthouse suite, she felt as though she was in a fairy tale.

She would make a real effort. The casino and hotel weren't officially open, but that night it was throwing open its doors for an intimate gathering of prospective investors, and she was going to be on-hand to ensure the smooth running of the place.

She poured herself a glass of champagne, and drew a long bath. Four hours to relax before the night kicked off.

Jermain and his two business partners, Andy Crabb and Jacob Cohen, were in the drinks lounge toasting their anticipated success before their guests arrived.

"I hope none of you object, but I've invited a friend to stay here while he's attending a convention in Marseilles," said Andy.

"The more the merrier." Jacob, the youngest of the three, had a glint in his eye. "Is he a good card player?"

"He's a doctor and his name is Bruce Levinstein," replied Andy. "And you know what they say, a fool and his money are soon parted."

A battered car rolled up the winding road towards the hotel and the three men watched as an elderly gentleman got out and leaned against the vehicle for a moment.

"Is that your friend?" Jacob asked disbelievingly.

"Yeah, that's Bruce," Andy replied as he went to let him in.

"Damn," Jacob said to Jermain, "that man looks like he needs a holiday!"

Within an hour, the years appeared to fall away from the doctor as he sat with the three men in the bar lounge. He had discarded his tweed coat, rolled up his shirtsleeves, and was making appreciative noises over the whiskey he had been served.

"I've worked for almost fifty years. I'm getting near my retirement. This is what it's all about." He leaned back in his chair. "Yes, I could get used to this life."

"We've all worked hard for this. I've been working since I was sixteen, now it's my time to enjoy myself," replied Jacob.

"You Yanks, always exaggerating. Working since you were sixteen!" Bruce sat up. "You can't be more than thirty!"

The demeanour of Jacob, who for the last hour had been polite and courteous, changed noticeably at Bruce's patronising words.

"Nearer forty, and I've worked damn hard, dodged a lot of bullets." He fixed Bruce with a stare. "Literally."

Bruce stared back, clearly overwhelmed. "Bullets?"

"Yes," replied Jacob, drawing the conversation to an abrupt close as he left the room.

Bruce turned to Andy.

"What is he, some sort of gangster?"

"No, Jacob's a decent sort, but his great grandfather was Mickey Cohen, the biggest gangster in twenties America."

Bruce gulped. "So it's not wise to upset the man?"

Andy laughed and slapped Bruce on the back. "He'll be fine. He's young, but thoroughly decent. That being said, don't make the mistake of thinking he's totally out of the game. Once connected, always connected."

As the evening of impressing the prospective investors kicked off, Jermain sat back and watched his daughter circulate.

"She's doing well, isn't she?" said Jacob, topping up Jermain's glass with champagne.

"Really well. It's fascinating watching her," he said, not taking his eyes off Kate as she charmed the men.

"You missed her." It wasn't a question so Jermain didn't answer.

But, yes, he had missed her, although he knew why she had gone away, and he knew it was his own fault. They had enjoyed the most idyllic lifestyle imaginable for the first fourteen years of Kate's life. South African Jermain and his English wife, Sara, had travelled since their wedding day and when their daughter came along they saw no need to stop. They had a boat, a beautiful forty-two foot Pacific Seacraft, originally called Sara and re-named Sara-Kate after their baby was born. On the boat they travelled far and wide and it could have been a lonely childhood for Kate, but she found her own ways to amuse herself. By the age of eleven she was fluent in Spanish and French, she could sail the boat that was her home, catch, gut and cook a fish and knew all the different woods and materials in the world that got the best campfire going. She never really attended school, instead learned ways and cultures that were far more useful than dead Kings and Queens or mathematics. But when she was fifteen their world was turned upside down when Sara was murdered during a mugging in

India. They had been docked in the Bay of Bengal and Jermain and Kate were off collecting wood for the nightly fire when the killer boarded the boat. Kate was first back on board upon their return and, to this day, Jermain remembered the stack of fire wood tumbling from Kate's arms as she looked down at where her mother lay, her throat slashed from ear to ear.

The killer, or killers, were never found and, after a long and painful time spent with the authorities, Jermain and Kate buried Sara at sea, and returned home to the farmhouse that Sara's father had left to his daughter in his will.

The farmhouse was a Grade II listed building, set in the Pennines. The actual town was a dot on the map called Appleby, the nearest town being Darlington. The scenery was pretty enough, but when they settled it was winter, the lakes had frozen over and snow covered the mountainside. Their nearest neighbour was five miles away in any direction, but the solitude didn't bother Jermain, it was just the sudden jolt of being plucked from the ocean and being dumped on land, with Sara missing from their little family of three. Kate refused to go to school or interact in any way with anyone, including her father. She seemed to hate the modern appliances with a vengeance, preferring to cook her meals on a fire in the garden. Social Services learned about her and came to visit. Baffled by her preference to live like a street child, they returned time and time again, until he became worried they would take her away. Not knowing how to handle her, he sent her off to a boarding school in Kent. The next two years passed in a battle of wills between the two of them, Jermain not knowing what to do or say without Sara's calming influence, Kate hating him for sending her away.

When the final term ended, she failed to arrive home. At first he was frantic, he even got the police involved and CCTV footage showed her boarding the Eurostar bound for France. Since she was officially an adult, they did nothing more. Eventually, he received a postcard, from India of all places, and fear shot through him at the thought of her being in the same land as her mother's killer. The postcards then came sporadically, from Africa, Greece, Thailand and Australia, where the messages finally got longer and warmer in their tone. Jermain, not without wealth, deposited money in her bank account every month and, although she barely touched the funds, he felt comforted by knowing she could get out whenever she wanted. Gradually he noticed Australia was where she stayed, growing mentally and physically stronger, it seemed, and so, finally, he took his own life off hold as he sensed she would soon return. Adventure had been missing for far too long, which led him there, to Cannes, and his new found friendships with Andy Crabb and Jacob Cohen.

"I'm sure glad we did all this," said Jacob, interrupting Jermain's reverie.

"You don't miss New York?" he asked, pulling himself back into the present.

Jacob sat back. "I miss the streets, the dusty hot streets, the noise, my family and friends, but not the constant wail of police sirens, the phone call that someone else had been shot, stabbed, or overdosed. I never wanted to go into the family business. Although it was all bona-fide, there were always elements of corruption and, after having a taste of it, I simply wanted a legitimate life. I'm done slumming it. I'll try some luxury living for a while," he replied.

Jermain was struck that those were almost the same words Kate had used. Maybe Cannes would be good for all of them.

Chapter Two

Zaire

As a child, Joe Palmer was the least likely person to discover the thrills of nature and culture. Born in 1975 in Brixton, London, his passions as he grew up were football and girls, in that order. As he entered his teens, vandalism and hooliganism were the order of the day, and a typical Saturday night was spent stealing the odd car for a joy ride, dropping tabs of acid, the drug of the eighties, or generally causing havoc with the other local gangs.

There was no psychological reason for Joe to go off the rails, no broken home or bad upbringing. It was simply Brixton in the eighties.

His parents worried over him, shouted, threatened, and eventually kicked him out at fifteen. That went over Joe's head like water rolling off a duck's back. He simply found an abandoned warehouse, kicked the door in and made it his home. The warehouse became the place to be, wild parties that went on for days, mad trips of sex and drugs that not even the police could stop. Of course, they tried in the beginning, but after a while they gave up patrolling the area.

It had all ended so suddenly. Joe and his friend Tyler left one of the parties as it entered its third night. Spotting a beautiful BMW convertible, they hotwired it and, within seconds, were roaring through the London streets. Joe laughed uncontrollably as Tyler, in the driving seat, swerved over the lanes of the dual carriageway. He laid out lines of coke on the mahogany dash and snorted it. Feeling the incredible rush, he licked the dash clean and sat back to enjoy the ride. A moment later, he pressed his hand to his forehead as a dull, intense pain began. He realised his nose was bleeding and, looking in the mirror, was horrified to see a blood vessel had burst in his right eye. He screamed as the pain turned into a volcano, splitting his head apart.

"What the fuck…?" Tyler turned, terror in his eyes as

well.

The scraping of metal as the car crossed the central reservation, then a spinning sensation, as the BMW flipped over, half way across Tower Bridge, were the last things he remembered.

He woke up in Brixton Hospital days later. The cocktail of drink and drugs should have killed him, his back was fractured and discs in his spine had shattered. Still, he fared better than Tyler. Joe, not wearing a seatbelt, had been thrown from the car. Tyler had been burned badly, and was in the intensive care unit. Even if he lived, which was not expected, he would spend the rest of his life in a wheelchair.

It was a living hell. Dealing with the thought of Tyler was bad enough, but he had years of painful physiotherapy ahead of him to try to make his shattered spine strong again. Eight months he spent in the hospital, enduring gruelling operations on his back and legs. The courts brought no charges as he was a minor, and community service was not an option, as he couldn't even stand on his own, let alone walk.

He sank into a deep pit of depression. No friends came to visit, his father refused to acknowledge him, and his mother, when she came, was falsely bright and optimistic.

Eventually, he was moved to a rehabilitation centre in Margate, Kent. He spent a lot of time by the sea. The centre was much brighter than the dismal hospital in Brixton.

He spent a year there. Each month the money came through, he never asked who was paying for it and, at first, didn't care. He presumed it was his mother, out of some misplaced sense of guilt for not visiting him too often.

It was at this junction in his life he first heard of Survival International. A man came one day with flyers for a charity run he was arranging. All patients who could were encouraged to participate, which at first was a joke to Joe, seeing as he had only just moved out of the wheelchair onto crutches. The Charity walk was to start at the centre in Margate, finishing at the centre's sister hospital in Canterbury, a good day's walk for those whose limbs worked.

Joe scoffed at the idea and crumpled the flyer, intending

not to give it a second thought. Until one day, as he made his way through the gardens on his crutches, he stumbled upon a girl of about sixteen. She had only one leg, the other was a stump that ended well up her left thigh. She was not in a wheelchair, though. On crutches, like Joe, she staggered her way up ahead of him, breathing heavily and snorting like a racehorse. Joe followed her around the grounds for hours, crying, although he didn't realise it at the time, and not really knowing why until months later. As she hopped and jumped haphazardly over the park area, she stumbled and fell. Joe's eyes widened and he made his way to her where she lay on the ground.

As he neared her, he heard her braying cries and he called out, "Are you okay?"

She rolled over, and he saw with astonishment that she was laughing.

"Who are you?" she asked as she sat up and retrieved her crutches.

"I'm Joe." He stuck out his hand, and she shook it solemnly. "That was quite a fall you took there."

"My name's Emily. I'm fine, getting used to falling over!"

He winced as she showed him the dark bruises, some old, and some fresh, that adorned her leg.

"I couldn't help noticing that you've been walking for hours," he said as he helped her up.

She leaned on him as she righted the crutches, and grinned.

"I'm practicing for the charity walk. I'm going to come in first, you know!"

He was stunned and deeply ashamed. He had scorned the walk, and here was this girl with one leg, who was not only determined to take part, but win it too!

"Are you going to do it?" asked Emily as they made their way back to the centre.

Joe looked doubtful. "Well I wasn't. Do you think I could?"

She beamed at him, all the encouragement he needed.

The fire crackled and died, bringing Joe out of his memories and back to Zaire. He fingered his St. Christopher necklace—it had once belonged to Emily—and smiled sadly as he remembered that first walk. He didn't like to think of it often, the recollection of the subsequent events of losing her was too painful. She had set him on the road to recovery, not just physically, but mentally too. She had taught him to love and care and, just as she had begun to help him make a fresh start, she had gone.

He kicked over the remains of the fire and stared into the darkness. Memories of his childhood dissipated, they would not help this tribe. Packing his compass and a couple of canteens of palm wine, he made his way onto the path and through the forest. About two miles down the track he stumbled upon a village. Not really a village, just an open plain with about a dozen mud huts standing around the edge. It might not be Chi's village, but Joe wandered up to the hut that obviously belonged to the chief and knocked on the door.

A woman came out and glared at him, letting off a stream of Swahili that he barely understood.

"*Jambo sana abadi?*"

Joe paused and tried to recall more of the local dialect and failed. "Chi?"

The woman grinned and waved her arms.

"*Abasi Missouri!*" she exclaimed and pointed to a hut directly opposite.

He took it the hut would be where he would find Chi, and he nodded at the lady and made his way over.

"Chi?" he called softly, standing at the open doorway.

Chi came to the door. His face lit up.

"Joe! Come in." He held open the beads decorating the doorway, and Joe entered.

Chi's home was simply one room. A bed, crudely made of wood, doubled as a couch in one corner, and various sized tables were all it held.

"Why so many tables, Chi?" asked Joe, sitting down.

"I make them. I take them into Kananga or Kisangani to sell them," replied Chi as he eagerly took the canteens of wine and set them on the open fire.

Joe knew this trick of old. Heating the alcohol made the herbs used to make the palm wine so potent it was almost like smoking pot. But it seemed Chi wanted some of that as well, as he brought out a huge intricate china bong and set about making their little party go with a bang.

After the terrible drug-fuelled accident, Joe had quit all narcotics straight away until, that was, he began his work in Africa. It was there he learned about the drugs that were pure, straight from the herbs, that lifted the taker and had no consequence of paranoia or violence.

As Chi worked with his herbs, Joe questioned him more about the land sale.

Chi told him everything he had heard on his visits to town. The Government were selling it, it meant more money for them, and it would give the tribal people work and produce more farming products or wood to sell abroad. It was a logical solution, for everyone except the Pygmies.

"Where's the nearest telephone I can use?" asked Joe.

"You would need to go to *Kinshasa.* There used to be telephones on the streets in *Bukavu* but the protestors have…" he groped for the right word "…killed them."

"Vandalised," Joe corrected him absently and took the bong that Chi handed him. "What are they protesting about?" he asked as an afterthought.

"Same as you, my friend." Chi grinned, taking a slug of the wine.

As a pleasant feeling came over him, Joe made a mental note to visit Bukavu as well.

Chapter Three

Cannes

In the Hotel Cannes Riviera across town, Linda Striker was also preparing herself for a night at Cannes Central. She was an English photographer, sent there to cover the night as part of a feature for *The Times* on New Businessman of the Year. She wasn't looking forward to the evening. After ten years in the business she wanted more, and was angry with her editors, who wouldn't let her go to the war zones. Instead, she was flown to the South of France for the photography feature on three businessmen, Andy Crabb, Jacob Cohen and Jermain Bryant. Then, in a month there was to be a shoot covering a birthday party in the same area for four girls, three who were twenty-one, the other eighteen. The girls were very prominent figures in society, two being cousins of Princess Stephanie of Monaco, one a Governor's daughter and the other, the daughter of the Prime Minister of Cannes. All four girls lived with their families in the same district, in huge mansions that stood up in the hills of Cannes. Normally Linda hated covering those sorts of shoots, she preferred more action to go with a good news story, but the reality of life demanded she take the work that was offered.

Instead of flying back to London she had decided to stay for a month between the shoots, taking advantage of the chance for a holiday.

Checking the location of the hotel on the map, Linda started to get ready. Black trousers, black vest top with her long, leather jacket slung over the top. Simple worked best for Linda, and she knew it. Brushing her long dark hair, she left it down and picked up her bag. She wanted to be early. If she was lucky she could get some quotes to use in her captions from the owners of the casino and rake in a bit more.

Kate was working the room, dressed in a floor length black halter-neck dress. Her blonde hair was long and wild and, with diamonds adorning her wrist and neck, she had never felt further away from the streets.

It's amazing how quickly things can change, she mused. One minute she was stalking through the African wilderness, trying to find a place to use as a lavatory that wasn't crawling with ants, and burying her tampax six feet deep, so lions didn't track her, now she was residing in the nicest hotel she had ever stayed in, part of which one day would be hers, wearing a two thousand pound dress, and talking with the high flyers of society.

She spotted her father making his way across the room, and she moved over to join him.

He handed her a glass of champagne as he hugged her and told her how beautiful she looked.

"Dad, who's that man?" she asked, gesturing over to a tall, dark-haired man standing by the bar, dressed in a black designer suit toned down by a leather jacket.

"That's John, John Campbell," Jermain paused and looked at Kate. "Bit of a playboy really."

"I was just curious. Come on, we've got to work the room." She gave him a quick hug and moved away, conscious of John Campbell's stare.

Mr Campbell, although being handsome and obviously wealthy, was the kind of man she wouldn't give a second glance. She preferred her men real, surfer types who were not afraid to get their hands dirty. She smiled to herself as she looked around the room. She probably wouldn't find many men like that there.

Several times during the evening, John Campbell met her eyes and raised his glass in a silent toast that said far more than she was comfortable with.

Linda stood halfway up the staircase and took some shots of the girl with her father. The girl, Kate, intrigued her. From all the research she had done on the investors, nothing much could be found about Jermain's family. The girl looked and moved like a model. *Anyone who looked like that and had a heritage like hers would no doubt be a bitch*, she thought.

She had to admit the hotel was quite something. And, from mingling with the guests, she knew the Bryant's would have no problem getting more investors than they needed.

Noticing everyone moving into the casino, she picked up her camera and followed the crowd. She had plenty of photographs of Jermain and the slightly aging Andy Crabb, but the third partner, Jacob Cohen, was proving harder to pin down. She had done her research, discovering his links to the New York underworld, and she knew he was elusive and inclined to keep out of the limelight. However, Linda was nothing if not persistent and, keeping her eyes and ears open, she moved into the main casino room.

She spotted Kate straight away, sitting at the bar, and speaking with the people who stopped to congratulate her. She made her way over and held out her hand.

"Hi, I'm Linda Striker. I'm a photographer with *The Times*, and I'd like to thank you for letting me come tonight."

Kate shook her hand warmly. "Hey, it's nice to see another English face. How are you enjoying the night so far?"

She was momentarily thrown off-guard by Kate's friendliness. It was not what she had expected at all.

"It's great. I got some good photos of you. I can send you a copy of the paper when they run it."

Kate pulled a face and told Linda to make sure she got her good side.

She laughed. "It doesn't seem to me you actually have a bad side!"

Suddenly they were in conversation, and all of her preconceptions flew out of her head. She actually liked Kate Bryant very much, and listened with interest to Kate's story of the history of the town. "So, how long are you in Cannes?" asked Kate as she got them both another drink.

"A month. After this gig I've got four weeks off, then I have a photo shoot to do on four little princesses who are having a huge birthday party."

"I've heard of that! That guy over there, he's the father of one of them." She pointed, and Linda recognised the Governor.

Before Linda could reply, a man moved across the room and stood in front of Kate.

Discreetly, Linda moved away and made a mental note to talk more to Kate later.

Kate saw the photographer go and gave her full attention to John Campbell.

"You're the most beautiful woman in this room tonight," he said in a strong American accent.

"Thank you," replied Kate whilst mentally gagging.

"I'm staying at the Cannes Riviera, penthouse suite." He leaned in closer and whispered in her ear. "I'll see you there later."

He was superficial, all hair and skin products—usually she liked her men a bit more rough and ready. It was apparent, by the cocksure way he stood in front of her demanding her attention, that he thought way too much of himself. Normally she would tell him in no uncertain terms where to go. However, he was a potential investor and she didn't want to ruin things for Jermain.

"I'm pretty much tied up here tonight, might see you around, though."

With that she slipped gracefully off her stool and, without a backward glance, she moved across the room.

Chapter Four

Bukavu

The very next day, Joe ventured out to Bukavu. He set out walking along the highway, with his backpack slung over his shoulder, and a promise to the Pygmies that he would return.

His first priority was to speak with his head office and inform them of the land sale in Zaire. Then he wanted to find the protesters and get all the information he could out of them. He was well aware that the protesters may not even care about the sale, and they were simply using it as a platform to state their grievances about the government or elections that were going on. Nonetheless, Joe was onto an adventure, and that was one thing about his job that he never shied away from.

He walked thirty miles that day. In Africa, a regular bus service could mean that transport ran regularly once a week, and he didn't intend to wait at the stop when he could walk it in that time.

Savannah temperatures meant that he was walking in almost unbearable heat during daylight, but when night came upon him they plummeted almost to freezing point. Several locals passed him and called out a greeting. He returned their waves, and sometimes walked alongside them for a few miles until they went off the track.

That night he made camp, lighting the fire first to get it going, and then pulling out some meals he had packed. The meals were pitiful, small silver bags that lasted fifty years in storage and tasted like the shite they were—chunks of processed meat with dry rice or noodles. The meals were mainly used for snow travellers or seasoned long-distance walkers. If Joe was not walking all day, he would be hunting his meat, but it was not feasible if he wanted to get to Bukavu as soon as possible, so the silver packages would have to do. Although, mused Joe, if he came across a deer in his path he would not hesitate to kill it.

Deer hunting was one of Joe's finest skills. When he was in Igarka, Russia, he had been on an expedition with some of the finest hunters he had ever seen. He watched them stalk the deer in the coldest environment he had ever experienced. When they brought the deer down, the work began. First they skinned it, slicing the skin so carefully that not an inch was wasted. The skin was then tied around the shoulders of the workingman to keep him warm. Next the innards were removed, not piercing a single organ, as this was their main source of meat for the next few weeks. The stomach contents were discarded, and the empty stomach sac was filled with snow and tied by the cartilages ripped from the deer's legs. This provided water for the hunters for the trip. But it was not only the meat they wanted—the entire deer, bar the stomach contents, was taken back to the women. Joe remembered watching in amazement as the women set to work, using the leg cartilages as cotton to sew together the best deerskin boots he had ever known.

It seemed gruesome to some people but, having seen it for himself, Joe felt differently. The Siberians used every part of the deer for their everyday needs, always remembering to give thanks to their God for it.

With the fire burning, Joe ate his meal heartily and lay back outside the tent. He knew he was in lion country and he should be trying to find a camp on high ground, but the fire should keep him safe.

He awoke the next morning to find the fire had died. He built it up again to make a cup of tea before he set off. As he crouched over the fire he rubbed his legs. Since the accident, he had been plagued by aches and pains that didn't go away until he had been up a couple of hours. Sleeping outside certainly didn't help, and sometimes it brought him down. When he felt bad about his weak back though, he forced himself to remember Tyler, and Emily, who managed to smile even though she only had one leg. It normally brought him out of his black mood and made him thank his lucky stars. One good point about the dodgy legs and back was that, while he worked in the mornings, he had to depend on his arms to practically lift him around while his legs worked themselves free. This meant he had incredible upper body strength, and he had no cause ever to visit a gym to keep in shape.

That day, he hoped he could cadge a lift that would at least take him a few miles down the road. After putting the tin on the fire, he made his way down to the lake and washed, pausing to watch a couple of bull elephants across the water. They ignored him as they frolicked, and he sat and observed them until he remembered his tea water and cursed for letting it boil dry.

Tea foregone, and rejuvenated by the sight of the beautiful elephants, he packed up quickly and made his way back onto the track.

He was deep in the heart of the Zaire Basin when the first vehicle went past him. He dropped his pack and raised his arms in the air. The Landrover stopped and he ran up to the driver's window. A middle aged English couple greeted him.

"Hi, how far are you going, mate?" asked the man.

"Bukavu, but if you're not going that far you can drop me where you leave the track," replied Joe.

"Your luck's in, mate, we're heading to Bukavu ourselves. Hop in."

Gratefully, Joe climbed in the back and introduced himself.

"I'm Suzie, this is Jack, and we're off to the Embassy to finalise a sale for a game reserve in central Zaire."

Joe's ears pricked up. Could that be the very land he was living on?

Politely, he questioned them until the full story came out.

Jack and Suzie, or 'Sooz' as Jack affectionately called his wife, had packed in their London jobs, she taking early retirement, and he voluntary redundancy from high paid jobs in the Stock Market that were making them miserable. They had cashed in their life savings, sold their home and come out to Africa.

They had looked at purchasing land in Niger and Libya, but they had discovered, upon their arrival, the unrest of the countries, constantly on the brink of war, which did not make for economical business sense. They tried their luck in South Africa, but whites were being driven out of their homes, and they had literally been forced out by gunpoint. Their experiences had not put them off, however, and they had moved onto central Africa, which was more settled.

There they had discovered the Government sale of the Zaire rainforests, and Suzie and Jack had the money and the contacts to be first in on, what now seemed to Joe, a spreading trend.

"Not just a game reserve, mind, pure luxury. We shall have the employees dressed in their tribal costumes. Imagine it, Joseph, divine!" Suzie made him cringe, as he pushed for more information about other sales that were happening.

"What about the locals, though?" asked Joe. "This is their home."

"Oh, we'll take care of them. We'll take them on, and they can live in the servant's quarters."

Jack found this highly amusing and Suzie joined in his laughter.

Joe clenched his fists and looked out of the window.

They had done it to Europe and America. Japan and Asia were well on the way to ruins. Foreigners were coming over to wreck this country with their funny ideas about buildings and technology, creating work, and getting them out of poverty. When were people going to realise this was the life the locals chose? If they wanted to be surrounded by televisions, computers and fax machines they would simply move across the Atlantic. When were Westerners going to realise that technology was slowly killing the planet?

Joe closed his eyes and feigned sleep for the rest of the journey.

When they arrived, he jerked awake, surprised to find he *had* slept most of the trip. Getting out of the Landrover, he thanked the couple, set his bag down, and sat for a moment on the side of the road. A five-hour journey in the car had been as bad for his legs and back as a night sleeping outside. The problem, which had never been diagnosed with a specific name, ranged from sciatica through to slipped discs, depending on which doctor he saw. None of them, whether private or NHS, had ever given him a firm diagnosis. Eventually, he had given up trying to find a cure, instead settling for the magic hands of Doctor Levinstein who, on a regular basis, manipulated his back to create a lull from the pain. Bruce Levinstein was past the age of retirement, but he loved his job so much that he would probably continue it until he dropped. Bruce was what Joe referred to as an old world gent. He had firm ideas about right and wrong and his language bounced between an almost Victorian speech to harsh cursing that never failed to amuse Joe. The Doctor had been a family friend before he was Joe's physiotherapist, and Joe was forever grateful that he could always find time to fit Joe in his busy practice. Dr Levinstein, however, was in London, and Joe cursed himself for not taking an hour to pay him a visit before he had flown out. He pondered the thought of returning to London for a fly-by visit before he went back to Zaire, and decided it was something he would have to consider seriously if he were going to be of any help to the Pygmies.

After a few minutes he got up and headed in the general direction of the Embassy, hoping that someone there would be able to give him details of the land sales.

He saw the tall building, a ridiculous sight among all the tin shanty homes that lined the dirt road, and had almost reached the door when a spasm shook his spine so hard he crumpled to the ground. Gasping for air, feeling as if ligaments were being torn from his spinal cord, he moaned and, thankfully, passed out with the pain.

He awoke in a hospital bed, and tried to sit up, but found he had no control over his lower body. He shouted for a nurse, and a striking black woman walked in.

"I'm paralysed," he gasped, and tried again to sit up.

"Relax, Mr Palmer, you have an anaesthetic in your spine. It has stopped the spasm that was causing you pain. Now we will find out the cause. Do you have medical insurance?"

He shook his head. He had the minimum cover provided by Survival International, but there was no way he was going to be treated in an African hospital that was severely understaffed, under-funded and under-managed. During his previous stay in Africa, he had been unfortunate enough to be bitten by a Saw-scaled Viper. The venom in this particular species of snake is highly hemotoxic, and Joe was lucky enough to get the treatment in time. However, he thought he might die, anyway, when he watched the needle plunge into his arm having just seen it come out of the patient next to him.

"I need to discharge myself. Get me my papers and find me a flight straight to England," demanded Joe.

"Mr Palmer, that is highly—"

"Now," said Joe. Calling upon all the strength he possessed, he levered himself upright, and swung himself to the side of the bed.

The nurse, seemingly not caring much anyway, did as she was bade. Within two hours the anaesthetic had pretty much worn off, and he was in the departure lounge in a wheelchair in Zambia Airport.

He had called Dr Levinstein's office from the airport, and had been informed he was in France for a medical convention, staying at a hotel in Cannes, so he had rung his personal number, and the doctor had told him to come immediately. Joe was a valuable patient but, more than that, he was a friend. Wheeling himself over to the ticket desk, he asked if he could transfer his open ticket to France instead of Gatwick.

The clerk checked the computer system and informed him there was a flight bound for Toulouse leaving in an hour, or he could wait overnight for the next flight to Nice. Joe took the Toulouse flight, although he dreaded the state he would be in when he actually arrived in Cannes, there being a good four-hour car journey from the airport. But it was far better than waiting another night, or taking the flight to Paris. Toulouse, although being near to the Spanish border, was closer to his destination.

Almost as an afterthought, he decided to call head office to tell them of the latest developments, and that he would be back as soon as he was on his feet again.

Back in Cannes, Bruce hung up the telephone in reception, and caught Jacob's arm as he walked past.

"Jacob, do you have room for one more? I have a patient coming, and I need to see him."

"Of course." Jacob clapped Bruce on the back, their cross words of the previous day put aside. "Is he a card player?"

Kate was going over the list of potential investors with Jermain when the reception phone rang.

"Cannes Central," said Kate.

"Kate? It's Linda, Linda Striker from London."

"Linda, how's it going?"

"Good thanks, I'm still in Cannes and I've got the photos from the party. They're being run in *The Times* and I wondered if you'd like to meet up and choose some?" Linda paused. "Of course, I understand if you're too busy."

"No, that would be great." Kate looked at her watch. "We'll have a drink here, and then, if you're free this afternoon, you can keep me company while I deliver some flyers advertising the hotel around the local areas."

"Sounds like fun. I'll see you in a bit."

"Who was that?" asked Jermain.

"Linda, the photographer from the party. She's coming over with some photos," she replied.

Jermain was pleased. Kate had never had close girlfriends, and it would be good for her to spend time with people her own age.

"I'm almost done here, and thanks for your help, I do appreciate it," he said. "Hey, when are you intending on taking the flyers out?"

"This afternoon. Why?" she asked as she started to clear away the books.

"Bruce has got a client flying in for an emergency. Any chance you could pick him up from Toulouse airport? I think he lands around 4 o'clock. Mr Palmer is his name."

"Of course, I'm glad to help." She smiled at him.

Jermain studied her for a moment and a warm glow of

happiness spread through him, as it did most days when he spent time with her. Over the years he had almost grown used to her being away, but the dark hole of loneliness in his heart had never closed until she had come back.

Kate barely seemed to glance at the photographs as Linda spread them out across the bar.

"What about going freelance?" Kate asked when Linda complained about her lack of opportunities in the editorial world.

"I've thought about it, but I need a regular wage. Maybe one day." Linda threw back her drink and smiled. "I shouldn't be complaining. I guess I'm lucky to have a job doing what I love."

"I never had a dream career," replied Kate wistfully. "I just wanted to live my entire life the way I lived my childhood."

"And how was that?"

"Travelling the world on the ocean." A dark shadow crossed Kate's face. "All good things come to an end, though."

Linda's journalistic skills told her to press more but, before she could continue, a tall, pale man walked into the bar. Looking at Linda, he stopped. She paused, stuttering over what she had been about to say. Mumbling a greeting, he backed out of the bar and vanished through the reception.

"My God, who was that man?" she asked.

Kate, who had her back to the entrance, swivelled round on her stool. "Who?"

"He was tall, pale, dark hair, my age." Linda leaned back to see if she could spot him outside. "Kate, he was the single most gorgeous man I've ever seen!"

Kate laughed, "That's Jacob, the other partner with my dad and Andy. You must have seen him the other night?"

"No, I couldn't find him. Damn! Now I wish I'd tried harder, instead of wasting my time on you!"

Kate joined in with her laughter. She considered the possibility of a holiday fling. After all, living in England and travelling on a moment's notice for work, she didn't have time for a relationship. Sometimes it was a lonely existence, but her work was her all and, so far, no man had come even close.

"Come on, let's go deliver those leaflets." Kate finished her drink and the two women walked to the car park.

Kate grinned as she saw the car Jermain had hired for her. It was a beautiful, brand new, bright red convertible Jaguar and just her style. Going over the map with Linda, they decided to start with Nice, and then work inland, taking the coastal road, hitting Marseilles and other towns along their route to the airport.

Speeding along, Kate put the top down and let the wind whip through her hair. The drive to Nice didn't take more than an hour, and she pulled over as they entered the town.

From first glance, they could see Nice was more tourist orientated than Cannes. Water sports seemed to be the game of the day and, for a while, Linda and Kate stood on the beach and watched the water-skiers. After a few flyers had been handed out to the locals, they walked around the town, checking out the restaurants and hotels, before stopping for lunch at a bistro in Saint Francois Square.

"Check this out." Linda pointed to a notice board advertising some medical conventions being held in Angels Bay.

"That's probably where Bruce's conventions are," replied Kate. "We should hit those. Doctors could probably do with an evening chilling out at the casino after a boring day of meetings."

"Good thinking. Hey, are you sure you don't mind me tagging along?"

"Heck, no, it's been really nice to have your company. Truth is, I've been on the road for so long I've not had many girlfriends since, well…ever!"

"Me neither, I'm based in London but I'm so often given assignments abroad I never really put down roots."

"In that case, we make a good partnership." They linked arms and made their way back to the car. "Let's go get Bruce's friend from the airport."

Joe limped off the eleven hour flight and attempted to straighten out his torso without much success. Making his way through Customs, he scanned the crowd waiting at Arrivals. Instead of Bruce, his gaze landed on a blonde lady, leaning on the railing looking rather bored. Her eyes met his, and she straightened up, a smile forming on her lips as he walked past. He lingered, returning her smile, hoping he didn't look too much of a fool as he limped along and, reluctantly tearing his eyes away from her, he kept on walking as he searched the group of people for the doctor.

"Kate, will this do?" Linda breathlessly arrived back with a makeshift sign she had just written, showing Mr Palmer's name.

"Excellent job. I can't believe we didn't think that neither of us knows what the other looks like. Here, I'll hold it up. Hopefully he won't be too long," replied Kate distractedly, her eyes following the tall, blond man, who had smiled at her before. "You missed a nice sight when you were gone, best-looking man I've seen in France so far," she added.

Suddenly she stopped talking and blushed as the blond stranger turned around, looked at the board that she held and started slowly towards her.

"Oh, he's coming over. Did he hear me? Don't look," Kate muttered and turned to face the other way.

"Hi."

Kate felt a heat travel down her spine as he greeted her and, hoping furiously she wasn't blushing, she turned around.

"Hello," she replied softly.

He gestured at the board, which now hung loosely by her side.

"I think you're waiting for me. I'm Joe Palmer. Did Bruce send you to collect me?"

The heat, which had been a pleasant tingle, now turned into total embarrassment, heightened by her friend's delighted laugh.

"I'm sorry. I'm Kate, this is Linda, we didn't expect you

to be so…young," she said helplessly.

"I don't feel very young," replied Joe as, with a slight struggle, he ducked under the rope.

"Yeah, I can see that." Kate took his bag. Joe appeared to be grateful to let her take it.

Joe stretched across the back of the car and watched Kate in the driving seat. In his line of work he avoided relationships. Travelling around the world for months at a time was not conducive to keeping any romance alive. Not that he was a saint. He had a fair few women in most countries across the globe who would meet up with him at a moment's notice if he was in town, but there had been nobody special in the ten years since Emily. There was something about this girl, Kate, though, that sparked something in him he thought he had lost when he said goodbye to Emily. Something more than lust or sex, something bigger, that was instantaneous and, if he wasn't mistaken, she had felt it too.

At that moment he caught her eye as she sneaked a glance at him in the rear view mirror and he smiled weakly, cursing the fact that he had left Africa so quickly and was still in his filthy bush gear. He made a mental note to ask Bruce to get him some decent clothes once he reached Cannes.

Kate blushed as Joe caught her last sly look at him in the mirror, and wondered what was going on to make her behave so out of character. It wasn't as if it had been years since she had been with a man. In fact, she had many male friends across the countries she had travelled, most of whom would be glad to meet up with her should she happen to be around. But although she had shared nights with some, it had never gone beyond anything deeper than companionship and the mutual need for sexual release. She wasn't sure what it was about Joe that pulled her with a magnetic force. He was incredibly handsome, tall and blond with the sort of tan that comes with spending a lot of time outdoors, just the kind she would normally go for, but there was something more, something she couldn't quite put her finger on.

She checked her mirror again, about to ask him what he was doing in Africa, but noticed he had closed his eyes and seemed to be sleeping. He had a slight frown across his features and she hoped he wasn't in too much pain. Turning back to the road, she jumped as Linda jabbed her in the ribs.

"I feel like a third wheel here," Linda whispered, trying not to laugh too loudly.

"Sorry." Kate glanced behind her once more, and then back at Linda. "I'm not usually like this."

Linda gripped her arm, her eyes ablaze with excitement.

"We'll let Bruce work his magic on him, get him back on his feet and then the three of us will go out and invite Jacob too!"

Kate laughed, appreciating Linda's agenda and, trying not to wake her sleeping passenger, she sped homeward.

As soon as the red jaguar sped up the circular drive and came to a halt outside the hotel doors, Bruce and Jermain fussed, helping Joe out of the car and into the hotel. Joe's back seemed to be even more seized up, and he avoided Kate's eyes as he shuffled past her like an old man.

Kate and Linda watched them disappear into the hotel and then looked at each other.

"Eventful day, huh?" said Linda.

"Sure was, things are getting interesting around here." Kate smiled. "Fancy staying for dinner?"

Linda nodded happily, and together they followed the men into the hotel.

Chapter Five

That evening, Linda and Kate ate a solitary dinner in the hotel. It was a sombre affair, with Kate disappointed that Joe was confined to his room where Bruce was assessing him, and Linda despondent that Jacob had not been seen since that morning.

"This is too sad. We're sitting here, pining for men who we don't even really know. It's too much. Come on, finish up and we'll go for a drink down by the water," instructed Kate.

Together they strolled down to the *Quai St Pierre* and ended up seated at a table outside the Irish Pub, overlooking the port.

A few people, recognising Kate from the Investor's Evening, stopped by their table. Kate, ever aware she needed to be gracious and courteous to the potential investors, invited them all to sit down, take a drink and, before long, they had a steady stream of visitors. Eventually, one by one they bade their farewells and vanished into the night, leaving Kate hoping she had left a good impression on them.

While Linda was away taking their empty glasses back to the bar and settling their bill, a shadow fell over the table. Kate looked up, startled, recognising the man from the investors opening who had spent the entire evening looking at her, and had then invited her to his penthouse suite at the Cannes Riviera. For the life of her, she couldn't remember his name, but she remembered his steely grey eyes.

"Good evening," she said politely.

"You didn't come and see me the other night." He sat down, uninvited, in the chair that Linda had vacated.

Kate sighed with annoyance. Pushy, she didn't appreciate, and this man was nothing but. She had been polite to the man just in case he invested in Cannes Central, but there was only so much she was prepared to take, plus, by the steady flow of traffic to and from their table all evening, the hotel had more investors than it could accommodate, anyway.

"I had other plans. I was busy. I have been since, and can safely say I will be in the future," she replied. "No offence, I'm just not interested in you Mr…?" she remembered too late that she had forgotten his name, and reddened.

"Campbell, John Campbell," he reminded her, his eyes flashing with irritation.

"Well, you have a pleasant evening, Mr Campbell," she replied, standing up as she saw Linda making her way back to the table. "Goodnight."

"John Campbell's after you, I see," stated Linda, as they walked around the port towards the hotel.

"You know him?" asked Kate.

"Everyone knows him. He lives off his parents' money. He's a playboy by occupation. He coasts from Cannes, Nice, Monaco, the entire Riviera, gambling and picking up pretty girls," replied Linda. "Usually, he succeeds when he has his eye on someone but, from the look on his face, I'm guessing you knocked him back."

Kate nodded, wondering about it. It wasn't that John Campbell was unattractive. He seemed attentive, courteous and polite, but he was also arrogant and full of himself. More sinister, however, was something lurking beneath his exterior, behind his cold grey eyes. It sent chills through her.

"Forget about him. Anyway, tomorrow, hopefully, Jacob will have appeared and Joe will be on his feet, and we can enjoy an evening with them," said Kate.

As the two women laughed in anticipation, Kate felt a chill again and, although she didn't turn around, she felt the eyes of John Campbell on her, boring into her spine.

The following morning, the hotel saw a full house for breakfast. Joe appeared, feeling much better after Bruce's master manipulation of his spine, and eager for a full English breakfast. He smiled to himself as he saw the hot plate housing eggs, bacon, sausages—in fact, everything he could have wanted. He saw a movement from the corner of his eye and spotted Kate standing by the window, looking out to sea, seemingly lost in her own thoughts. Freshly shaven, wearing new clothes and, feeling really clean for the first time in months, he moved towards her.

"Good morning," he said, startling her out of her reverie.

For a moment she stared at him as though she had no idea who he was, then her eyes widened in recognition.

"Morning," she said and offered him a bright smile. "You look better."

"I feel it. Bruce is the only man who can help when I get a seizure like that." His eyes, although happy to linger on Kate, moved over to the buffet.

"Oh, you must be starving. Come on, help yourself," she said, leading him over to the hot plates.

"Only if you'll join me?" he asked, handing her a plate.

Their fingers touched as she took the plate from him and he felt the same jolt run through him that he had experienced the day before at the airport.

"What were you doing in Africa?" she asked once they were seated with their breakfast.

And so Joe began to explain—how his job had taken him to Zaire, how he had heard the news of the land sales and gone to Bukavu to learn more about it, right up to his collapse on the steps of the Embassy and his nasty experience in the hospital.

Kate wanted to know what sort of job took someone out into the wilds of the rainforests, so Joe told her in depth about his career with Survival International.

"That's incredible," said Kate when he had finished. "How did you get into all that, then?"

Joe's face clouded over for a moment. He shook his head. "Now that really is a rainy day story."

Kate sensed not to push it and was about to change the subject when Jacob, Bruce, Andy and Jermain arrived.

Remembering Linda's interest in Jacob, she pulled out a seat and patted it before addressing both Jacob and Joe.

"Linda and I were thinking about going out tonight and we wondered if you two would like to join us—dinner, drinks and dancing?"

Jacob was in agreement, and Joe agreed to dinner and drinks, but perhaps not dancing.

"Well, take it easy today. I'll contact Linda and we'll all meet here at 7 o'clock, okay?" Smiling brightly, pleased that she had been more on form in front of Joe than yesterday, Kate left the hotel, stopping briefly to greet Jermain, then hurrying over to *Rue d'Antibes* to peruse the fashion boutiques in preparation for that evening.

At 7 o'clock they met in the hotel bar, compliments were exchanged, a bottle of wine was quickly finished off and, half an hour later, the foursome headed out to the Rue Louis Perrissol and dined at Le Salon Independents. Immediately the food started to appear, course after course of tasty dishes. Vodka flowed freely and, before long, the four were chatting as though they had known each other all their lives.

Over dessert, Kate questioned Joe more about the land sale that had him so concerned, and the ways that it would affect the Pygmies.

"All they want is a bit of land. They don't want to build on it or pull the forest apart, just live there in peace." Joe shook his head. "But the Government has different ideas. Some of it has already been sold."

"Why can't you buy the land?" she asked him.

"Survival doesn't endorse that. Even if they did, they don't have that sort of money. Remember, they're a charity, they receive no government funding," he replied.

Kate understood his frustration. During her travels in Africa she had realised that the country was happy how it was, and it did not wish to be changed by Westerners. She had seen the Africans as they lived, how the women sang as they worked in the fields, their children alongside them and their babies on their backs, and the men who hunted for their families, feeling like men because they were keeping their wives and children alive.

But in the villages where the white man had been, the women were silent as they loaded up their labour-saving devices. Not having to work hard to achieve anything, they had no satisfaction at the end of the day. And if the food was already there, there was nothing for the men to do but sit and drink all day.

She explained this to Joe.

He nodded and threw her an admiring look. "That's exactly how it is."

"There's so much more peace there, if you go to the right places. Australia, too," she said.

He asked her about her time in Australia and she was happy to share the year of her life where she had really found peace. Peace that had eventually led to her return home.

She had started her journey in a dusty town near the Nullabor Plain. There she did not have to search for Aborigines as she had planned, they were out in force. But they were not the Aborigines she had wanted to see. They were the new generation, the generation that could not live in the wilderness and were not yet town folk. They had become lazy, not quite belonging anywhere, sitting in the Laundromats drinking the days away. She hated to see this, so deeper she had gone, heading toward Adelaide, further north, further into the wilderness. And there she had found them, brown faces, winding their way across the plains, making a journey for no other reason than they felt the need to. Kate was familiar with The Songlines, the Aborigines special religion, and wanted to hear the story of how the people came to walk their own Songlines of hundreds of generations. And so, with them she walked, her hair bleached blonde in the sun, muscles defining with each further mile. Sometimes she would walk alone and pick up a trail left by another, sometimes they walked in groups, right through the night. The Aborigines taught her to glean honey from the bees, which fruit to eat, which was good for medicine, and how to relax and enjoy their country. She grew to understand their language, and when they would sit quietly, a peace grew in Kate that she never had thought possible.

"Now I'm here, and it feels really good to know there's somewhere out there like that." She ended her story and Joe smiled at her tale.

The evening had been wonderful, and when they were ready to go home Kate suggested they all go out again the following evening for a meal.

Joe was in agreement and, whilst Linda and Jacob walked ahead, Joe hung back.

"Are you busy tomorrow? During the day I mean."

"No, not really, why?" she replied.

"Well, it would be good to get out of the hotel, see a bit of the area before I leave." His eyes shone brightly and her heart leapt at the chance to spend more time with him.

"I'd like that. We can go out straight after breakfast if you like?"

"It's a date." He slung his arm casually over her shoulder and together they walked back to the hotel.

High on the events of the evening, and less cautious than usual, neither of them noticed the figure of John Campbell lurking in the shadows by the marina. Even more unaware were they that he had shadowed the foursome all evening.

When they parted company in the reception of the hotel, he with a chaste kiss to her cheek, Kate had no time to replay the memory as Linda hauled her into the bar.

"What a great evening! Did you have as much fun as me? I can't wait until tomorrow, I'm just so gutted I have to go back home eventually," Linda rattled off. "Drink?"

"No, thanks. Joe and I are spending the day together tomorrow and I want to look fabulous, so no alcohol for me." Impulsively she leaned over and planted a kiss on Linda's cheek. "Night, hun, see you tomorrow."

On the way to the door a thought struck her and she stopped and turned around. "Why are you not back at the Riviera hotel?" Even as she asked the question, she realised why Linda was in such a heightened state of excitement. "You're staying here, with Jacob?"

Linda's face said it all. Laughing, Kate took the wine glass from Linda's hand and pushed her up the stairs.

"See you in the morning." She smiled.

"This wasn't supposed to be a holiday for me, you know," Joe stated as they strolled down the Quai Saint-Pierre onto the Jean Hibert Boulevard the following morning. "I thought I'd be laid up in a crummy old hotel room with just Bruce as a visitor."

Kate smiled at him and, taking it as a sign, he grasped her hand.

They walked for a while in comfortable silence, until they turned off the main road, onto the soft sand and down to the waterfront.

At that hour of the morning the alfresco dining areas lining the beachfront were deserted, but when they reached the last one before the Boulevard du Midi, they saw in the far corner a single table set with a crisp white tablecloth, upon which was an ice bucket with champagne and fresh strawberries, thoughtfully placed under netting.

Joe noticed that Kate looked stunned. He hoped he hadn't overdone it. He wasn't usually one for hearts and flowers. Maybe it had something to do with the romantic setting he had found himself, after spending so long with so many stresses and struggles in Africa. *Or, maybe,* he told himself, *it was simply the way she makes me feel.*

"I don't know what to say," she squeezed his hand. "I'm not sure if I've had champagne at this time of the morning before!"

He decided to play it down a little. "I'll tell you a secret, it's as much for my benefit. I don't get much luxury out in the wilds."

She laughed, and together they sipped at the champagne and relaxed in a companionable silence as the beach gradually came to life when the surfers, shoppers, joggers and dog walkers came out.

After a long breakfast, they walked back the way they had come over to the Quai Laubeuf and watched the ships coming in and out of the harbour. There they talked for hours, taking a break occasionally to run to the shop for iced cokes, resuming position, bit by bit finding out pieces about each other's lives.

She told him more about her travels, but avoided talk of, or questions about, her parents. She started her story where it suited her, from the time in Africa and Australia and how she had come to be in Cannes. Joe answered her questions about his line of work, but she noticed that when she tried to find out how he had got into his kind of lifestyle he uneasily evaded her questions.

Not feeling she had the right to challenge him over things he obviously didn't want to talk about, she changed the subject.

"Actually, we should get going if we're still going to dinner tonight."

"Oh, okay." He helped her up from the quay wall and kept hold of her hand as they walked leisurely back to the hotel.

As Kate reached the Penthouse suite, she collapsed on the bed and looked up at the ceiling. It had been a perfect day, utterly perfect in every way. So why did she feel so desolate? It was a question she knew the answer to. No matter how much fun they had together, eventually, be it hours, days or a week, Joe had to leave. She heaved a sigh. *It's like a holiday that goes too fast*, she thought, *but, there's still tonight.*

Summoning a smile, she rolled off the bed and threw open the wardrobe doors, energy refreshed, eager to look her best.

In his hotel room, John Campbell became steadily drunk. He had called Kate at the hotel to invite her to dinner. He had a fascination with her. He wasn't sure if it was the fact she had turned him down twice, or simply that she was a stunning lady. Whatever it was, John Campbell was not a man used to being given the brush-off and he did not appreciate it. Now it had happened a third time, as he had been told she was already out for the evening. To make matters worse, he had also called Janine Finch, an ex-girlfriend of his, and she had told him in no uncertain terms where to go. Feeling drunk and reckless, he pulled on his jacket and headed out to town by himself.

Later that night Joe, Kate, Linda and Jacob sat on the terrace of the Riviera Bar and traded stories. Jacob had finished his tale of growing up in New York, and the problems and privileges of being raised in such a prominent family.

"I'm thinking of following you back to Africa," said Linda. "God, can you imagine the stunning photos I could take there! I could do a feature on your charity." She was thinking out loud but Joe high-fived her.

"Anything that highlights Survival, I'd be up for."

"Don't you ever take time off?" laughed Kate.

"I'm serious, I've had more fun and stimulation with you guys these last few days than during my entire life in London."

As they resumed their chatter, a shadow fell over their table and they looked up to see a tall, dark-haired man standing over them, clutching a bottle of tequila in his clenched fist.

Kate was startled. She recognised him, how could she not? He seemed to be everywhere she was these days, but again she couldn't remember his name.

"I see you've forgotten me already," he growled, his bloodshot eyes moving away from Kate and coming to rest on Joe.

"John!" Her brain dredged his name up from somewhere. Relief poured over her. "John Campbell, this is Joe Palmer, Jacob—"

"Fuck off, bitch," interrupted John. He took a swig from the bottle.

Whilst the four looked at him in shocked silence, John leaned in suddenly over Kate, and grabbed the front of her shirt. As Joe moved in to help, Kate acted upon instinct and, pulling back her fist, she hit John hard in the stomach. He doubled over.

Jacob and Joe exchanged glances, a wary look synonymous to the male species that clearly read, *we're going to have to deal with this in the good old-fashioned way.*

Together they rose, one on each side, and steered John Campbell outside. He didn't go quietly, but both men were strong and, eventually, Linda and Kate could no longer hear his shouts.

"What was that about?" Kate was more angry than upset. She slammed her fist down on the table. "How dare he? I knocked him back. I was polite. I should have told him to go fuck himself," she snarled.

Linda's eyes widened. Since she had met Kate she had witnessed only the sweet side of her, this was almost scary. Still, she reasoned, she would no doubt feel the same if someone she barely knew had spoken to her in that manner.

Linda, ever mindful of the fact that Kate was the new face of the newest hotel and casino in Cannes, suggested they leave, after noticing the stares of the other patrons. They met Joe and Jacob coming back up the street.

"He's gone. Who the hell *was* that?" asked Joe.

"He was investing in the hotel. He came on to me, twice. I knocked him back, twice," replied Kate, her cheeks pink, whether with embarrassment or anger, Linda wasn't sure.

"He's a major player, not used to being turned down," said Linda, looking down the street in the direction he had gone. "Maybe Jacob and I should go back, make sure he's not hanging around the hotel."

And so they separated, Linda and Jacob hurrying in one direction, Joe and Kate, determined to continue with their date, taking a more leisurely long way back to Cannes Central.

"I'm sorry, Joe, I'm not normally this much trouble to take out," said Kate guiltily.

"Well, it's not your fault, is it?" he replied, and pulled her down to sit on the sea wall.

He put his arm around her, the tips of his fingers brushing lightly against the lace outline of her bra that peeped through her low cut shirt.

Her heart leapt. She was sure he would feel it drumming under his fingers. Standing up, she pulled him off the sea wall onto the beach below. It was urgent now, for her at least, knowing that with each minute that passed, the future rushed towards them to take him away. Thoughts of how to behave flew out of her head. She wanted him to know just how much she wanted him, liked him, *needed* him. They crouched like animals where they landed in the soft sand, staring warily, drinking in the sight of each other. Joe moved first. With fingers like lightening he undid her shirt. She shrugged it off and moved towards him, lifting his T-shirt, and pulling it over his head. That one fluid motion was the starting signal, the mutual consent that had been exchanged. His strong arms swallowed her up as he enveloped her, and lowered her down onto the sand.

Living such a carefree life, and being raised the way she had, Kate had never been sexually shy. But, as she lay on the sand, still warm from the blazing sunshine, she felt like she was on the brink with Joe, on the edge of something that could be special. She ached at the thought of him leaving and, propping herself up on one arm, she turned to face him.

"When do you have to leave?"

A cloud came over his face and he shrugged. "Soon, a week maybe, perhaps two if I can get some holiday leave from work."

Two weeks! Kate smiled and settled back down into his arms. Two weeks was a long time, not as good as forever but better than him leaving within days.

"Are we going to sleep here tonight?" he asked.

She laughed and helped him to his feet. Secret looks exchanged as they brushed sand off each other, and hunted around for discarded garments.

Climbing back up on to the road, she grabbed his arm and he turned to face her.

"Promise me two weeks," she demanded.

He wrapped his arms around her. "I'll try my best," he replied.

Linda and Jacob had filled in the others on the behaviour of John Campbell, so when they arrived back at Cannes Central, Jermain questioned Kate about the incident as they stopped by the bar.

"It was strange. He *was* really drunk but, still, I don't know if he would be a good investor." She planted a kiss on

Jermain's cheek. "But this is your hotel, you do what you see fit."

Jermain shook his head fiercely. "We don't want him, or anyone like him, having any links to this place. We've got enough people without him." He gestured to the empty seats between Andy and Bruce. "Join us for a round of cards?"

Kate and Joe exchanged a look, one that Jermain didn't miss.

"I think we're going to…" She trailed off and cleared her throat. "Good night all."

Jermain sat back in his chair and watched Kate and Joe make their way up the stairs hand in hand.

The boy was good for now. He liked Joe a lot, but he knew he would have to leave sooner or later, and he hoped Kate realised that too.

Across town, preparations were going on for the biggest party Cannes had seen in a long time. Janine Finch, Marie DuPont and twins, Ester and Sienna Martinez, were going through the guest lists and discussing themes and decorations. In usual circumstances, preparing a party for four girls would be hard enough, but for four young ladies of Cannes celebrity royalty status it was almost impossible.

The girls had lived their whole lives in the hilly region of Cannes, in a cul-de-sac that was home to their villas. The Villas in the Hills were a well-known secret, far enough away from the seafront to provide a little privacy, but in a residential area equivalent to Park Avenue. Now the street was to see the biggest party, certainly in its history, and all the important people in Cannes and its surrounding areas were attending.

The sprawling gardens of the houses were adjoining, and in each of the gardens a huge six-foot square portrait of the girls as babies was erected.

The girls had known each other their whole lives, and were best friends as well as neighbours. It was coincidental that their special birthdays were all within days of each other and it made sense to them and their publicity-mad parents to share a party.

Janine Finch was secretly hoping that John Campbell would come to her party. Her plan, when they had been dating, had been to scare John into a marriage proposal by threatening to leave him. John, however, didn't take kindly to threats and her plan had backfired. She had been furiously plotting to get him back ever since. Of course, Marie, Ester and Sienna were not aware of this, as Janine was sure that Ester had designs on him herself.

The previous night, when the girls had been round, she had been in the bathroom when her phone had rung. She had heard Ester answer it, telling the caller to leave her alone. Knowing it had been John, she had been furious that Ester had masqueraded as her. But of course, she couldn't show the girls she wanted him back. That would be weak and, although they were her best friends, in a society such as the one they were raised in, there was a certain amount of rivalry.

Her widowed father, Colonel Roberto Finch, now the Governor of the state, had raised Janine in the strict old-fashioned way, the only way he knew. Her routine had been as regular as clockwork—up at six each morning, even on weekends, no shouting, no running, no playing in an inappropriate manner. Now, on the brink of adulthood she knew this was not normal, but she thanked him for her upbringing. Never had she cried in front of him, or shown her emotions and, in Janine's mind, this made her stronger than the other three girls put together. Deep down, she knew in her heart that her demeanour pushed a lot of people away, John included. Although a lot of men pretended they liked the challenge of an ice maiden, she knew all they wanted was a real woman, soft-centred and there at their beck and call.

But Janine had also had confidence instilled in her from an early age. As far as she was aware there was nothing she couldn't do, and nobody she couldn't have. Again, that included John. And on the night of her party she was going to get him back.

"Do you think John will come?" asked Marie, tossing her perfect blonde hair over her shoulder and fixing her gaze on Janine.

Janine shrugged. "Who cares?"

John Campbell was not feeling his usual suave self as he crouched behind the garden wall of his hotel, projectile vomiting into the bushes and trying to save his Gautier suit from the tequila flavoured regurgitation. When there were only dry heaves left he wiped his face, wincing as he felt the bruise on his upper arms from being manhandled away from Kate Bryant.

John's fury rose again like bile and he spat on the ground. He would get them back! Nobody made John Campbell look a fool and got away with it. And while he was on a revenge course he would fix that conniving bitch, Janine Finch, as well.

Feeling slightly better, he made his way back to his room.

The sun was just beginning to show over the horizon, but Kate had been up for hours. Sneaking away from the bed where Joe peacefully slept, she sat at the computer in reception, a mug of cold black coffee next to her, and an ashtray filled to overflowing. Smoking was usually reserved only for when she was troubled or feeling down, but in the last few hours she had smoked through nervousness. She couldn't help but wonder if Joe would get his leave, but even if he did, he would leave eventually.

Reaching to switch off the computer, her hand hovered at the button and she changed her mind. Logging back onto the net she typed "Survival International" in the search engine and immediately printed off all the information that came up.

Lighting up another cigarette, she started to read. That was how Linda found her two hours later as she came down to the lobby with Jacob.

"Hey!" Linda wandered over as Jacob called out a greeting and went into the kitchen. "When did you get back?"

Kate looked up from her papers.

"Hi, Linda, last night." Seeing the look on her friend's face, she smiled. "He's still sleeping."

"You mean you've left that lovely man in bed alone?" Linda moved the computer screen towards her. "In favour of work, as well."

"Not work, I'm just checking out what he does, it's real interesting,"

Linda smiled. "So what's really up?"

Kate sat back down at the computer.

"I know it's crazy. We only just met, I don't know that much about him, but I feel like I know everything," she paused to light another cigarette. "I wish in a way I'd never even met him because I know that every man I meet in the future I'll be comparing to Joe and in a couple of weeks he has to leave."

"Well, come on, don't talk like it's already over. He's still in your bed, for Christ's sake. Come on, let's eat, it'll make you feel better."

As, one by one, the hotel occupants made their way into the restaurant, Kate helped Jacob serve up his famous New York breakfast.

"My father was stupid to get you as a partner. You should have been head chef," she laughed.

"We New Yorkers can cook, kid, don't you forget it," he replied, and together they carried out the last of the feast.

Kate saw Joe on the telephone in reception. He raised a hand in greeting. She smiled back, ridiculously happy to see him, wondering if he was on the phone to his office, and hoping he had managed to get a little more holiday leave.

She saved him a seat and listened to the chatter around the table. *This is a happy place*, she thought. It was a miracle everything had come together so soon—her relationship with her father, new beginnings with Joe, new friendships with Linda and Jacob and wonderful grandfatherly figures in Andy and Bruce.

"Hey." Joe slipped into the seat next to her and poured himself a coffee. "I spoke to work on the phone about getting some holiday."

Kate's face lit up in excitement and she clutched his hand. "What did they say?"

He sighed and shook his head. "I couldn't get two weeks."

She crumpled in her chair, aghast to feel tears threatening.

"Really?" she said softly and looked down at the table.

"Really." He took her chin in his hand and forced her to look at him. "I didn't get two weeks—I did get a month, though."

She gasped and threw her arms around his neck, causing the rest of the table to break off their talk and stare at them.

"A whole month," she whispered in his ear. "I'm so happy."

Chapter Six

The Calm before the Storm

The next month raced by. For everyone at Cannes Central it was a month of perfection.

The preparations for getting the hotel off the ground were running smoothly. The three owners had not rushed things. Instead they had taken their time, all having enough financial stability not to have to get the hotel opened in a hurry. Their laid-back attitude, instead of causing unrest among the locals, had built a steadily growing frenzy of excitement in the vicinity. Staff had been hired, the opening night was planned for the first week in May which was a strategic move by the owners, seeing as the Cannes Film Festival ran from the sixteenth of May for twelve days, and then for a couple of weeks after the Grand Prix. The hotel had started taking bookings in March and, within two weeks, it was fully booked for all of May and June.

Linda had no intentions of returning home to London just yet. Finally, she appeared to have found that one man who made her work not her sole priority, for once. She applied for, and received, a three-month visa, and decided to see what happened after the ninety days were up. In the meantime she was working in the reception at the hotel, and staying with Jacob in his room. For one always so organised and work orientated, she had thrown caution to the wind, and was taking each day at a time, knowing that the safety net of London was always only a few hours away.

The only one of the original group missing was Bruce Levinstein. After having the best time of his life, he had received a call from his wife back in England. Knowing the medical convention had finished, she had wanted to know why he was still in France. Bruce, feeling chastised, had returned home reluctantly, with an invitation from Jermain to return anytime he liked.

Kate and Joe were in their own world. For the first three

weeks they spent every day together. They hired a classic 107 foot Schooner and she taught him to sail around the Riviera and, by the end of that first week, he was taking it from Cannes, through Juan Les Pins up to Cap Martin and back. In return, he taught her how to surf, starting in the relatively calm waters of Beauvallon and then taking five days to visit Lacanau near Bordeaux, where they rode the high waves during the day and spent the early evenings wandering around the local vineyards, before spending cosy evenings in the villa they had rented.

Sometimes they spent time with Jacob and Linda, occasionally with Jermain, but never apart.

Three weeks had passed and on the Monday of the fourth week Kate awoke with a heavy feeling in her heart. It had been growing steadily over the last month, knowing that with each new day it was closer to Joe having to go back to Africa. They had not spoken about it, except for one time. The day he had told her at breakfast that they had a month together, they had agreed to enjoy every second and not talk about what would come after.

Now, however, the end was looming and, as she made her way out to the balcony and lit a cigarette, she heard him stirring.

"Hey," he called from the bed. "What are you doing out there?"

"Just taking in the view," she replied, trying to swallow back the tears that threatened.

He came out onto the balcony, resplendent in jeans and a bare torso. He watched her smoke and, knowing her well by then, he raised his eyes.

"Feeling troubled?"

"Kind of," she replied and turned to face him.

The sight of her huge sorrowful eyes haunted him and he came to sit opposite her and gestured for her cigarette, from which he dragged deeply.

"Feeling troubled yourself?" she asked, amused.

"I guess time's going too fast, right?" he said, handing the cigarette back and staring out at the gardens of the hotel.

She shrugged and stubbed it out.

"You could come with me," he said.

It had not been the first time he had said that. Always before, he had mentioned it in a light-hearted way, although she knew he was serious.

A year before, when she had still been travelling, she would have jumped at the chance, but since then things had changed. She knew those ten years had been spent running from the demons of her childhood—the way her mother had died, the thoroughly depressing way she and Jermain had attempted to live afterwards. Now they had moved on and had found a new life, in a new place and, after his joy at having her return, she couldn't leave her father again so soon.

"You could stay," she retorted.

But they both knew this also wasn't a real possibility. Joe was a master at his work. His skill and training were in huge demand, and it wasn't only what he did for a living, it was who he was.

"Shit." He got up and leaned on the balcony. Eventually, she came up behind him, wrapping her arms around him, feeling his frustration and matching it with her own.

"No more of this," she said and kissed his bare shoulder. "There's another seven days for us."

He turned around and wrapped his arms around her. In silence, they stayed together like that for a long time.

The arrival of Bruce was a welcome distraction. Worn out and dishevelled, he appeared late morning in the same battered old car with a matching battered attaché case.

"I am in need of another holiday," he announced as everyone greeted him. "My wife and I, we're not getting on too well."

Linda and Kate fussed over him while the men herded him into the bar, and Jacob eagerly pulled out a deck of cards.

Bruce sat back in a chair and regarded them.

"This is more like it, and you—" He pointed a finger at Joe. "When do you leave?"

Joe, feeling Kate's eyes on him, sat down opposite Bruce.

"In a week, why?"

"I'm coming with you. My wife needs a break. I'm semi-retired and it's not suiting either of us." He patted his battered case. "I want to find out about natural remedies. I'm not ready to hang up my stethoscope yet. Is that all right with you?"

Joe smiled. Having Bruce along on his return to Africa could provide a diversion for him and the way he would no doubt feel being without Kate.

"It's fine, more than fine," he replied.

All too soon it was Joe's last day. Kate awoke with tears on her cheeks and turned over to find Joe already awake and watching her.

"I can come back. You can come and visit. It's not the end," he whispered.

They spent the day alone together, wandering around the port, watching the boats sail in and out of the harbour, and sitting on the wall above the site of their first magical encounter. They laughed about it, the sand, and their inability to wait for a more appropriate place to make love.

In the early evening Joe and Bruce bade farewell to everyone, and Kate drove them to the airport.

She hugged Bruce goodbye and he vanished discreetly through to Departures, leaving her with Joe.

"This is really shitty," she said, determined not to cry.

"Yeah." He took her hands and looked so deeply into her eyes it was as though he could see her soul.

"If you knew your land was safe, the place for the Pygmies had been bought and wouldn't be built on or developed ever, would it make you stay?"

She had never told him she had thought about buying it. She didn't want him to think she had used her wealth to make his problems in Africa go away so he would be free to stay with her. Now she was using the land sale in a way she had promised she wouldn't.

"If anyone buys it, then they will build on it and, even if not, there's always other land, other tribes, always problems," he replied.

She pulled him to her in a fierce hug and breathed in every part of him.

"Go," she said, knowing tears were close and not wanting that to be his final memory of her.

She pushed him, knowing nothing more could be said or done to make the parting any easier. He turned and walked quickly through to Departures, where Bruce met him and raised a hand in a goodbye gesture.

She waved to Bruce, the lump making her throat sore, watching them walk away.

Once they had disappeared from view, she collapsed onto a chair and put her head in her hands. The tears she had just about managed to control flowed freely until she felt a hand on her shoulder and looked up to see Linda standing in front of her.

"What are you doing here?" she choked out as Linda hugged her.

"We knew this would hurt, honey. I thought you could do with a friend," Linda replied. "Come on, Jacob's outside with the car. He'll take your car home and you can come with me."

As they walked to the car, she handed her keys over to Jacob, realising it did hurt, so much more than she had feared, and he really had left. As Linda helped her in, she took her hand and squeezed it, knowing that, although she'd lost Joe, she had a very good friend who was there to stay.

Chapter Seven

The Storm

Joe and Bruce arrived back in Africa, both feeling very different emotions. Joe was tired and depressed, Bruce revitalised and buoyant, eager for adventure.

Once they arrived in Zaire, the following day, Joe realised that having the doctor around was turning out to be good therapy, as well as good fun. After Joe had told him a brief history of the Pygmies, Bruce was anxious to get as much information about their natural plant medicines as he could.

Even though they had been away a month, nothing had changed on Joe's return to the camp. The Pygmies welcomed him back, and did not ask where he had been. They had accepted him, and accepted that he had needed to make a journey. He introduced Bruce, and watched as the doctor solemnly shook hands with the tribe.

Later that evening, as they sat once again around a campfire, Joe told Bruce of his plans to visit Chi, to see if he could find out anything further of the land sale. He wondered if Jack and Suzie, his taxi into Bukavu, which seemed so long ago, had managed to buy the land.

Bruce, looking decidedly uncomfortable sitting on the ground, said he would go with Joe to the village. He grumbled on the way that it was no wonder Joe's back was buggered, if he sat on the cold ground all day and night.

"Good job you're here then, Doc," said Joe grimly as they started their walk.

Chi was easy to find, still perched in his hut, lounging on his floor with his enormous bong at hand, as always.

"Joe, my good friend!" he exclaimed. "And you brought a guest."

"Hey, Chi, good to see you, buddy," said Joe, trying not to laugh at the look of horror on Bruce's face. "Relax," he whispered to Bruce.

"The land sale, you heard anymore yet?" asked Chi as he

poured a generous amount of palm wine for his guests.

"No, that's why we came, to see if you'd heard anything else," replied Joe.

"No, it may have been sold, people have been talking. I do not know more than that."

"Well, we can't do anything tonight. Tomorrow I'll see what I can find out," replied Joe as, ruefully, he downed his palm wine and took a hit from the bong.

They awoke the next morning, still in Chi's hut. Joe looked around for Bruce. From his foggy recollections, he remembered a lot of wine and a lot of pot but not much else.

He heard a noise from outside the hut, and stumbled outside to find Bruce drinking from the trough that stood in the square.

"Hey, Bruce," Joe said. "How are you feeling?"

Bruce waved him away. Joe grinned. The poor doctor hadn't known what he was letting himself in for when he proposed to join him.

Chi was nowhere to be found, so Joe settled down in the shade of a tree to wait for Bruce to liven himself up. As he sat there, he remembered Chi telling them the land might have been sold. He groaned at the prospect of another trip to Bukavu to call head office. Although the trip was a nightmare, it had to be done, and the sooner he could find out, the sooner he could start a plan of action.

Standing up, he called out to Bruce and told him to get a move on.

"What's the hurry?" asked Bruce as he staggered over, obviously hung over.

"We need to go to Bukavu today, we need to call Survival and find out more about this land. If somebody is going to roll in here with bulldozers then we have to be aware," said Joe. "I've been away too long, I've neglected my work."

"Why?" asked Bruce wearily. "If the sale has gone through, then they've won."

Joe looked at him in amazement. "Bruce, this is only the beginning. There'll be protests, fighting, and we have to be prepared."

Joe disappeared into the forest. He heard Bruce muttering, "Jesus Christ," as he followed.

Back in Cannes, Kate made her way back to the hotel after collecting the papers officially naming her as the owner of the Zaire land from the bank in Nice where they had been waiting for weeks. It was official. She was now the proud owner of roughly five hundred square miles of rainforest in Zaire. Not for long, though. When she got back to the hotel, her first job was to courier the paper to London to the head office of Survival International. She had been speaking with Steve Chapman in London for the past couple of days, and although he was aware of whom she was and what she had done for them, he had no idea of the real reason why.

Well, when Joe got wind of it they would all know, and she didn't care who knew. She was in a position to help someone she cared for, and she had done it. Her fears that her actions may ruin their relationship no longer mattered. It was already ruined.

Linda was waiting in the lobby when she got back, Jacob was hanging around as usual, and Kate felt the usual pang when she saw them together.

Since the day she had said goodbye to Joe, she had embraced the tough exterior she had possessed during her troubled teenage years. She knew it, Jermain knew and everyone else who had been around her recently, although nobody mentioned it. It seemed to be her survival instinct, to fold in on herself when she was let down.

She forced a smile and told Linda she would be five minutes. Even though she didn't feel in the mood for a party, she had promised her friend she would go along with her for the photo shoot on the birthday party up in the hills. Since her business was now finalised, and there was nothing for her to do at the hotel, she couldn't really back out. She supposed she welcomed the distraction, anyway.

Upstairs in her room, she pulled a brush through her hair and slipped a black T-shirt on with her black jeans. She didn't feel like dressing up and, with four princesses on the loose, she supposed nobody would be looking at her.

Picking up her bag, she went downstairs to meet Linda.

When they left the hotel, Kate complaining that they were miles too early for the party, it was already dark. After a fifteen minute drive around the coastal road, Linda made her way up the cul-de-sac and parked outside the houses.

Kate got out of the car and looked around.

"Not much action yet, is there? I'm gonna find the party."

By the time Linda had got her camera equipment out of the boot, Kate had disappeared.

The whole street was in darkness. Linda was sure that it wasn't a surprise party. Everyone had been talking about it for weeks.

Slinging her camera bag over her shoulder, she made her way up to one of the houses. As she walked, she raised her camera and began taking random shots of the beautiful houses. Some of her best work came from those sorts of photos, and she especially liked the ones of celebrities when they were not posing. Natural photographs were Linda's forte, and those would come out great. As she snapped away she realised she had missed it, and thought about trying to get some freelance work while she stayed here.

The houses appeared totally empty, so she went around the back with the intention of getting a close-up of the portraits of the girls that she could see in the gardens. If she angled her camera correctly she could get a shot of each photograph. She found herself on the rear patio. Something seemed very wrong. A horrid feeling came over her.

One of the portraits had been slashed, and a red liquid that looked like blood was running down the edge of the frame.

She lowered her camera and looked around. The street should be alive with festivities, but the darkness and the still of the night had her badly spooked. Then she heard a shriek from one of the neighbouring houses, making her jump. All at once she felt vulnerable and very scared.

Feeling as though she was being watched, she turned and sprinted into the house, through the open patio, through the lounge and bolted for the open front door. Racing toward the car, calling for Kate, she heard a sound behind her and, like Lot's wife, she knew it would be bad news if she turned around. She jumped in the car, leaning over to lock the passenger door. Almost shrieking in her terror, she quickly scanned the back seat to make sure nobody was lurking there. She reversed down the narrow road and spun the car around, letting out a scream when she saw a man standing in the road, watching her. Stepping on the pedals with feet that felt like they were encased in roller skates, she stalled the car. Not de-clutching, or even going into neutral, she restarted it and raced down the hill until she reached the coastal road.

When she reached a point where she could get off the road, she stopped and fumbled for her mobile phone.

She misdialled a couple of times before Kate's phone began to ring. It rang for a long time, Kate wasn't going to answer. As her breathing returned to normal, she sat back in the driver's seat and wondered what the hell had just happened. She had panicked completely, which was most unlike her. But she had been spooked, badly, by the feeling she had experienced, just by being in the house.

Once her heart had settled back to its normal pace, she started the car and, feeling a bit foolish, she turned it round and headed back the way she had come.

Linda pulled up minutes later. Flashing blue lights and the road being cordoned off, made her blood run cold. Her first thought was of Kate. She jumped out of the car and ran to the nearest policeman.

"What's happened?" she asked, her voice high with fear.

He held her back and said she could go no further.

Knowing she wouldn't get any more out of him, she peered into the road, shouting out as she saw Kate being taken out of the house.

Kate glanced in her direction. As Kate passed within range of the headlights of the police car, Linda could see that her face was smeared with blood and tears. But whose blood was it? Kate didn't look injured, that was for sure.

A crowd of police gathered. Linda knew that, sooner or later, they would want to speak to her. She saw the man who had watched her drive away earlier glance in her direction, and approach one of them. She melted away into the gathering crowd, and made her back to her car, trying not to attract too much attention.

Driving well over the speed limit back along the coastal road, her head spun. Why had they taken Kate? And what had she seen in that house that had shaken her so?

She ran into the lobby shouting for Jermain. He came out of the kitchen, and stopped short at the sight of her.

"Jesus, Linda, what's wrong?"

"It's Kate, the police have taken her away. We got to the party and there was nobody there, and when I went back, the police were everywhere and they were taking her into a police car."

He put his arm round her and led her to a chair.

"Calm down. Tell me everything, slowly," he commanded.

Linda told him everything she knew.

Jermain stood up, a grim look on his face. Taking Linda's keys from her, he told her to wait by the car while he roused Andy and Jacob.

Five minutes later they were on their way to the police station in Cannes centre.

The policewoman stared at Kate. She stared back. The tape was switched on, the time and date recorded, and the policewoman reminded her of her rights before asking her to start at the beginning.

Kate began her story in a wavering voice.

"I went into the house. I tried the light switch but it didn't work so I went into a room on the right. I called out but nobody was there. Then I saw a girl, she was on the floor and I went over. I said something to her, I asked if she was all right, I think, and she didn't answer." Kate felt bile rise in her throat as she recalled the image. "I shook her, and my hand was wet when I touched her."

"Where did you touch her? What part of her body?" snapped the policewoman.

Kate stared dumbly at her for a moment before resuming her story.

"Her shoulder, and her hair was down her back and it was wet and I looked around. I could see a poker, it was wet as well. I called for my friend and then everything seemed to happen at once." Kate felt dazed now, incredulous that she had got out of the situation with her own life intact.

"What happened 'all at once'?"

"My phone rang, it made me jump and then something, *someone* was there, someone ran past me and I picked up the poker but I couldn't see whoever it was. I thought they were still there so I ran."

She hadn't got very far until her legs gave way and she crumpled to the floor, still clutching the poker and curling herself into a ball. That much she remembered. She didn't know how long she stayed like that, curled in a ball with her eyes closed until the police came and lifted her up like a rag doll.

The poker had dropped from her hand, and she vaguely remembered a police officer picking it up carefully and placing it in a plastic bag.

The policewoman still stared.

"Who was she?" asked Kate as a male colleague joined them.

"The lady in question was Janine Finch," he replied, sitting down and leaning in close. "We understand you have been seeing an ex-boyfriend of hers. Tell me, Ms Bryant, did you kill Janine in a jealous rage? Had you had a fight over Mr Campbell?"

What did they mean *seeing* her ex-boyfriend? "No!" Kate protested, although it sounded hollow to her ears. His statement whizzed around her head. They thought she had murdered the girl! They thought they had the killer already! And how did they know about John Campbell?

"What do you mean 'No'?" The man was in her face again. Kate struggled to stop her tears. "Do you mean you didn't kill her in a rage, or you didn't fight over John Campbell?"

"I didn't kill her, and I didn't fight with her," Kate moaned. "I never even met her and I certainly wasn't seeing *him*."

"We have your fingerprint, Ms Bryant. Your *blood-stained* print. And you were holding the murder weapon," said the policewoman. "You're not on the party list, and you're not exactly dressed for a party, are you?"

There was a long silence in the room. Kate felt her heart pounding.

Where was Jermain when she needed him, and what had happened to Linda? And Joe—thoughts of her lover ran through her mind. Her lip trembled.

She looked up and swallowed hard.

"Switch that tape off," she ordered in a voice that was steadier than she actually felt. "Get me a solicitor."

The policeman on reception told Jermain he couldn't see Kate at the moment, as she was being questioned.

"But what for?" he asked in frustration.

The policeman stared up at Jermain coldly. "Murder," he responded. Jermain staggered back to Andy, Jacob and Linda.

"Someone's been murdered," he said in hushed tones.

"Shit!" Linda swore and put her head in her hands. "I knew, as soon as I walked in that house, something bad had happened…" She trailed off, guilt hitting her at fleeing the scene.

As if sensing her thoughts, Andy looked at her sharply.

"Why did you drive away without Kate?"

"I'm so sorry, I panicked…" She closed her eyes, and tears crept from under her lids. "I'm sorry."

"It wasn't your fault. Nobody knows how they would react unless they were in that situation," Jermain said, throwing Andy a look. "We have to find out what's happened to Kate. She must have seen something."

"Linda said she had blood on her. Do you think she was hurt too?" asked Jacob anxiously.

"I've got a bad feeling," said Linda slowly. She pictured the police leading Kate to the car, the way they had roughly pushed her head down as she got in the back seat. She knew that they were not questioning Kate as only a witness.

Chapter Eight

Outside the room being used to question Kate, the two police officers talked rapidly in French.

"I want the other one in here, she's an accomplice and I want her questioned now," said Detective Dupree as he lit a cigarette.

Officer Marron nodded and headed for the reception area.

She was surprised to see Linda already there. She marched up to her.

"Linda Striker?" she asked. Linda looked up. "We need to ask you some questions, if you'll follow me."

Linda paled and looked at Jacob.

"Wait, what about a solicitor—?" he started, but Officer Marron cut him off.

"Please come with me."

Linda stood up and turned to the others, who stood and watched helplessly as she was led away.

Officer Marron paused at the door and turned to address Jermain.

"Your daughter wishes for you to call her lawyer. Please advise him accordingly and leave his name at the front desk so we know when he arrives."

Andy took out his phone before she finished speaking and dialled the number of his solicitor in London. Jacob whispered to Jermain that he was heading over to the Finch mansion to see if he could find out any information. Jermain nodded his consent and concentrated on Andy's phone call.

Andy snatched a pen off the front desk and scribbled a number on his hand. He dialled again and looked at Jermain.

"He gave me the number of a good solicitor who lives in Nice. He won't come cheap but he'll be worth every penny."

Jermain heaved a sigh and sat back down. With Linda and Kate under arrest, Jacob off doing his detective bit, and Andy sorting the solicitors out, there was nothing left for him to do but sit and wait.

Bruce had pulled out all the stops and somehow found a trader willing to loan them his car for a small fee. The journey to Bukavu took no time at all and, as they arrived, Joe glanced ruefully at the embassy steps where he had met his fate the last time he had been there.

Bruce had gone into the embassy to find out if Joe could use the phone to call England. Now he came hurrying back and beckoned for Joe to follow him.

"You can use the phone. I paid for it already," said Bruce as they went through the embassy doors.

"Thanks, Bruce," said Joe. "I won't be too long."

As he dialled the number for the office in London, he thought about the fight that lay ahead. Never in a million years would he turn away from the Pygmies. He would change tactics and teach them to fight for themselves instead of fend for themselves. It would be tough. The Pygmies were not natural warriors, preferring a peaceful life to wars and fighting. But he knew the importance of their home to them, and if he got caught in the cross fire then let it be.

The voice of Steve Chapman came on the line, greeting him like a long-lost friend.

"Joe, my buddy, how are you doing out there?"

Joe, ever mindful that this was long distance, skipped the pleasantries and got straight to business. "Hi, Steve, we just got word that the land sale might have gone ahead. I need you to find out who bought it, and what my next move should be."

There was silence on the other end of the line. When Steve spoke, Joe could almost hear him grinning. "There's no sale. From what we can gather, the land rights have reverted back to the government, some technicality, red tape, you know how it is. So your guys are safe for the time being at least."

When Joe hung up he repeated the conversation to Bruce.

"So your land is safe, at least for the moment?" Bruce smiled and slapped Joe on the knee.

Joe nodded and leaned back in his chair.

Bruce chattered away, excited for Joe and the Pygmies of whom he had become very fond. Joe wasn't listening. Although in body he was in Africa, his heart was back in Cannes, with Kate.

Linda put her head in her hands and felt like tearing her hair out. The police had questioned her time and time again, the same questions over and over, hoping to trip her up. They had nothing on her though, and they knew it. At three in the morning they let her go. She looked anxiously around for Jacob and rushed to him when she saw him waiting in reception. He took her arm and almost dragged her to the car.

"Jesus, Linda, I thought they were never going to let you go," he muttered as he helped her into the passenger seat.

She tried to light a cigarette, but her shaking hands failed her.

"What about Kate?" she asked him as he held her hand steady and lit the cigarette for her.

He shook his head and remained silent.

"Jesus." Tears came to her eyes and she took a deep drag. "This is a nightmare."

"I know. And there's nothing we can do now, so I'm driving you back to the hotel."

Driving at high speed, he raced back to leave her with Andy and Jermain.

"You're not coming in?" Linda asked as he drew up at the hotel, keeping the engine running.

"I've got business." He kissed her quickly and, leaning across, opened the car door for her.

Feeling frightened, she nodded and ran up the driveway, where Jermain was waiting for her.

Jacob watched her go inside and revved the engine. He drove slowly to the main street and parked the car. Stepping out, he glanced around before jogging over to a black Fiat Punto parked in the long stay section of the road. He jammed a length of wire down the driver's window, and was in the car in less than thirty seconds. In another ten seconds he had ripped the ignition out and hot-wired the Fiat. Pulling on his seat belt, he headed towards the police station.

On his arrival, he parked the Fiat and circled the perimeter of the building. It was hardly Alcatraz. In Cannes nobody expected serial killers to be on the loose, thus the relatively crime-free town had no need for a high tech security-ridden police station. He waited until one of the officers came out and lit a cigarette. Creeping up behind him, he brought a hand down hard on the back of the officer's neck. The officer went down with a thud and Jacob moved him off to the side of the building.

Entering the station, he was relieved to see nobody on the reception desk. Taking out his .9mm, he held it ready and moved toward the door leading to the cells and the interview rooms. He looked through the glass, saw the two rows of cells, and moved back to the front desk. Leaning over it, he could see hooks holding numbered keys. He grabbed all five bunches, and went back to the door. By the power of elimination, he eventually unlocked the door and made his way in, closing the door softly behind him. He was in a corridor, about five cells on each side. At the end of the hall were two doors that he presumed led to the interview rooms. Keeping low, he moved silently down the hall until he found Kate. He looked into her cell, and saw her sitting on the edge of the bed, looking toward the window.

He rapped once on the bars of the cell with the keys. She jumped and turned around. Her eyes widened and, as she opened her mouth, he made silencing gestures to her. The key to her cell was the fourth one he tried. She came to the door and scooted out. He motioned for her to be quiet again, and pointed to the door he had come in. She understood and ran to it, peering out of the little glass section to keep watch.

Jacob unlocked all the other nine cell doors, seven of which were occupied. There was uproar. Drunks were stumbling out into the corridor, whooping and yelling with glee. Two young prostitutes tottered out into the hall, looking bewildered. Seeing a movement in one of the interview rooms, Jacob pulled his hood over his face and ran back up the hall to

Kate. As he ran past the two prostitutes, he shouted to them, "Can you let us get a head start?"

The girls, up for more action and a chance to get back at the police, nodded enthusiastically. Grabbing a few of the drunks by the hand, they blocked the hallway.

As Jacob grabbed Kate by the hand and pulled her out into the reception, he glanced back and saw Officer Marron trying to get past the crowd of prisoners in the hall.

"Hurry…the black Fiat," instructed Jacob. They sprinted to the car. It was unlocked. She got in the passenger side and sunk low down in the seat, as the crowd of people spilled out into the parking lot.

"Hang on, this could be the drive of your life," Jacob said through gritted teeth as he spun the wheels on the gravel and pulled out of the parking lot.

On the coastal road heading toward Nice, he remembered the gun tucked in his waistband. Steadying the wheel with one hand, he put the gun under the dash.

"Jesus!" Kate seemed to be in shock as she clung on. "I can't believe you just did that. I don't know you at all, do I?"

He favoured her with a penetrating stare. "Nobody really knows anyone, Kate."

She caught his message and frowned. "You think I did it?"

"That doesn't matter, but whether you did or didn't do it, I don't think you would have been found innocent. That's why we're getting you out of here." He turned off toward a private airstrip on the outskirts of Cannes.

"Where am I going?" She sounded like a little girl, and he reminded himself that she wasn't used to that sort of caper.

"To Joe and Bruce," he said. "I know roughly where they are. You'll be safe there."

"Do they know about this?"

"No, at least, not yet, and they probably won't find out. My guess is they don't read the newspapers where they are."

"If you thought I'd killed her, would you have still done this?" she asked.

"Yes," Jacob answered truthfully.

"But why? If you knew I was guilty, then surely you should leave me behind bars?"

"It's complicated, Kate. It's the way I was raised. You're not stupid. You know things are done differently where I come from. You look after your own, no matter what. Now listen, there's a plane taking you to Zaire. It's going to drop you in Cameroon, which is the only place we can get, without needing landing clearance. Here's a map, it's an Ordnance Survey, so you can't go wrong." Still driving, he hand her piles of paper. "It's a three day journey to Zaire on foot, or if you can get a lift you can make it in a day."

"What about my father?" she asked. "Does he know what's happening?"

"No. I thought it best not to tell anyone. That way he won't have to lie to the police," replied Jacob.

"They'll realise you were involved."

"I know." He pulled off the road and headed toward a small aeroplane parked in the shadows by a small runway.

"Will you tell him I love him? And I didn't do it, Jacob. You have to try and find out who did this. I'm innocent, I wouldn't kill anyone." Kate's voice rose as she realised it was nearly time to leave, and she had so much to tell him.

She was more frightened than ever, more so than when she had been arrested. A hundred questions ran through her head. How long was she going to be away? When would she see Jermain next? What happened if they caught her in Zaire?

Jacob stopped the car and his arms were round her. He tried his best to soothe her. Eventually, she quietened down and he asked if she was ready.

She nodded and vowed that, from this point on, she would do her best to be strong. She was heading into the unknown, which would have excited her before, but this time she was on the run, running from the police, and she was damned if they were ever going to catch up with her.

"Thanks, Jacob." She hugged him tight as she got out of the car. "Look after Linda and everyone else."

"I will. Come on, your lift's waiting," he said, taking her

arm and guiding her toward the plane.

"Who's he?" whispered Kate, spotting a man standing beside it.

"He's your pilot. He's fine, he's a friend."

As Kate stepped aboard, she threw one last glance at Jacob, and managed a small smile.

* * * *

The others were gathered in the restaurant. As Jacob took off his jacket, he heard the distant wail of sirens.

"Linda, upstairs," he ordered and held his hand out to her.

She rose and hurried over to him. He threw a glance at Jermain and Andy.

"We're going up to my room. I think the police are coming to speak to you. When they ask you, tell them that Linda and I have been here since I brought her back from the police station."

"What?" Jermain half rose out of his chair but Jacob shook his head.

"We've been here all the time. Right?" He made sure they understood and, satisfied, he pulled Linda up the stairs, taking his coat with him.

"What's happening now?" moaned Andy. "This is all beyond me. I mean, I came here to run a business."

"Shut up." Jermain held up his hand and strained his ears. He could hear sirens, heading in their direction.

In less than a minute, the police were swarming all over the hotel and casino. Jermain sought out Officer Marron and asked her what they were doing.

She favoured him with an icy stare and narrowed her eyes

"Your daughter has escaped, Mr Bryant. Earlier this evening, she was helped to flee the prison. You will need to be interviewed."

His heart leapt at this news, and his thoughts turned to Jacob. Was he the accomplice who had helped Kate escape?

"I know nothing of this," Jermain replied calmly as Andy sat beside him open-mouthed. "And you won't find her here."

Officer Marron didn't reply, instead she made her way up the stairs just as Jacob and Linda started down them. Jermain noticed that Jacob had changed into white running shorts and a black T-shirt. As Officer Marron passed them, she raked her eyes over Jacob. She let him pass, however, and continued along with her other officers to search the hotel.

The police left an hour later, Officer Marron promising to catch up with them all the following day, to speak with them individually. Her words were loaded, but Jermain nodded and thanked her as she left.

When the door closed behind her, he turned to Jacob and fired off a string of questions.

"Where is she? How did you get her out? Is she safe?"

Jacob held up his hand and motioned for them to go into the bar, where he poured everyone a drink.

"Kate's safe. I'm not going to tell you where she is, but she is in good hands."

Jermain exploded, "She's *my* daughter and I have a right to know where she is!"

"If you don't know, then you won't have to lie to the police when they question you tomorrow. It's logical, Jermain. You don't have to worry about her," Jacob said.

Andy looked relieved. He clearly didn't want to be involved in this. He enjoyed leading a simple life and all this business was not good for his heart.

Jermain nodded and downed his drink. He knew vaguely of Jacob's past and the way he worked. He would get nothing further out of him.

"Just tell me you're sure she's safe."

"Safe as houses," confirmed Jacob. "It's been a long day. We're going to bed."

Leaving Andy and Jermain downstairs, he took Linda's hand and went back to his room.

As she shut the door, Linda scanned the room to make sure it was empty. Paranoia had hit and she saw nothing strange about the odd police officer hiding to eavesdrop.

"Did you really help her?" she asked.

He nodded and started to undress.

"What happened? You have to tell me, Jacob," she begged and sat next to him on the bed.

"Nothing to tell, honey," he said. "Kate's safe. We just have to leave it like that."

"But where is she?" cried Linda.

He turned to her and took her face in his hands.

"Please, Linda, it's best if I don't tell you. The police would get it out of you, eventually, if you knew." He paused and smiled gently at her. "She did ask me to take care of you, though."

She was happy with that but, as she lay in the bed with Jacob sleeping beside her, she couldn't help but wonder where Kate was, and what she was doing.

As the occupants of Cannes Central prepared to turn in for the night, Kate flew over Sardinia, heading fast towards the continent of Africa. She inspected a bag that Jacob had provided, emptied the contents onto the floor of the plane, and rooted through them. A couple of jumpers, clothes suitable for where she was headed, a carton of two hundred cigarettes, a thermos of tea, and a hip flask filled with whiskey! She sent him a silent message of thanks, and sat back to wait.

The pilot had not spoken two words to her, but she was bored now and too wired to sleep, so she picked up the bag and made her way to the cockpit.

"Would you like a drink?" she asked him, feeling foolish at playing the hostess.

He grunted. She took it as a yes, poured him a tea and passed it over.

"I'd rather have some of that," he replied, eyeing the open bag and nodding towards the hip flask.

"Oh, okay," she replied. Taking back the tea, she passed him the whiskey.

"And one of those." He nodded at the cigarettes and, obligingly, she lit one for him.

"Do you do this a lot?" she asked curiously.

He turned to face her. "Only when Jacob calls me," he replied.

She nodded and sat back to study him. The way that he almost folded himself into the cockpit suggested that he was a tall man, probably over six foot, and must have weighed over two hundred pounds, although she could see it was all muscle. and his black, bald head gleamed like polished marble.

"What's your name?" she asked tentatively.

"You don't need to know my name." His voice was deep and gruff but he softened his words with a wink.

"I was just curious as to what to call you," she said defensively. "Are you not curious about me?"

He shook his head. "I know all I need to."

"Which is?" she asked, determined to get this silent ogre to have a conversation with her.

"That I have to take you to Cameroon, and then meet Jacob's brother to collect my money," he replied.

"Why Jacob's brother?" She took the hip flask from him and took a sip.

"Well, I know this ain't legal, and anyone who knows Jacob will be watching him, so if I turn up and he gives me ten grand, then that's going to look a bit suspicious, right?" he explained.

"Ten grand!" she squeaked. "I owe Jacob more than I thought."

"So you're with Jacob, huh?" He gave her the once over.

"No, he's just a friend." Ten thousand pounds flashed through her mind. She smiled to herself. "He's a very good friend indeed."

He nodded and turned his back. With nothing more to say, she made herself comfortable and tried to get some sleep.

* * * *

Bruce had kept the trader's car, finally managing to persuade him to sell it for the equivalent of three hundred pounds. Although a wreck—it stalled whenever it rained and the petrol cost more than the car was worth—Bruce needed wheels. Every day since his arrival, he had made the trip from their base in Zaire to Kinshasa, a relatively westernised town that gave him the fix of real life he needed to continue living in Africa. It wasn't ideal. Any newspapers were at least two days old by the time they got there, but at least Bruce could keep up with what was going on elsewhere in the world.

Joe complained to Bruce about his seeming obsession with the outside world.

"We come here to forget all that shit, Bruce. What the hell is so important that you have to drive two hours a day just to get a newspaper?"

"You have to remember, Joe, I'm not used to all this. I need to ease myself in gently," said Bruce as he set off for another trek. "Is there anything I can get you?"

Joe shook his head and waved goodbye, but as Bruce pulled away, he put his hand on the driver's side window. Bruce unwound it and stared, dumbfounded, as the window fell out and smashed on the ground.

"Well, will you look at that!" he muttered.

Joe laughed. "Can you get us some drink? Anything you can lay your hands on, as long as it's alcoholic."

Bruce nodded and, still swearing about his car that was now one window short, he started the drive to Kinshasa.

He drifted into a daydream as he drove. No matter how much he complained to Joe, he was growing to like it there. The simplicity of life was ideal. The Pygmies came in and out of their lives every day, greeting them, wanting to learn more skills from Joe, and thanking him time and time again for the land that was now theirs. Each time Bruce caught sight of the Pygmy Elders he would pounce on them, begging them to teach him more of the healing plants he planned to take back to England and teach their remedies to his colleagues. He supposed that he should leave soon. He had twice spoken to his wife, who was now under the impression he had left her for good. He would give it another couple of weeks, and then he supposed he would have to return.

On his arrival in Kinshasa he made his way directly to the

shop where he had become quite a well-known customer. He picked up his normal daily buy, a pot noodle, which was his only comfort from the shit that Joe served up. Bruce knew that no matter how long he lived in this place he would never get used to eating plants and boil-in-the-bag meals. Just in time, he remembered Joe's request for some alcohol, and picked up a litre bottle of some unknown brand of whiskey. Finally, he turned to the newspaper rack and scanned the headlines. They roared out at him, making him blink in case he was imagining it. When he opened his eyes they hadn't changed. He edged forward and picked up the previous Sunday's edition of *The News of the World* and read the headline.

Nightclub Owner Does Moonlight Flit From Jail.

He looked at the photo of Kate and recognised it from one Jermain had shown him, taken the night of the opening for investors. She was smiling, and looked quite stunning in her black dress and diamonds. He tucked the paper under his arm and picked up *The Times.*

Cannes Murderer Escapes.

"Murderer?" he scanned the story quickly, unable to believe what he was reading.

Kate was the sweetest girl he had ever met. How could she kill someone? *Who* had she killed? The stories were much the same—naming a Janine Finch as the victim of a brutal murder, for which Kate had been held. Then, in the early hours of Saturday morning, an unknown accomplice had broken Kate out of the prison, along with all the other prisoners that had been in residence that night. No trace of Kate had been seen since, but the getaway car had been discovered—a black Fiat Punto—which had been stolen from the long-term parking bay in the town centre.

Hurriedly Bruce paid for his goods, and started the drive back to Zaire.

* * * *

It was Tuesday, and Kate had been on the road since Saturday afternoon. Jacob's friend had dropped her off, as promised, in Cameroon and had gone over the Ordnance Survey maps, so she was sure of where she was going. She had not dared cadge a lift. A few wagons had passed her, but she was afraid to hail them for fear they would recognise her. She was in no doubt her face would have been in the press, and wasn't prepared to risk being noticed. So, alone on the road, she walked.

It all came back to her, her days and nights hiking in Australia, and the peaceful feeling she had long since forgotten. There was no thinking, no noticing the blisters or the heat of the sun, simply ambling along to the beat of her heart. She developed a pattern, mainly walking through the night until about lunchtime. Then she would eat what she could find. The knowledge came flooding back of what she could eat, and what would harm her, as she foraged around the forests, trying to identify the plants and mushrooms that didn't look very appetising, but that she knew would nourish her until she reached her destination. She would sleep until late afternoon in the shade of a tree or building before starting again.

That day she had been walking for over eighteen hours without stopping to sleep. She had slipped into some sort of trance, scuffing along, ignoring the pain in her feet, and the flies buzzing around her face. Now she felt the change. Instead of running away from Cannes, she was walking toward Joe. He was what she was there for, not because she could no longer live in her home. In some distant part of her mind she knew that was untrue, but it kept her going. Somewhere between crossing from the Savannah into tropical rainforest climates, she knew now she was near.

She realised, almost too late, she was bordering on dehydration, which can creep up quickly. The climate was not going to help her. Stopping in the shade of a tree, she took out the last of her water and smoothed it over her body, knowing it would take too long to rehydrate herself by drinking it. Studying the map through eyes that were nearly closed by bites, she saw she had fifteen miles to go. Fifteen miles on no water was going to be tough but, if she could sink back into her thoughts, and find that pain-free zone where her body moved of its own accord, she could do it.

She stood up and, thankful the sun was sinking, started walking to the east, towards water, towards safety, and towards Joe.

* * * *

When Bruce arrived back, he found Joe crouched over the campfire, building a frame in which to cook the two rabbits he had slain earlier. Bruce grimaced and thanked God for his pot noodle. He was unsure how to broach the subject of Kate, so didn't. Joe rarely mentioned her, and Bruce had made the mistake of thinking the lack of talk about her was because he was getting over her.

Putting the papers in his tent, he set about boiling water for his pot noodle.

"I had a good idea," said Joe. "I'm going to build a place here, somewhere we can sleep and stay dry."

"What a splendid idea," Bruce said. "Shame I won't be here to seek comfort in it."

"You're not leaving?"

"In a couple of weeks. My practice needs me." He gave a small chuckle. "It even seems like my wife needs me."

"You should bring her here. It would do her the world of good."

"Somehow, I can't quite see it," laughed Bruce. It wasn't until he lay his head down to go to sleep that he remembered Kate.

Kate stumbled upon their camp at sunrise. Never in her life had it taken her all night to walk a mere fifteen miles, but the last night had been the worst she had ever experienced. She had started to hallucinate. Mirages appeared before her, beautiful blue streams that she used all her energy running to, only to find they were not really there.

But she had arrived. She knew it must be them by the two tents nestled together. She spotted a full bottle of water lying beside one of the tents and pounced upon it, drinking so much so fast she almost vomited it back up again.

Joe heard the commotion outside his tent and reached for his rifle. The previous day it had been the rabbits rooting around, and he had managed to catch dinner. Maybe it was a larger animal today, something that could keep him in food for a few days. Sliding out of the tent he moved stealthily around the corner. Rifle poised, he squinted, aimed and pulled the safety catch off. He adjusted the vision to see… a girl!

He lowered the rifle and wondered if he were still dreaming. A dirty, bruised girl in torn clothing was drinking his water. He peered closer. She was white under the mud and bites that adorned her, and her dirty hair looked…blonde. She stiffened and, still kneeling on the ground, turned. Their eyes locked. Under the bruises and the bites and the swollen lips he still recognised her.

"Kate?" he whispered.

She stood up and swayed. He ran to her and held her steady. She tried to speak but all that came out was a squeak as she clung onto him.

"Christ," he muttered, as he sat her down and shouted for Bruce.

At first Bruce didn't appear to recognise her either. He ran and inspected her as she tried to sit up.

"She needs water, badly." He snatched the water bottle and poured some into a cup, motioning for Joe to do the same.

While she sipped eagerly, he poured the rest over her shivering body.

"Those plants, the ones for the midge bites, get some," he ordered Joe.

When Joe came back, Bruce had carried her into his tent. She was out cold.

Bruce took the plants and crushed the leaves in his fists to get the healing sap. He rubbed it onto the bites and covered her with his blanket.

"She needs to sleep," said Bruce. "Rest is all she needs now."

Joe pulled Bruce out of the tent and threw a glance back

at her.

"I can't believe she's here. Why is she in such a state?"

Bruce paused as if he was about to say something, but he just shrugged. "I don't know any more than you." He cast a look at Kate, who was sleeping soundly. "I guess we'll know everything when she wakes up."

It didn't look like that was going to happen anytime in the near future, so they set upon gathering food and water in preparation for when she awoke.

Chapter Nine

Cannes Central was doing badly. Every single investor had pulled out and hate mail had landed on the mat of the lobby every day since the murder. Jermain sat and read each piece in the deserted bar. The opening had been set for May, just a couple of weeks away but, bar some miracle, that was definitely off.

He was a lost man, his dreams shattered in the wake of the tragedy that had rocked Cannes. He didn't believe Kate had done this. But somebody had, and somebody had managed to get Kate in the frame as well. Now, on top of the hotel going down and the money lost, he had her to worry about. Jacob had refused to tell him where she was, just that she was safe. Linda swore she didn't know either, and Jermaine believed her.

Andy entered the room and patted him on the shoulder.

"How you feeling today?" he asked and sat down opposite.

Jermain raised his eyes to meet Andy's and shook his head. "It's finished, Andy. Before it even started. All that work, effort and money, all gone."

"Don't say that! We never needed the investors, that was just to attract people. We can still do this on our own."

Jermain laughed. It was a harsh and brittle sound. "But who will come here? And it's not just the casino. I need to know where Kate is. She can't hide forever, and running almost proves her guilt."

"She hid from you for years," commented Andy.

Jermain shrugged and stood up from his chair. Looking like a man twice his age, he shuffled out of the room.

* * * *

Kate awoke to the feel of cold water on her forehead. She opened her eyes and saw Joe sitting beside her, a concerned look on his face.

"Hey," she croaked and smiled, grimacing as the action made her lips crack.

"How are you?" he asked, and helped her as she tried to sit up.

"Okay. How long have I been asleep?"

"About eighteen hours. You were exhausted." He handed her a cup of water and she drank gratefully. "Do you feel up to telling us what happened, and how you got here?"

She nodded, and Joe called Bruce in.

As they settled down, Kate studied both men. Neither appeared aware of what had happened back in Cannes. Would they believe her? The evidence against her was damning, she knew that. She took a deep breath, and lied.

"I missed you too much, I wanted to see you. I misjudged the distance and shouldn't have walked from Cameroon, but I'm feeling much better now."

"You walked here from Cameroon?" Joe was shocked.

"It was okay at first. I did a lot of walking in Australia when I was with the Aborigines. I had good training." She smiled wistfully. "But then I finished my water, and just had juice from plant leaves the last night."

"I'm glad you're here. You're so stupid, risking your health and your life that way, but I'm really glad you're here." Joe pulled her to him and held her tight.

Discreetly, Bruce left the tent. It was apparent Kate didn't know he was aware of the real reason she had come to Africa. Should he tell Joe? Or mention to Kate he knew she had been branded a murderer?

He didn't know what to do for the best, so, taking his drink, he wandered off into the bush and left them alone.

Kate sat with Joe by the campfire, lost in her own thoughts, realising this hadn't been planned very well. Although they were solitary there, how long could she stay without telling him the truth?

"How long can you stay?" he asked as he got up and started to collect the firewood.

"I'll stay for a while, if that's okay?"

He dropped the firewood and took her hands, obviously ridiculously happy to see her.

"Stay forever," he said.

She laughed.

He hunted for the last of the tinned food, then looked up shocked when she took the wood and built a campfire.

"That's a good fire," he said as she stood back with a proud look and wiped her brow.

"But wait, you've not seen my best bush skill yet," she said and produced a bundle of brush and grass from behind her back and a couple of fat sticks. Then she crouched on the ground, and proceeded to light the fire using the sticks and tinder. He was mesmerised, and when it burst into flame he shook his head in wonder.

"I've never met anyone apart from me who could do that," he said. "Where did you learn?"

"Australia," she said and took the cans of food from him. "Let's eat."

And so they shared a dinner together, not quite the Ritz, but it was the happiest Kate had been since this state of affairs had begun. Joe had a calming effect on her and made her situation seem not quite as hopeless as she had thought. The fact that there was still a murderer on the loose in Cannes disturbed her, and was always at the back of her mind. As she munched on the beans, she decided to get in touch with Linda as soon as possible, and see if there had been any more developments back home.

"I feel bad that Bruce has disappeared. Where is he, anyway?" asked Kate as they cleared up after their meal.

"Probably getting drunk with Chi." Joe grinned at the thought of Bruce being let loose with the palm wine again. "He'll be happy enough."

Kate yawned and smiled regretfully at Joe. "Do you mind if I turn in? I'm shattered again."

As Kate got up to walk to the tent he caught hold of her hand.

"I'm really pleased you're here," he said.

"So, Joe," she said and tugged the front of his shirt playfully, suddenly not feeling so tired anymore. "Why don't you show me just how grateful you are?"

He returned her smile and allowed Kate to pull him into the tent.

The tent was cool and together they fell upon the floor, each anticipating the roller coaster ride that they had both missed since their separation.

When Bruce ambled back to camp in the early hours, he saw their shadows by the light of the oil lamp and, smiling to himself, he went quietly into his tent to sleep.

As he joined the couple around the breakfast campfire the next morning, the atmosphere was buoyant and positive. Joe still appeared oblivious as to Kate's real reason for being there, and Kate seemed happier than when she had arrived.

She asked Bruce if she could come along for the ride to Kinshasa and, eager to get her alone and question her, he readily agreed.

After breakfast, Joe waved them off. They climbed into the wreck of the car and started the journey to town.

As they drove along, Bruce couldn't think what to say about the killing and subsequent arrest, and Kate seemed so normal that he started to wonder if he had imagined it all.

"I'm going to call home, just to let them know I got here all right," she said, not looking Bruce in the eye and he watched her as she crossed the phone to the telephone booth.

As he watched her dial, he realised the hotel back in Cannes could well have a trace on the line, and he followed her to the phone box, unsure of what to do.

Linda sat at the reception desk, brooding about the events of the past few days. She had spoken to her Editor at *The Times* and had officially handed in her notice. Once all this mess was sorted out she was going freelance. For the moment she was staying with Jacob. He showed no signs of wanting her to return home, and she was more than happy to stay here and help out Kate's father and the doomed hotel. The telephone rang and she picked it up, expecting it to be one of her colleagues from the newspaper.

"Hello?"

There was a crackle and a beep, which she knew from experience was the trace setting the police had put on the line. Another pause, then a voice came over the wire that made Linda's heart leap.

"Linda, it's me."

She stood up, knocking a pile of papers onto the floor in her excitement.

"Kate! Where are you, no don't answer, but are you okay?" she asked frantically.

"Yes, please tell my dad I'm okay. I can't say where I am but I'm safe."

"God, Kate, its manic here, police everywhere." She lowered her voice. "I know you didn't do it, Kate, but the police won't listen to us."

"You have to help me, Linda. I'm innocent. Can Jacob help in any way? There must be some evidence they've missed." Kate's voice broke.

"The police are not even investigating it anymore," Linda said. "They think it was you and that's the end of it for them. You must be careful, Kate."

Back in Africa Kate sagged against the side of the phone box. She didn't notice Bruce getting increasingly agitated outside, until he opened the door and hissed at her.

"Hang up!"

She started but, before she could reply, he reached an arm in and cut off the phone connection as she stared at him in horror.

In Cannes, Linda hung up the phone and picked up the pile of papers she had knocked to the floor. She looked at them absentmindedly. They were the details of the land sale in Zaire. Thinking back over the phone call and the male voice that had spoken to Kate, she realised where her friend had fled to.

Kate cried, big tears that slid down her face, as Bruce led her out of the phone box and across the street.

"You know, don't you?" she sobbed as he sat her down on the dusty roadside. "Does Joe?"

"No, I didn't know whether to tell him. I didn't know what to do, so I did nothing," he replied.

"I didn't get to speak with my father," she wept. "And Linda said they're not even contemplating that anyone else killed that girl."

Bruce wrung his hands helplessly. "Are you going to tell Joe?"

"He might think I did it," she said, her tears slowly receding. "And I didn't. I swear to God I didn't."

"All right, come on now, let's get some supplies and get back to camp. It'll figure itself out." He took her hand and together they walked back to the car.

Linda was still pondering the telephone call when Jacob came in.

"Hey, you all right?" he asked as he came up to the reception desk.

"Kate called."

He put his finger to his lips. Pulling her around the reception desk, he motioned for her not to talk, and led her out into the hotel grounds.

When it was clear they were alone, he sat her down on the edge of the fountain.

"What did she say?" he asked. "Is she okay?"

"Yes, she said she's safe."

"And?"

"Nothing else. She could only speak for one minute. I think she knew about the trace on the line," said Linda.

"She shouldn't have called. They'll catch her," he muttered.

"She's with someone, isn't she?"

Jacob didn't reply.

Linda pressed further. "It's not your family. The man spoke with an English accent."

"He spoke to *you*?" Jacob asked, a concerned look coming over his face.

"No, to Kate. He told her it was time to hang up." She narrowed her eyes at him. "I knew the voice. It was Bruce, wasn't it?"

Clearly not seeing the point in hiding it any longer, he nodded.

"So she's in Africa with them?"

It felt like a huge weight had been lifted off Linda's shoulders as Jacob confirmed her suspicions. Joe and Bruce would take care of her, while they did their best to find the real killer. She outlined her conversation with Kate and told him he had to try to find the murderer.

"Linda, I've done all I can," he snapped. "You know that. There's no other evidence. The police are certain they had the right person." At the look on Linda's face, he threw up his hands in a gesture of despair. "What else can I do? Huh?"

Before she could reply, she noticed a man making his way up the drive.

"God, it's that John Campbell," she whispered as he approached. "What can he want?"

What John wanted was to find out was where the hell Kate Bryant had disappeared to as, without their prime suspect, he was being questioned by the police almost daily and he wanted them off his back.

Linda had been wrong when she thought that the police were not looking into the murder any longer, they were still checking out all the people that Janine Finch had contact with and, John knew, without Kate in the frame, he could well be at the top of the list.

Putting on his most charming smile, he greeted Jacob and Linda who eyed him suspiciously.

"I wanted to offer my sympathy about what has happened to Kate," he said as he reached them. "I feel so bad about the night I behaved so terribly. I was drunk, and I've regretted it ever since." He paused to make sure he had their full attention. "Since she isn't here for me to apologise to in person, I wanted to see if there is anything I can do to help."

"There's nothing to help with. She's done a runner. Nobody knows where she is," said Jacob. "Had you not heard?"

"I had. I just thought…" John trailed off and shrugged. "Well, if you do need anything I'll be in Cannes for a while yet. Is Mr Bryant here, by the way?"

"No," said Linda sharply. "Can I give him a message?"

"Yes, I just wanted to make sure everything was still going ahead with the casino. I'm ready with my investment, you see, so whenever he wants to go over the papers, I'm available."

Jacob and Linda exchanged glances. They were both aware that almost all the investors had pulled out of the deal. John Campbell was one of the last people still interested. Although Jermain seemed to have lost all interest in the casino, if they could get things back on board, it could be what he needed to get him back to his old self.

Jacob also remembered that Kate had specifically instructed that John Campbell was not to be an investor after the situation between them. But Kate wasn't there.

"I can draw up some papers now, if you want," Jacob said hesitantly.

John smiled politely. "That would be fine by me. Do you mind if I wait?"

"No, that's fine." He gestured to Linda. "Get Mr Campbell a drink, would you?"

Rolling her eyes, she stalked inside to the bar with the men following her.

"I need to make a call. Are you okay to wait here?" Jacob asked John as they came into the reception.

"Of course, take your time," said John, and sat in one of the chairs by the reception desk. As Jacob disappeared into his office Linda asked him what he wanted to drink.

"Whiskey would be fine, thank you," he replied. As soon as Linda returned to the bar, he stood up and examined the other side of the reception desk. It was littered with papers, and he shuffled though them. Most were invoices for goods purchased for the hotel, but there was also a stack of letters, addressed to Jermain, from investors all pulling out of the deal. John smirked and put them back where he found them. Another pile of papers, half hidden under two grey folders, caught his eye and, leaning further over the desk, he pulled them out and scanned them quickly. They were pages of articles and advertisements about Africa, Zaire in particular, and a couple of exposes about a charity called Survival International. His brain started ticking, and, knowing he was onto something, he folded the pages quickly and tucked them into his inside jacket pocket as Linda came back with his drink. She handed it to him without a word and went back into the bar.

Jacob, unable to get hold of Jermain, had spoken to Andy on the telephone, who agreed it would be a wise move if they accepted John's investment in the casino. If people saw John Campbell going ahead they would be more likely to follow, and the hotel might stand a chance of living to see the opening night, after all. So Jacob returned to John with the papers, which he signed with a flourish.

"We'll be in touch, when things have settled down a bit, let you know what's happening," said Jacob as he handed John his copy of the contract.

"No problem." John shook Jacobs's hand. "Everything will be fine, and remember, if I can be of any help, please call me."

Jacob nodded and, with a growing feeling of unease that he couldn't explain, he watched him go.

When John got back to his hotel room he pulled the papers out of his pocket and read carefully through each one. Something niggled at him, a hazy memory he couldn't quite latch onto, which frustrated him because he knew it was something that would help him find Kate.

Unable to think what it was, he left it and decided to go downstairs to the Internet café to try and find out more about the charity.

When he returned an hour later, he had gleaned a lot more information than he could have wished for. In his hands he held a few more pages he had printed off the website. One of them contained a photograph of Joe Palmer and an article about his latest expedition in Zaire. He had recognised Joe instantly. He was the guy who had dragged him out of the Riviera bar, the one who had been with Kate. John felt immensely satisfied as it all sank into place. Joe Palmer had gone back to Zaire; Kate had fled to be with him. Grinning to himself, he reached for his jacket and, collecting up all the papers, he prepared himself for a visit to Officer Marron.

Chapter Ten

An Arrest

The day had gone rapidly downhill on their arrival back to Zaire. The heavens had opened and a tropical rainstorm had descended upon camp. The tents were down and the fire wood was damp. Joe, used to such occasions out in the bush, got to work sorting out the camp so it was liveable again. Bruce sat on a log under a sheet of canvas, planning his escape back to England, and Kate sat miserably with Bruce pondering her future.

When she had fled England before and lived in Africa, she had not wanted to return home, but the difference between then and now was she'd had a choice. She tried to explain this to Bruce, and he nodded his understanding.

"Who would want to live in this wet mud bath when you've got a luxury penthouse suite in Cannes?" he mused.

"I always preferred Australia, anyway," Kate said. "At least the weather was predictable."

Bruce took her hand. "What are you going to do, Kate?"

She thought for a moment before answering him.

"Make the best of a bad situation, I guess."

Joe watched them as they sat quietly talking. Something had changed in Kate, but whatever it was she wasn't telling him. He wondered if she felt out of her depth in his environment, and resolved to give her some sort of project. There were so many things to do. With all the coming and going since he had arrived, he had barely started on sorting out the education side. A cabin needed building as well. Maybe that was something Kate could help with.

When he finished tidying up the camp he approached her and told her about the cabin.

"A cabin," she exclaimed. "A week ago I was building the biggest casino in Cannes, now I'm building a shed in the jungle!" She smiled as she said it, but her words confused him.

If she wanted to be back in her Cannes hotel why had she come here?

"It'll keep you busy and help me out." Joe hugged her briefly. "Think about it, yeah?"

When dawn broke, the new day found Kate and Joe surrounded by the Pygmies. Before they had gone to sleep the night before, wrapped in the safety of each other's arms, Joe had told Kate it was time for him to do some serious work. So, with a resolution to help him as much as she could, they had started the day with the Pygmies, watching Bruce as he gained as much knowledge from them to take back to England with him. Language, they realised, was no barrier as it simply wasn't needed. The pygmies demonstrated which plants they used for which ailments and Bruce filed it all away in his memory.

They had just started to build up the fire to make some tea when there was a commotion in the trees surrounding their camp. The Pygmies scattered at once, as about six men in military uniform burst into the clearing. Kate knew instantly the game was over, and she froze as they started towards her.

"Wait a second." Joe was on his feet and Bruce stood protectively in front of Kate as they descended upon the camp.

They ignored Joe and reached out to grab Kate. She struggled and broke free of the soldier's grip. Turning wildly, she sprinted for the forest, but she was no match for six men. They caught her and, within seconds, snapped a pair of handcuffs on her wrists. She turned and called to Joe frantically as, without speaking, the soldiers marched her out of the clearing to their waiting truck.

Joe ran behind them, pleading with the soldiers to explain what was happening.

They ignored him again, and continued walking in stony faced silence.

As they bundled her into the truck, Joe kicked the tyre in frustration. Kate looked at him through her tears.

Before Joe could stop the truck it was gone, leaving in its trail a dusty cloud.

As Bruce came running, Joe turned to him with a look of shock on his face.

"Bruce, what the *fuck* is going on?"

When Kate could see Joe no longer, she turned back and looked out of the front windscreen. She knew the danger she was in with the African Military, and was well aware of their reputation for raping and robbing. She eyed their weapons uneasily. The prison back in Cannes would be a safe haven compared to where she was now. Her only hope was that the soldiers were working on direct orders from France and, therefore, she would remain safe. She closed her eyes and leaned her head back against the chair, contemplating her fate.

Jacob wandered aimlessly around the hotel foyer, waiting for Linda to get ready so he could take her out to lunch. Every day he was surprised at what he felt for her. He had been married once, to an American who had broken his bank and his spirit, and he had not expected to find anyone else to share his life. Though it was still early days for them, he had high hopes for Linda and himself. As he glanced at his watch, the telephone rang. He leaned over the desk to pick it up.

When Linda came down the stairs he hung up the phone. From the grim look on his face, she could clearly tell it was bad news.

"Who was that?" she asked.

"The police. They've found Kate."

She put her hand to her mouth. "Oh, no, how?"

He shrugged. "I have no idea. They put two and two together and came up with the right answer, I guess."

"Where is she now?" asked Linda.

"En route here. We'll skip lunch and bring the others up to date, okay?"

She nodded and sat down to wait for Kate to return.

"So where the hell was she, anyway?" yelled Jermain as Jacob filled him in.

"Zaire, with Bruce and Joe. She's on her way back now.

We should get to the police station so we can see her."

Jermain nodded grimly and picked up his coat. "Some good plan," he snarled as he stormed out of the room.

Linda came up behind Jacob and hugged him.

"He's not angry at you, just the situation," she said.

"I know." Jacob sighed. "But it's gonna get worse, now they've found her."

"Something will come up, new evidence…" Linda trailed off. She knew as well as anyone that Kate running made her look guilty. All that they could do now was support her.

Within the hour they sat in the reception area of the police station where Kate had made her escape two weeks earlier. Andy and his lawyer, Thomas King, arrived and greeted the three of them.

"Is she here yet?" Thomas asked.

"No, they said she should arrive soon," said Jermain.

As Thomas began to explain what was likely to happen, the door opened and two officials led in Kate.

"Dad!" she cried. He ran to her and enveloped her in his arms.

The handcuffs prevented her from hugging him back and Jermain felt the tears rising. Thomas stepped forward and introduced himself.

"Thank you for helping me," she said.

"I'm not sure that running away has helped your defence, but we'll do the best we can," said Thomas.

Officer Marron appeared and, taking Kate's arm, she cast a look over the group and led her out of the room.

"That's that, then," said Linda morosely.

Even though Kate was back, things moved slowly. The hearing was set for three weeks' time but the murder trial would not begin for many more months. Thomas King worked with Kate almost every day. He was sceptical and not entirely positive, which did not put her into a secure frame of mind.

She sat in her cell and thought about Joe, wondering how the building of the cabin was going, and if Bruce was still there. Thomas had advised her it could be unlikely she would get bail. Murder was a serious offence, and there would be no community service for her. And there would be no Jacob to rescue her this time. She was all cried out, bored, depressed and slowly going mad from living in the one room. Sinking down onto the bed and staring blankly at the wall, she felt more helpless than she had ever done in her entire life.

"My life's over," she whispered to herself and, once more, the tears came.

After much deliberation, Linda had decided to attend the funeral of Janine Finch. Jacob had tried to talk her out of it, but she urged him to accompany her; at the very least they could take a good look at Janine's friends and family.

"You won't find anything, honey," said Jacob. "The person who killed her is hardly likely to turn up, is he?"

"I don't care, I'm going. Are you coming with me or not?" she replied as she dressed in her black suit.

"Okay, I'll come," said Jacob, and, with a resigned sigh, left the room to get some breakfast.

The funeral wasn't the only thing on Linda's mind. The absolute last thing she needed at that moment seemed likely to have happened. As Jacob left the room, she pulled the pregnancy test out of her bag and carried the box into the bathroom. How she could have been so careless, she didn't know, and she didn't know how Jacob was going to take this latest news, either.

It was the first time she had ever had to take a pregnancy test, and she followed the instructions to the letter. When she was done, she laid the test on the sink and sat on the edge of the bath to wait.

She was still waiting five minutes later, unable to get up off the bath and look at the result. It was Jacob who unknowingly banged on the bathroom door that pulled her out of her trance-like state as she jumped up from the side of the bath and snatched up the test, holding it behind her back.

"Honey, what are you doing?" he asked.

"Nothing." She tried to smile but failed. "I'm coming down now."

"What's that?" He nodded to her hands behind her back.

"What?" she asked, edging away from him.

"This." He spun her round and took the test out of her hand. "Oh." He looked at it, then at her. "Are you…?"

She snatched it and put it back on the sink.

"I don't know," she snapped, annoyed at being caught. "I was doing the bloody thing when you came in."

For a few moments they looked at each other. Jacob made the first move. He drew her out of the bathroom and sat her on the bed.

"Linda, I know this is all very recent, and we've only just started seeing each other and all that. But I think we're going to be good together, and if that stick in there is positive then you'll make me very happy. If it's negative, then we've all the time in the world to plan things like that."

"Really? But a baby is such a huge commitment, expensive and…" she trailed off, realising she could think of no negative aspects about bringing a child into the world.

"Go look at it, Linda. We've no worries about money, you know that." He patted her back, and she stood up and walked slowly into the bathroom.

As he watched her go, Jacob grinned to himself. His miserable marriage had never produced children and he had a burning desire to be a father. Linda would make a wonderful mother and, if this test turned out to be a false alarm, then it was something he felt they should consider in the future.

"Well?" he called out, unable to contain his excitement any longer.

Linda stuck her head round the door and held up the test. She read it once more, as if to make sure she wasn't mistaken, looked up at him and grinned.

Her face told him all he needed to know.

With a whoop, he lifted her up and spun her round. She shrieked and hugged him tight.

"Can we tell Andy and Jermain?" he asked eagerly.

"Sure." Linda smiled and took his hand. "I think they could do with some good news today."

They ran down the stairs, and hailed a greeting as they went into the restaurant, where Andy and Jermain were dining.

"Well, you two are in good spirits. What's up?" asked Andy as he helped himself to more coffee.

"We've got some news," said Linda, almost bubbling over in her excitement.

Jermain stood up. "You're getting married!" he exclaimed.

Linda and Jacob exchanged glances.

"Uh, no," said Jacob. "It's bigger than that."

"I'm pregnant," said Linda.

"Oh, but that's great!" Andy came round the table to shake Jacob's hand.

"Yes, yes it is." Jermain hugged Linda. "Kate will be thrilled."

There was a lull in the atmosphere as they all thought of Kate and the pending trial.

"I'm going to see if I can visit her, maybe after the funeral," said Linda.

"You're still going to the funeral?" asked Jermain.

"Just to the service," replied Linda, taking Jacob's hand. "We'll see you later."

The church was packed to the rafters and television screens had been set up outside so members of the public could pay their respects as they watched the service. Janine Finch had been an important part of the society, always in the limelight, and her public had loved her. As well as sadness, Linda detected anger in the crowd and, as Jacob led the way to the church, Linda caught his hand and held him back.

"Let's hang back here, yeah?" she said nervously.

He understood, and they found a place near the church door.

When the funeral cortège drew up, and the coffin was bought out, a wail went up from the crowd. It chilled Linda to the bone. As the coffin moved past, Linda scanned the faces of the family who gathered around it. She recognised Janine's father, the Governor, and the three other girls whose party it had been. Following a few feet behind, she saw John Campbell. He raised his eyebrow at her and nodded.

"I've seen enough," said Linda. "Let's go see Kate."

As they walked back to the car, Linda was deep in thought.

"There's a lot about that night I don't understand," she said.

"Like what?" Jacob asked.

"Well, for one thing, it was so dark, deserted even. It was supposed to be a party, but where was everyone?"

Jacob shrugged as she continued, "And the painting of Janine had been slashed. Kate wouldn't have had time to do that and then move onto Janine's house and kill her."

He stopped. "Have you told the police all this? Did they put it in your statement?"

"Of course I did. It just doesn't add up."

"Let's hope it comes out in the trial," said Jacob as they reached his car.

Kate stood by the opaque window, trying to see out, when her cell door opened. An officer stood in the doorway.

"Visitor for you, Bryant," she said, standing away from the door to allow Kate to pass through.

Wordlessly, Kate went out into the corridor and followed the officer to the visitor's room. She expected it to be Thomas King. He had been coming to see her almost daily to question her in preparation for the hearing and the pending trial. She was pleasantly surprised when she saw Linda and Jacob sitting at a table waiting for her.

"Kate!" Linda stood up and hugged her.

"No contact," snapped the officer, who stood by the far wall, idly swinging her key chain.

Kate scowled and sat down opposite them.

"Did you go to the funeral?" she asked.

"Yes, but not for long, it was a dismal affair," replied Linda. "But how are you bearing up?"

She shrugged. Prison life was neither here nor there. She was in a cell on her own, it was clean, small and quite possibly the worst place she had ever lived. "And I've lived in a lot of places," she told them, trying, but failing, for some humour. She hoped every day that another prisoner would be moved into her cell, so she would at least have somebody to talk to. She was bored, restless and chain smoking until she had almost lost her voice.

"I'm sorry." Linda touched her hand. "We brought you some cigarettes but they have to check them over first."

Kate nodded. "Thank you. So what's going on in the outside world? How's Dad? And how are you two getting on?"

Exchanging a secret smile with Jacob, Linda bounced up and down on her seat. "Well, we have some good news," she said.

Kate clapped her hands together. "You're getting married!"

Jacob rolled his eyes and Linda laughed.

"No, but it does involve a commitment of some kind." Her hand went to her stomach and she raised her eyes.

"Oh, my God, a baby!" Kate shrieked. "That *is* good news!"

Linda linked her arm through Jacob's and smiled.

"We're happy."

As Linda talked on about the baby and their plans for the future, Kate felt incredibly lonely. It should be her with the plans, making a life for her and the hotel, and maybe Joe. That would never be an option now.

"What am I doing, telling you all this when you're stuck in here?" Tears sprung to Linda's eyes and Kate shook her head fiercely.

"You enjoy it while you can, Linda, don't feel bad. I need to hear this. I need to hear about other people's lives and what's going on." She laughed, a humourless sound. "I need to live my life through other people now, don't I?"

"Thomas is doing the best he can for you, Kate," said

Jacob. "I'm just sorry Zaire didn't work out. We still have no idea how they found out."

"No matter," said Kate and, glancing furtively around, she lowered her voice. "They asked me how I got there, who broke me out of this place, but I told them I'd never seen the people before."

Jacob winked sagely, bringing a wry smile to Kate's face. "We're all here for you, and we'll be at the hearing."

Kate looked up and took a deep breath. "Have you heard from Joe?"

A huge pause gave Kate her answer, and she smiled bravely. "Doesn't matter," she said. "He has a lot on his plate."

Idle chitchat resumed and, all too soon, it was time for her friends to leave. Ignoring the stern reprimands from the officer, they hugged Kate.

"We'll see you soon," Linda promised.

"At the hearing," confirmed Kate. Waving, as she watched them leave the building, she felt worse than ever as she followed the officer back to her cell.

Later, Thomas King arrived and, as he waited for Kate, he checked out his reflection in the window of the interview room.

He was young for a lawyer, only thirty-five and extremely nervous, though he hoped his posture did not show it. Painfully aware, at five foot six, he was shorter than average, he stood up straight, hoping that his stance would exude confidence.

Or would that simply look like he was trying to be someone he wasn't? he worried, and turned away from the window.

Thomas had wanted all his life to be a lawyer, having grown up in London—poor and impoverished, wearing the same clothes all term until his mother could scrape enough money together to buy new ones by working double shifts at the packing factory, or his father had a win on the horses, which wasn't too often.

Thomas King Senior had very nearly destroyed the young

Thomas's dream before it had begun. A crook, small time burglar and general con man, he had thought he had a reputation but, in reality, he had been a sad, old man who just couldn't deal with the seriousness of a steady job. Thomas Junior would have had some respect for him had he been part of the mafia clan, or a big jewel thief, but no, knocking off the local post office was about as big as it got.

When they had learned of his past in Law School it had nearly been the end. The son of a petty thief, wanting to be a lawyer, was out of the question. But Thomas Junior had learned a lot in his short life and, kissing his mother goodbye, had dropped out of Oxford and flown to New Jersey in the U.S.A. In America, things had been totally different. Most of his fellow students had been the sons or daughters of Mafioso families, drug barons or known criminals. Here he had found, for the first time in his life, that he fitted in.

At twenty-five, he had finished his education and looked around for a job. He had finished his finals with the second best grades in the class and a lot of job opportunities had been offered to him. He had chosen wisely—a small but respected law firm where he'd had an outside chance of making partner in less time than a larger firm would have ever deemed possible. So, Thomas King Junior had begun his working life handling small cases for Sarenden & Pullman. After seven years, the firm had branched out overseas and opened up an office in Nice and, with Thomas being trilingual in French, English and German, it had made sense to offer him a position. Then he had faced a big choice—wait there in case he made partner in the near future, or relocate to the south of France where the money was good, the accommodation first class and the crime was low.

There had never been any real choice.

And so, there he was. For three years he had had it easy, handling small cases and generally raking it in for not doing very much at all. Well, that had changed. He had been called in by Andy to handle a murder case—his first murder case.

Something else bothered Thomas. He had always felt it the most important thing to have absolute faith in one's client and in their innocence, and the trouble was, he did not have that faith in this case, not at all. But, worse than that, possibly the worst scenario that could happen between a client and a lawyer—he had fallen for Kate Bryant. He certainly hadn't seen that coming. When Andy had called him, he had arrived, all professional lawyer, and had been knocked out by her. At first, he had been sure he could control it, after all he would have to be dead, or a priest, not to find her attractive, but then, he had begun to get to know her, and had found her fiery spirit irresistible. Then, suddenly, his perspective had changed. He didn't give a damn if this lady was innocent or not, he just wanted to get her the hell out of that prison.

Reflecting upon it now, he knew he should have got out at the start, handed the case over to one of his colleagues. But it was too late.

It was always too late.

Shaking his head, he turned to the reams of papers that lay over the table and picked them up. The jury, he mused, could be a problem. The judge had specified the jurors must not be local, so they had all been drafted in from surrounding areas, the furthest away being Lyon. That, however, was not far enough away for Thomas. Press coverage of the murder of Janine Finch had been huge, worldwide as opposed to nationwide, and right now Kate Bryant was on everybody's hit list.

His thoughts were interrupted when Kate entered the room and, as usual, he was thrown at the mere sight of her. How someone could look so good in prison attire was beyond him, but somehow she pulled it off.

She greeted him and sat down at the table.

"I just wanted to check you were ready," he said.

"As I'll ever be," she replied and smiled wanly at him.

"I'm going to get you out of here. I swear it," he said, and she looked up, obviously startled by the intensity in his voice.

"You know I didn't do it, right?" she asked. "You have to know that, or I really am done for."

He studied her intently for a few moments. Then it sunk in.

Yes, he *did* know she hadn't murdered Janine Finch. Just that one split second, when her tough exterior had vanished for a moment and he had seen the truth in her eyes, he knew.

He began to nod slowly, and then he smiled. "Yeah, I know it."

Breathing out, she grinned at him, dazzling him with her smile as she reached across the table and took his hand. He looked at it, her hand on his, and for a moment he let himself forget they were in a prison and that he was her lawyer. For just a moment it didn't matter.

The clanging of a distant cell door brought him back to reality with a bang, and he snatched his hand away.

"I'll get you out of here," he repeated as she stood up and, with a last glance in his direction, she left the room.

For a long time he stood, watching the place where she had been, until he gathered up the papers and left the prison.

Back in her cell, the door locked behind her, Kate resumed her position by the window through which she still could not see anything.

Chapter Eleven

The Hearing

Joe watched as Bruce packed up the last of his belongings and checked around the camp to make sure he had left nothing behind.

"I kind of got used to having you around," he said.

Bruce stopped what he was doing and came across.

"I might be back," he said. "Chances are looking good that the wife has filed for divorce, then I can come back here and live out my retirement eating pot noodles and getting ants in my arse until I die."

Joe laughed. "Your wife will be waiting for you, you know that."

Bruce grimaced. "Got a present for you." He gave a sheepish grin as he held out the keys to the car.

"Nice one." Joe took them and tossed them from hand to hand with a thoughtful look on his face. "At least I can drive into town and get the papers, keep up to date with whatever's going on in France."

After Kate had been taken away, Bruce had told Joe everything, and shown him the newspapers he had stashed. Joe refused to read them, and her name had barely been mentioned.

"I'll look in on her. My first stop is Cannes, and I'll get word to you on how it's going back there."

"Thanks, Bruce, I appreciate it," said Joe. "How long do you think the hearing will last?"

"Not long, it's just really a bail hearing," said Bruce as he put the last of his luggage in the car.

Joe nodded and looked around the camp. An idea was beginning to form and he sat down on a log to think it over as Bruce finished loading the car.

"That's the last of it," called Bruce. "I'm off then, back to civilisation!"

"Hold on." Joe stood up. "I'm coming too!"

Bruce nodded, as if he had expected all along for Joe to leave with him.

"Come on then, we'll miss the plane," yelled Bruce as he clambered in the passenger seat.

"I need to pack a few things," said Joe as he disappeared into his tent.

"No need, done it all for you," laughed Bruce as he held up Joe's bag.

"You sly old—"

"What? You think I don't know you, boy!" Bruce leaned over and opened the passenger's door. "Now get in and stop dallying."

On the journey to the airport Joe was silent, thinking about Kate. It hurt him to think of her locked in a cell somewhere. It hurt him, and confused him even more that occasionally he found himself wondering about her innocence.

"What if the hearing doesn't go well, Bruce?" he asked suddenly. "What are we going to do then?"

Bruce patted his leg, "Chin up, old chap. We'll keep fighting, is what we'll do."

Joe nodded, not very reassured, and looked out of the window.

The groups had gathered and were waiting in the lobby. Jacob had herded everyone together. He noticed Jermain's worried look and took his arm.

"Your girl is tough. She'll be fine." He glanced at his watch. "We need to leave in five minutes. Everyone ready?"

"We're ready," said Linda.

"Okay," Jacob replied. "We'll get the cars out."

Kate was nervously pacing her cell. She had not slept at all the night before and, no matter how hard she tried, she couldn't stop trembling. For the hundredth time, she wondered how this had happened to her just when everything had been going so well in her life.

"'Morning, Kate," a voice startled her, and she turned to

see Officer Marron letting Thomas King into her cell.

"Hey, Thomas," she said wearily.

"Got you the suit," he said and handed it to her.

She took it without speaking, and threw it on her bed.

"Do you have a cigarette?" she asked him.

"Um…here." He dug around in his pockets and came up with a crumpled packet of camels.

Kate was impressed.

"You don't look like the type to have such a bad habit," she said.

"I have many vices, Ms Bryant," he retorted. "Most I like to keep hidden."

She shrugged, not believing him for a moment, and held out her hand for a lighter.

"You looked miles away when I came in. Were you thinking about the hearing?" he asked as he handed it to her.

"Wondering how the hell I got here." She lit the cigarette and blew smoke rings towards him. "Do you know what I was doing a year ago, Thomas?"

"What were you doing?"

"I was in Australia, living with Aborigines, learning from them, sharing their lives. They're so free, Thomas, the whole of the country is what they call home, and they can go anywhere they please." She stopped and looked around the room. "Now look at me. I had the whole world, and all I have now is one room." She swept her arm out angrily and dragged on the cigarette.

There was silence for a few moments and then Thomas took a tentative step forwards and crouched down in front of her. "I'm going to do my best for you, you know that, right?" he said softly.

She caught it in his voice, and knew right then what he felt for her. It was written all over his face and in his tone of voice. She was so touched she felt a lump rise in her throat. It could be bad, his feelings may get in the way of forging a strong case, but on the other hand, if she was not mistaken, he might try that little bit harder to save her.

She put her hand over his and nodded.

"I know you will, Thomas."

They stayed that way, just touching and looking, until Marron banged on the door to say it was time to go.

As they led Kate away, suit in hand, she looked back and saw Thomas sit down on her bed and put his head in his hands.

The courtroom was packed. The press were gathered upstairs in the gallery, pens poised to get every detail. Janine Finch's family and friends sat to the right of the dock, stony-faced and silent. Jermain, Jacob, Linda and Andy filed in and looked away from the glares Mr Finch threw at them all. They sat to the left of the dock and waited nervously.

A hush descended over the room as Kate was led in, handcuffed, by two officers. Thomas marvelled at the difference in her. Earlier, she had been frightened, almost childlike in her fear, and it had been written all over her face. He had felt her hand shake when he had held it, and had been worried how she would cope. This lady in front of him now was like a different woman. She was poised, avoiding the stern glare of the Finch's, and nodding to her family. She looked… strong.

He nodded to her and she smiled as one of the officers removed the cuffs. She sat down and raised her head directly towards the gallery. One reporter, ignoring the "*prohibido fotografica*" sign, snapped off a couple of shots, and heads turned in his direction.

"All rise," a courtroom official bellowed, and feet shuffled on the wooden floor as they all did so.

The trial was to be conducted in French, with an English interpreter on hand.

The Judge entered.

Inwardly, Thomas groaned.

His Lord Justice Alveraz was commonly known as one of the hardest judges on the southern coast. Thomas had met him a few times before and had always been in awe of him.

"Be seated," the same official called out, and the hearing began.

Despite the request for the English interpretation, the judge spoke rapidly in French. Kate, being fluent, tried hard to keep up, but found she couldn't concentrate. The English interpreter shrugged his shoulders and sat back, redundant. After about five minutes the judge slammed his gavel down and rose. Kate looked around, unsure of what was happening, as the officers came and led her back down to her cell.

"Thomas, what's happened?" asked Jermain, wondering if they were just taking a break.

Thomas came over, his face ashen.

"No bail," he said quietly.

There was nothing else to say as they sat back and wondered what would happen next, and how long they would have to wait.

Fury had replaced Kate's sadness and she sat seething on the bed in her cell.

"I'm so sorry," Thomas said.

"You said you'd get me out. You fucking promised me." Kate knew her words were harsh, but she couldn't stop the abusive words that spewed from her lips.

"I warned you bail would be unlikely. Kate, this isn't the end. I will get you out, please, please, believe me."

She wrenched her hands free. "When will the trial be?"

"A few months, maybe six," he replied.

She turned towards the window without replying.

Joe and Bruce landed in Nice at noon. Joe called the hotel on the chance that someone would be there as Bruce sorted out a hire car for them.

He hung up as Bruce came across the arrival lounge.

"No answer."

"They'll all be at the hearing," replied Bruce, and dangled the keys in front of Joe's face. "Come on, our chariot awaits."

Outside, the heat hit them, and Joe unbuttoned the top few buttons of his shirt. The man from Hertz was waiting for them and he gestured to a bright red Ford.

"Do you think she's okay?" asked Joe as they sped away towards Cannes.

"I never met anyone as tough as Kate," Bruce replied. "Except maybe my wife—she's not impressed with me, you know."

"Did you call her?"

"Yes, I did, and said sorry but I was going to a hearing for a girl I met in France who is charged with murder. Yeah, she's not happy."

Joe laughed, although it wasn't funny.

Halfway to Cannes, Joe instructed him to stop the car, jumped out of the passenger seat and forced him over so he could drive.

"The hearing will be over by the time we get there at this rate," said Joe and revved up the engine.

Bruce buckled his seat belt with an alarmed look, and they resumed their journey.

Linda sat on the front courtroom steps when they arrived, smoking a cigarette. They parked across the road, and she stood up and waved.

"Hey, Linda," Joe greeted her with a kiss and Bruce hugged her. "How's it going in there?"

"No bail," she said almost in a whisper. "It's over now, at least until the trial."

Frowning, Joe sat on the steps. "I'm sorry." He banged his fist on his leg in anger. "If I'd have known, maybe I could have kept her safe, hidden her somewhere better."

Linda rubbed his arm. "Everybody's done everything they could. They're in there now, talking to her solicitor. We just have to wait."

"What do they even have on her, evidence-wise I mean? Why is she even in the frame?" asked Joe.

Linda threw the cigarette on the ground and watched it burn out. She told them about Kate splitting when they reached the party, the slashed photo in the garden, the frantic phone call from Kate, and her subsequent arrest.

Joe listened carefully, horrified.

"So she did do it? She *killed* that girl?"

"No! Come on, Joe, it's just circumstantial," she snapped.

He stood up and looked at Bruce. "It doesn't sound very circumstantial. Jesus, Linda, all this time I thought she was…"

"Thought she was what?" Linda stood up and faced him head on.

He looked at her for a long time, emotions boiling up inside him. "I thought she was innocent," he said eventually and, returning to the car, he climbed in, started up the engine and leaned out of the window. "Bruce, are you coming?"

"No, I'm staying. Joe, where are you going?" Bruce shouted.

"Back to Zaire." Joe threw a bitter look at Linda. "Back where I belong."

As he sped off, Linda turned to Bruce.

"Kate must not know about this," she said. "Do you understand?"

He nodded his agreement and, shaking his head, they both returned to the courtroom to wait for the others.

* * * *

The next few weeks were a waiting game. Some things provided a welcome distraction—Linda's pregnancy for one—and the hunt for a home for herself and Jacob took up most of their time.

Many meetings were held over the opening of the hotel, and the verdict was still open. They argued back and forth and then, once one person came around to thinking a certain way, somebody else changed his or her mind.

A month after the hearing, a date was set for the trial, in two months' time, the first of September.

Once more, things began to move. Thomas King took up residence in Cannes, but declined Jermain's invitation to stay at the hotel. No matter how hard everyone tried to include him, he never quite felt like one of the group. He visited Kate a few times a week, or stayed at the château he was renting, sometimes feeling foolish for rattling around in the big home by himself. But it was in a peaceful area, a few miles away from the bustle of Cannes, in the town of Mougins. He worked hard on Kate's case, reading previous case files, going over and over the police records, and making his defence the best he could possibly make it.

Bruce had returned to England but had promised to be back for the trial. He had heard nothing from Joe, despite leaving numerous messages with his people at Survival International. He felt at odds with the pending trial and the effect it was having on his friends. He was living a life in the middle, not really wanting to return home to his wife, but not yet belonging in Cannes. But life went on, and he muddled through as best he could, desperately hoping Joe would reappear once more before the trial began.

All too soon the trial arrived and, once more, everyone waited in the courtroom as the judge made his entrance. Jermain was nervous and fretful, and Linda stayed by his side and did her best to calm him.

Kate stood in the dock. Much like the last time she had been there, she kept to her personal vow to remain strong and positive. She looked at Thomas, who smiled at her, and she wondered how she would have got through the last few months without him. He had become her saviour and, although he had not yet saved her, he had given her hope, and they had forged a bond.

"Let the jurors be sworn in," said Alveraz. Everyone watched silently as, one by one, the jurors laid their hands on the bible and read out their vows.

When they were done, the Judge nodded to the prosecution lawyer, Liam Kane, who stood up and approached the front of the courtroom.

Thomas knew Liam Kane. It didn't help that he actually liked the guy. When he had first come to France, Liam had been working for the same firm and had shown him around. He was older than Thomas, in his forties, with a confidence that came with never having lost a case.

As Kane turned and faced the courtroom, everyone in attendance sat up expectantly.

The trial had begun.

The first witness called to the stand was Pierre Rodriguez, the man who had seen Linda driving away, and who had called the police when he had found Kate on the floor of the Finch's hallway.

After he had been sworn in he turned to Liam, who began.

"Can you please, for the court, state your name, address and occupation?"

Pierre did so, claiming he was a widowed, retired doctor, and had lived at the same address for over forty years, the last ten of which he had lived on his own.

"Mr Rodriguez, can you tell us, in your own words, what happened the night of August twenty-ninth?"

Pierre nodded and, speaking in careful English, he began his story.

"I had been invited to the party. I was about to leave my house, which is six doors away from where Mr Finch lives, and was just locking my front door, when some of the lights in the street went out. At first, I thought it was a power cut, but then I noticed the lights from the main road were all on, and those in most of the houses as well, and they would not have been if it had been a power cut." He paused to take a sip of water, before continuing. "I looked over at the Finch house and lots of people were coming out, and going into Marie Dupont's house, just across the street. The Dupont house still had power, you see."

Liam nodded and made a few notes on his pad.

"What happened next?"

"Well, I went over there, too. The whole party was gathered while the caretaker went over to the power-box at the end of the road to find out what had happened."

"Was Janine Finch at the Dupont house?" asked Liam.

"No," replied Pierre.

"Objection!" Thomas stood for the first time and

addressed the judge. "That's speculation. If the whole party was there, which I believe to be about thirty people at that point, how could he have known if the girl was there or not?"

"Over-ruled," the judge said. "Continue."

Thomas sat back down and Liam turned back to Pierre.

"Please, in your own words, sir."

"So, when I realised I had left the girl's gifts at my home, I decided to go back for them. As I left the house, the lights went out in the rest of the street, and part of the main road as well. I didn't think too much of it. After all, the caretaker was onto it and should have had it fixed before long. So I went to mine. As I went inside, a car drew up. I didn't take much notice of it," he said almost apologetically.

Liam nodded and gestured for him to continue.

"I went into my house, fumbled around in the dark for the gifts and, as I was about to leave, I remembered I had left the light on in my kitchen, so I went in to turn it off. If the power came on, and there was a spark, it could be dangerous…" he trailed off, clearly wondering why he was telling them this, and tried to pick up the thread of his story.

"So, I turned it off, got my torch and, as I switched it on, I noticed the portrait in the Finch's garden. It had been slashed, so I went out the front to tell the others about the vandalism."

"What then?" Liam said.

Kate glanced around the courtroom to see that everyone was leaning forward, hooked on the story.

"I went down my drive, and saw a woman running from the Martinez house, which is next door to the Finch's. She got in the car that had pulled up when I went in, and reversed erratically down the road. I went into the road and watched her go. The band that had been hired for the party was coming into the road, and they scattered as she drove through them. It was a miracle none of them was hurt," he finished and fixed a stern gaze on Linda, who blushed.

"What did you do next?" Liam asked softly.

"I started to head over to the Dupont's. Then I heard a scream from the Finch house and went over there. The front door was open, and there was a lady lying on the floor near the front door." He stopped to drink some more water. "She was unconscious. She had blood on her hands and was holding… holding a poker, which also had blood on it. I started to tend to her, and then I saw Janine, in the lounge, on the floor…" His voice broke, and the court stirred uncomfortably. Pierre took a few seconds, and then continued. "She, too, was very bloodied, and I knew then not to touch anything, so I called the police."

Liam walked around to the front of the room and shuffled through his papers. "You were a doctor for thirty years, is that correct?" he asked.

"Yes, that is correct," said Pierre.

"Have you ever attended a murder scene, before, in your career?"

"Once, yes, that is how I knew not to disturb anything," said Pierre.

"No further questions, your Honour." Liam sat down and Thomas stood up, looking more confident than he felt.

"If I may call on your medical background, Mr Rodriguez?" Thomas asked and, after a glance at Liam, Pierre nodded.

"The weapon, an iron poker, was quite a heavy instrument. How much force would have had to be used?" asked Thomas.

Liam stood up. "We have an expert witness from the Medical Centre for this purpose, your honour, who will be in attendance during this trial!"

The judge pondered for a second and looked at Thomas. "I'm allowing it," he said gruffly.

"You may answer," Thomas directed at Pierre.

"Quite a lot of force. It is a slim instrument but potentially deadly," replied Pierre.

"If you would take a look at my client, Miss Bryant—would you say she is capable of handling said *instrument*, with enough force to kill another human with one stroke?" The courtroom turned to look at Kate, and she lowered her head against the scrutiny.

"With all due respect, sir, we all know Miss Bryant is quite a strong lady and, if I may say so, quite capable of harming another human," Pierre said.

The crowd chortled.

Kate blushed. Word on her hitting John Campbell in the Riviera Bar had obviously got around.

"Harming, yes, but *fatally* harming?" Thomas shot back.

"Enough," said Liam and rose from his seat.

The judge nodded, as if bored with this line of questioning.

Thomas changed tack. "You said, yourself, it was dark due to the lights being out in the road?"

"Yes," Pierre confirmed.

"So it's quite possible you didn't see if anybody else had been involved in this attack?"

Pierre hesitated, and then nodded. "It is possible…yes," he replied.

Thomas sat down. "No further questions."

Alveraz raised his eyebrows at Liam, who shook his head.

The judge banged the gavel, and declared that the court be adjourned until nine o'clock the next morning.

The court stood as Alveraz left the room, and Kate was led down the stairs.

When they got back to the hotel, Linda went straight up to her room. She sat on the bed and wiped her face free from tears. She knew it wasn't looking good for Kate, and felt a terrible guilt that if she had not driven away from the scene of the crime in a panic she might have been the witness her friend needed.

"Honey, we're gonna get some dinner on. You hungry?" Jacob called from outside the door.

Linda wiped her face and choked back the tears. "I'm not hungry at the moment, babe. Save some for me, yeah?" she called.

"Okay."

She listened until his footsteps had faded and reached for her camera.

In times of stress there was one thing guaranteed to sooth her—developing prints. Since that awful night she had not touched her camera, and she had reams of film to develop. Picking up five films, she opened her case, took out her developing kit and made her way downstairs. Everyone was gathered in the lounge—Jacob, Andy, Jermain, even Thomas. She watched them all for a second, her gaze landing on Jacob as he poured a whiskey for everyone, and she smiled to herself.

As if he felt her eyes upon him, he looked up. "Hey!" He smiled and came over. "Changed your mind about dinner?"

She shook her head and accepted the small glass he handed her.

"You need it after today. A bit won't hurt the baby." He poured her a little whiskey, mixing it with a lot of soda water.

"Thanks." Linda downed her whiskey, and turned to Jermain. "I wanted to ask a favour, if I could use your cellar for a bit." She held up the handful of film. "I want to develop these or they'll pile up forever."

"Of course, it's unlocked. Feel free," said Jermain.

Linda thanked him and said she would see them later.

Reaching the cellar, she set out the trays and filled them with the developing fluid. Working in no specific order, she unravelled the film from the first canister and set to work.

Three hours later, Jacob came down the stairs with a dinner tray.

"Hey, you've been working for hours," he said as he set the tray down in front of her.

She glanced at her watch and was surprised to see he was right.

"I didn't realise the time," she said, taking some orange juice. "I should be done in about half an hour."

"Me and the guys are setting up a card game. Want to join in?" he asked. The telephone rang on the reception desk, and he glanced back up the stairs.

"Nah, you go ahead. I'll be up in a bit," she replied and smiled as he made his way back up.

She had a tendency to get lost in her work. Like any artist or writer, once she started she got so involved, sometimes a whole night would go by and she would not even be aware until dawn filtered through the blackout curtains. Almost all the prints were done. There had not been many of any importance, and the majority of the photos were of the opening night when the investors had attended the hotel. Her gaze lingered on one of Kate, standing with her father and John Campbell. Putting it aside, she gathered the last batch off the pegs on which she had hung them to dry—scenery of Cannes, more of the hotel, the hotel exterior, the opening night, and Jermain giving his speech. She stopped as she came to the end of the line and squinted at the last three photographs. They had obviously been taken in darkness and the general shot was of a house. She drew in a sharp breath as she recognised the prints as those she had taken when Kate and herself had arrived at the party. They were of the Martinez house. On the first print she could just make out the portraits of the four girls in the gardens behind the house, including the one of Janine that had been slashed. Looking at the second photo, she could see it was the same as the first, except…

She snatched the photograph down off the peg and looked closer. In the right hand of the frame there was a figure, disappearing around the side of the house. It looked like a male, dressed in black, with a flash of red, as the inside of his coat flapped open in the breeze.

"Jesus," she whispered. Goose bumps adorned her arms as she snatched up her digital camera.

She flicked through the images and zoomed in as far as she could on the one after those she had printed. The man could be seen more clearly on this one. He had his back to them and was totally unidentifiable except for one very important feature. It was more in focus than the other one and, if she looked very hard, she swore, on the red lining of the man's coat, she could see tiny letter 'G's.

Gucci.

A Gucci jacket.

A leather Gucci jacket.

She dropped the print and turned on her heel, running back to the first stack of photos. She flicked through them until she came back to the one of Kate standing with her father. Jermain, resplendent in his black suit, had his arm around Kate, who was smiling for the camera, and John stood in the background, one hand holding his champagne glass, the other hand in his pocket, exposing the red lining of his black leather jacket, adorned with… little letter 'G's.

"Holy shit!" She stared at the photos again, one by one. "Bloody hell!"

When she got to the lounge there was nobody there.

"HEY!" she shouted in frustration, jumping when Thomas appeared with Andy in tow.

"You okay, Linda?" Thomas asked.

"No! Yes!" she squealed. "You have to see this!"

Thomas put down his glass and took the photos from her. He squinted at the prints, then looked at the image on the camera.

"Where the bloody hell is everyone?" she asked.

"Jermain and Jacob went to get some Chinese," replied Andy.

"Linda, what is this?" asked Thomas as he leafed through the prints.

"Okay, when Kate went to the Finch's house I stayed behind to take some photos. These are the pictures and, see this?" she pointed to the male figure in the two shots.

"Christ, someone else was there?" asked Thomas.

"Yes, but not only someone else—look at this photo." She handed it to him and pointed out the design on John's jacket.

He stared in silence for a while, gazing from one photo to the other.

"Well?" she demanded. "What do you think?"

He looked up, shaking his head. "I think we've found ourselves the real killer."

"John Campbell?" The colour drained from Andy's face as it registered.

"Do you have copies of these?" Thomas stood up and pulled on his coat.

"Yes, I have the original film."

"Good, keep it safe." He snatched up his car keys and made his way to the door. "I'm off to the police station with these."

Linda stood up. "I'm coming, too." She looked back at Andy. "You stay here and explain to the others when they come back."

She had never seen Thomas so hyped up as he was on the drive to the police station.

"This is great, new evidence at the very least. They'll have to call the trial off. There'll be a re-trial, and this time Kate will be a witness instead of the accused!" he said.

"Such good news. What do you think will happen now?" she asked.

"They'll arrest John Campbell, and hopefully Kate will be released. That's what I'll be pushing for, anyway."

They drove the rest of the way in silence, Linda's heart beating with excitement and Thomas clearly elated.

On arrival, Thomas strode up to the reception. As luck would have it, Officer Marron was there, and she looked from Thomas to Linda in surprise.

Thomas slapped the photographs down on the desk and grinned at her. "Here's some new evidence, Officer, possibly leading to the arrest and conviction of the *real* murderer," he said, folding his arms.

She took the photos out of the envelope and looked at them carefully. After a time she looked up. "Come with me," she said and, coming round the side of the desk, she opened the door that led to the interview room.

Thomas winked at Linda and, trying hard to keep their excitement under control, they followed her through.

At eight thirty the following morning, John Campbell was arrested in his hotel room. The incriminating jacket, encrusted with blood, was found in a plastic bag under his bed. It was all they needed. By half past nine, faced with the new evidence, he had confessed all, and at ten o'clock, Kate was given the news that she was free to go.

Chapter Twelve

The Shooting

All hoping to get the first photo of Kate Bryant as she took her first steps to freedom, members of the press pushed their way to the front of the noisy, raucous crowds that had gathered outside the courthouse,.

Bruce and Andy stood in the centre, still unable to believe this latest turn of events. As the door opened and flashbulbs exploded, Bruce felt an arm on his shoulder. He turned around. "Joe!" His friend pulled him into a hug and, just as quickly, released him. "What are you doing here?"

He had asked himself the same question on the flight over. Despite his misgivings, he had been unable to stop himself following the trial, and had moved into Central Africa to get the information on the Internet. Once he had seen the reports from the first day, along with a photo of Kate leaving the dock, he knew he had to be there.

When he had left after the bail hearing, he thought he had hated her. Such evidence stacked against her meant that she was guilty, right? But, more than that, he hated the fact that he had been foolish enough to think she had turned up in Zaire because she missed him. His place, his home, had simply been a place for her to hide because she was in trouble and, if he were entirely honest, that hurt more than finding out she was a killer.

But it was unfinished between them. She was never out of his thoughts and he knew if he witnessed her being sent down, it might provide some sort of closure for him.

The flight and car rides since he had last checked the news meant he had no idea what had happened in the last twenty-four hours. Now he stood next to Bruce before the courthouse, wondering why everyone had gathered there.

"Bruce, what is all this?"

Bruce was about to reply when the courtroom door

opened, and Kate stepped out amid a blast of flashbulbs and microphones.

It had all happened so quickly. One minute she had been preparing herself for another excruciating day in court, and then Thomas had appeared at the door of her cell.

She had been dressed in her suit when he had arrived.

"You're late," she said as she spotted him standing in the doorway.

"You're free," he replied, unable to keep the grin from his face.

She walked towards him and looked into his eyes, thinking it was a joke and not getting it at all. "*What*?" she asked when he offered no further explanation.

Taking her hand, he sat her on the bed and gently explained everything to her.

It took a while to sink in. She had so many questions, but could think of no way to ask them.

She took a deep breath and walked over to the window.

"I can really go home?" she whispered, with her back to him.

"Yes," he answered, standing up.

She turned to him and, as the tears began to fall, he moved towards her. She stepped into his arms and he held her tight until she had gained some control.

"There'll be press outside. Are you ready for them?" he asked as she took a last look around the cell that had become her home.

"I'm ready," she said and linked her arm in his. "Let's go home."

Thomas stared in horror at the scene that unfolded before him. He had been trying to control the crowd when a hush descended. He had been a few feet away from Kate, to her left, and the people in front of him prevented him from seeing the girl that approached her with the loaded gun. Then he saw her and the glint of steel in her hand, and he froze.

He heard the click as she removed the safety catch, and it

was as though that small noise propelled him into action. He stood up and sprinted towards Kate, not thinking, just knowing the girl was moving ever closer with her gun and, if he could get to Kate in time, he would take that bullet for her. Before he could reach her, the bullet punched through Kate's white shirt. Thomas let out a strangled cry as she was thrown backwards. There was silence for a second, and then the police arrived and fired at the crazed woman. She went down, not far from Kate. Madness descended upon the crowd. Thomas battled his way through the people and reached Kate at the same time as Joe.

Joe knelt down and stared at her inert body. She was conscious, still alive. His heart leapt with hope. He watched as her eyes grew heavy, and her gaze shifted towards the man who had slumped next to him. He drew in a ragged breath as his eyes locked on hers. Her eyes closed. He fell back, looking up to the sky, tears coursing down his face.

In due course the ambulance arrived and, as they loaded her onto the stretcher, a medic sat astride her and performed chest compressions.

Jermain, who must have witnessed everything from the back of the crowd, fought his way to the ambulance and climbed in with her. It sped away, leaving the two men standing in bewilderment.

Not knowing who the other was or his connection to Kate, they looked at each other with matching expressions of despair.

Joe ran a hand over his face and shook his head. "How did this happen?"

Thomas swallowed his tears and faced him. "Are you a friend?" he asked.

"Kind of." Joe shrugged. "Friend, boyfriend. I don't know."

Thomas backed off and realised this must be the famous Joe Palmer he had heard about. Kate had never mentioned him, but he knew that Joe had unknowingly sheltered her in Zaire before her arrest. He also knew from Linda that he had come to the hearing, heard all of the evidence and walked out on her. Distaste rose but he swallowed it back. Focus must be on Kate now.

Bruce reached them at that moment. "We have to tell the others," he said and led Joe and Thomas to his car.

Linda, Jacob and Andy had stayed at the hotel to prepare a special meal for Kate to welcome her home.

Joe shuddered at the thought of telling them what had happened. "I need to go to the hospital. I need to be with her," he said as he dug in his pockets for his keys.

"You're in no state to drive," said Bruce, taking the keys. "I'll drop you off at the hospital and go back to the hotel. We'll meet you there."

Joe nodded and choked out his gratitude.

Linda was just putting the finishing touches to the dinner table when Thomas and Bruce burst in.

She looked up, startled. By the look on their faces, she knew instantly it wasn't good news.

"Jacob!" she yelled, rushing over to Thomas, who looked close to passing out as he leant against the wall.

Jacob and Andy came into the foyer and exchanged glances.

"Thomas?" Linda took his hand and sat him down. "What's happened?"

He took a deep breath and clutched onto her. "Kate was shot," he said.

Linda's mouth fell open. She shook her head. "Shot? By who? Is she…is she…?" she trailed off and put her hand to her mouth to stifle the bile that rose in her throat.

"Bruce, what the fuck happened?" Jacob asked, as if hoping he would get more information from him.

"She was at the front of the courthouse. Thomas was going to release a statement to the press and then this girl, uh… Ester—I recognised her from the photos in the papers, friend of Janine Finch—she came up with a gun…" he broke off. "She shot her," he finished quietly.

"Oh Christ, did she…is she *dead*?" Linda whispered.

"I don't know," said Thomas.

"Right," Jacob pulled Thomas out of the chair. "We have to go the hospital, right now." He ushered them all out of the front door.

"This is unreal," said Bruce as Jacob drove them to the medical centre. "Everything that's happened, now *this*." He turned to Linda. "Joe turned up as well, saw the whole thing. We dropped him off at the hospital. Jermain went with her in the ambulance."

"Please, God, let her be okay," said Linda, but it was an empty plea made to a God she wasn't even sure existed anymore.

Kate couldn't see. It was as though she was underwater. Voices and sounds were muffled and she panicked, trying to get to the surface. Eventually, realising it was a futile struggle, she lay back, drifting and listening…

Jermain pleaded, tearfully, as someone squeezed a plastic oxygen bag in and out, in and out, forcing life into her failing lungs. Jermain, again, telling her to fight, she had to fight. She wanted to tell him she couldn't, she couldn't do *anything*.

When Jacob, Linda, Bruce and Thomas arrived at the hospital, Linda broke away from the others, and ran to where Jermain sat, slouched in a chair. "What's happening? Is she okay?"

"She's in surgery. They need to remove the bullet." Jermain broke off as tears coursed down his face. He clutched her hand. "She's ripped to shreds, Linda, so much blood…"

She burst into tears, hugging him.

Kate was expected to be in theatre for around eight hours, and there was nothing anybody could do but sit and wait.

They each dealt with their emotions in their own way. Andy, who had found the last few weeks a huge struggle after his former quiet life, sat in the hospital chapel, so he told them, not praying, just thinking, hoping for a small miracle.

Bruce, always a good one to have around in a crisis, gleaned as much information as he could from the doctors hurrying in and out of the operating theatre. He listened grimly and kept the others up to date.

At one point, he took Joe aside. "The bullet passed through her stomach, through to the back. It's lodged in a vertebrae near her spinal cord. A false move could be dangerous," he explained. "Not a word to Jermain, he doesn't need to know this yet."

Joe went white. "Paralysis?" he whispered. After his time in the hospital with his spine problems, surrounded by people like Emily, paralysis was a dark nightmare that lurked in the back of his mind.

"She needs support, Joe," said Bruce in a harsh tone. "Not pity, or shock. You, as well as anyone, know this."

Joe nodded and drifted back down the hallway to sit next to Jermain.

Linda and Jacob walked hand in hand around the hospital grounds. Under the circumstances, he had lifted his no smoking ban and Linda was grateful. Her nerves were frayed and her emotions raw.

As they walked around the front, Jacob spotted Thomas sitting by himself on the fire escape steps. He started towards him, but Linda held him back. He looked at her questioningly and she shook her head at him.

"Leave him," she said.

Jacob looked over to Thomas and back to Linda. "Why?" he asked, genuinely confused.

"He's feeling this, too, right now," she said. "We all care for Kate, but Thomas thinks he doesn't have the right to show how he really feels."

Jacob raised his eyebrows. "You mean him…and Kate? Ha!"

"Don't laugh, he loves her," protested Linda and cast a pitying glance at Thomas.

"Bullshit!" Jacob laughed. "You're nuts, lady!"

"Yeah, well, we'll see. And shut up about it, okay?" she demanded as they turned around and made their way back inside.

At six o'clock that evening they wheeled Kate out of the theatre and into the Intensive Care Unit. As the surgeon approached them, he took off his mask and looked at them all with weary eyes.

"The bullet was removed, but Kate lost a lot of blood. The good news is that the bullet missed any major organs, but it did lodge in her spine preventing an exit. It's just a case of waiting now, I'm afraid."

Jermain nodded. He had not expected anything else. "Can I see her?"

"Just for a second. She is unconscious, sir, so please, not for long," replied the surgeon.

Jermain took a deep breath and followed the doctor down the corridor.

Kate was underwater again. For a long time there had been nothing, like sleep. Now she was back in her cotton-wool world where she couldn't quite wake up.

There was a lot of speculation about whether unconscious people could hear. Kate could verify it was true. She found she had to concentrate hard and, even then, for a while there was just muttering, muffled sounds she could not distinguish. Then she heard Jermain clearly, and strained to listen to his words.

"I'm so sorry, baby." His voice was thick with tears, and she tried to get past them to listen to him. "I saw it all, but I couldn't get to you, it happened so quickly. You must fight, my darling. I can't lose you as well."

I'm trying, Dad, I really am, but I don't know what to do.

At midnight, Bruce persuaded everyone to go home and rest up for the night. Kate was stable, and they would all be more use to her if they had at least a few hours' sleep. He elected to stay and keep an eye out until they all got back.

When Thomas arrived back with fresh coffee, he was surprised to see everyone had vanished.

"I'll stay and finish this," he said and eyed the door to Kate's room.

Bruce nodded and leaned back in the chair.

Sometime later, Thomas awoke with a start and looked around him in confusion. Then he remembered where he was and sat up straight. The hallway was empty, except for himself and Bruce, who was sleeping soundly.

For a few minutes he sat there, sipping at the cold coffee he had bought before he had fallen asleep. Eventually, he stood and, checking Bruce was still sleeping, walked over to Kate's room. For a while he watched her through the window. Glancing over his shoulder, he saw nobody was around and quietly let himself in.

She looked like she was sleeping. Her chest rose and fell in a steady rhythm, and he watched it for a second, taking comfort from the fact that she was breathing, albeit with the aid of the respirator.

Later, maybe hours, days, possibly weeks, for there was no time structure in Kate's world, she heard Thomas. Strange that he should be there. Where was Joe? Why could she not hear Joe?

Silence again, and in the part of her brain that could still hear, she realised she wanted to listen to Thomas.

She sensed rather than felt him take her hand and she tried to squeeze her fingers, close them around his, but it didn't happen.

So she settled back, and listened carefully.

"You knocked me out the first time I saw you. I remember, you had been brought back from Zaire, and I was harsh to you, telling you how you had made it difficult for yourself by running away. It was a defence, Kate; it was my way of not letting you see how you affected me.

"But I did in the end, didn't I? I couldn't hide it anymore. And I think you knew.

"At first I was sceptical, and I wasn't alone. Andy, even Joe—they weren't convinced you were innocent. But you convinced me that day, before the trial. I knew, really, really knew you hadn't done it.

"I loved you that day, before then, since then. Every day for the rest of my life, I'll love you. And I wish so much I'd told you, but I can't tell anyone, nobody at all."

A long pause, too long, and she thought he had gone. Then he spoke again and, had she been conscious, his next words would have brought her to tears.

"I tried to get in front of you. I tried to take that bullet for you, Kate. And I would have managed it, if only I was faster. I would have died for you."

When Kate felt Thomas leave, she had no time to speculate on his words, as she suddenly fell back another level in her world. A jolt, a distant beeping noise, and then nothing…

The telephone awoke Jermain at once. He snatched it up.

"Hello?"

"Jermain, you need to get here. Kate's taken a turn for the worse," Bruce said.

He sat up and clutched the phone so hard his knuckles turned white. "Worse? In what way?"

"She's arrested, that means—"

"I know what it means. I'm on my way." He hung up, and pulled on the clothes he had taken off only hours before.

As he sprinted down the stairs, he called out for Joe.

Joe, who had not been sleeping, was in the lounge, nursing a large glass of whiskey, deep in thought, emotions running through him, making his head spin and his brain hurt. The truth was, he couldn't bear to see Kate, couldn't face the thought of sitting by another hospital bed watching another girl he loved slowly fade away. Because that was what would happen. It happened to them all—Emily, Kate, Tyler. Even if it were not death it was sometimes worse. What way was that, to live without an arm or a leg, or in a wheelchair? He felt he had brought nothing but bad luck to all of them, and maybe it wasn't too late for Kate.

He was seriously contemplating leaving France to let her recover on her own. In his traumatised state, he thought if he did leave, maybe she *would* recover.

Jermain interrupted his train of thoughts, and he looked up as he ran past.

"Her heart's stopped, we need to be there," said Jermain.

Joe slammed his glass down and followed Jermain out of the hotel.

Arriving back at the hospital, they found Bruce pacing the corridor. He ran up to them.

"She's stabilised, she's breathing but not unaided, and…" he tailed off and led Jermain to a chair. "She's in a coma."

"Jesus." Joe slumped against the wall.

Jermain paled and tugged at Bruce's sleeve. "What are her chances?"

Bruce shrugged. "It's not my case. The doctor will be speaking with you."

"Don't give me that shit," Jermain said through clenched teeth. "You're a bloody doctor. I'm sure you know the statistics on people in comas, so bloody tell me."

"It depends on a huge variety of things, age, fitness, previous medical history. Kate has everything on her side," he said comfortingly.

Just then Linda and Jacob dashed in.

"We heard you go. We thought something must have happened," said Linda breathlessly.

Bruce took them to one side and explained what had happened to Kate.

"Christ," said Jacob. "Now all we can do is wait?"

Bruce nodded in confirmation.

A few minutes later the consultant on duty arrived, and led them all to a separate room.

"Whilst Kate is in her current condition, this room is for your use whenever you want to be here," he said and waited for them all to sit down.

The doctor repeated everything Bruce had already told

them, and that Kate was being constantly monitored.

"You can sit with her, all of you. It's been proven that coma victims can often hear what's happening around them, and familiar voices may help," he said.

"Can I see her?" Linda asked.

The doctor nodded.

Before she followed him out of the room, she turned back. "Is that okay? I mean, if I sit with her for a while?" she directed her question at Joe because he hadn't yet seen her.

He nodded, and Bruce gave him a sharp look before speaking. "I'll get us some coffee. God knows we could all use it. Joe, you'll help me?"

Joe obediently followed Bruce out of the room and waited for what he knew was coming.

"So you don't want to see her? Is that it?" asked Bruce as they walked toward the coffee machine.

"It's not that simple," Joe said. "I don't think I'd be good for her."

"Emily, right, and Tyler, this is about what happened to them?"

"I can't help how I feel, sort of responsible in some way," replied Joe.

"But you weren't, and you know it!" exclaimed Bruce. "*She* needs you in there." He pointed down the corridor to the room where Kate lay and, with his free hand, grabbed the front of Joe's shirt. "She needs to *hear* you."

He pulled away and turned. "I can't see her. You have to understand."

"Oh, shit." Bruce sighed heavily.

"I'm sorry." Joe turned toward the exit. "Tell them I'm sorry." Without another word, he jogged out of the door and into the night.

Forgetting the car he had parked in the lot, he ran out into the balmy night, in no particular direction, as long as it was away from that stinking hospital.

After a while he found himself on Quai St. Pierre.

He sat down heavily on the pavement and stared out to sea, thinking of Kate, how she had looked at him, when she had been shot, and the blood that had pooled around her as she lay on the ground outside the police station. Even if she lived, she would be a ruin, possibly paralysed, a cripple.

Just like Emily.

Just like Tyler.

Partially, like himself.

He was not stupid. He knew he should have continued with the therapy they had offered him over the years, but he had thought he was fine, thought it was in the past, forgotten.

But it wasn't forgotten, it was simply buried, and now it had surfaced—the old feelings, the guilt and the shame, not being able to protect those he loved, or make things better for them.

As he stared out onto the moonlit ocean, he knew there was only one person who could exorcise his demons.

He had to visit Tyler.

* * * *

It was another eight days before Kate came round again. Eight days of hell for those who loved her and made the hospital their home.

They settled into a routine. Linda—who was having trouble sleeping—and Jacob sat with her most of the night, talking to her. Jacob had been uncomfortable with this at first, but had soon overcome his qualms.

Jermain, always a naturally early riser, took over from dawn until mid-morning, when either Andy or Bruce would come in.

Thomas had vanished. Andy had settled his payment on the day Kate was released, but the cheque had still not been cashed.

Joe had also gone, along with his clothes, and everything he had left at the hotel. He had left no word for Bruce, and nobody had heard from him in over a week.

"I'm so grateful for your presence," Jermain told Linda. "You're a real trooper." When it became apparent that Kate was not going to wake up any time in the near future, she had arrived at the hospital armed with lotions, brushes and all sorts of women's things that had made Jacob roll his eyes.

"You think she wants to look like that when she wakes up?" Linda had hissed at him and nudged him away from the bed.

"S'long as you don't expect me to help," Jacob had retorted, and let her get to work.

But even Jacob had been impressed when she had finished. With the help of the nurses, she had washed Kate, powdered and perfumed her and shampooed her hair until it gleamed.

Jermain had thanked her with watering eyes, and she had held his hands. She had never been in a close family environment; her parents had been in their forties when she had been born. 'An unexpected surprise' was how her mother put it. She felt grateful to Jermain for letting her into his family circle.

It was the graveyard shift, and Jacob dozed in the chair in the corner. Linda talked to Kate while she filed her friend's nails, not that there was much to file. They had been bitten down to the quick, but the body doesn't stop whilst in a coma, and they were growing through.

At first she thought she had imagined it, a slight pressure on her hand from Kate's fingers. She stopped filing and stayed dead still, closing her eyes, waiting for it again.

Kate knew it was time to go, but which way? That was the question.

For the last few hours, or days, she couldn't tell, she had been rising steadily up through the levels she had sunk past when her heart had stopped. Now she was in the middle and, in her world, she sat up and looked around.

She seemed to be in some sort of tunnel, or a hallway, maybe. It was white, bright white, almost clinical in a way.

She turned to her left and looked down the length of the tunnel to see some figures waiting patiently. They were very beautiful in a way that made Kate want to meet them. Before walking towards them, she looked to her right and saw the world. It seemed she could see the entire world, parts she had visited in her other life, and places she had yet to see.

She knew she was in control now. It was her choice. She knew what she had to do. With one last glance in the other direction she turned, and started the journey back home.

"Christ," Linda whispered.

She had definitely felt something that time. She clutched Kate's hands and leaned over her.

"Come on, honey. You can hear me, can't you?" Linda glanced over her shoulder at Jacob who still slept soundly. "Time to wake up, Kate. *Now.*"

She could feel it, something pulling her onwards. Suddenly, unable to wait any longer, she ran.

Back in the real world her heart monitor began to bleep louder and louder.

Linda took a deep breath. Something was happening. She could see that on Kate's monitor. She didn't need to be a nurse to understand Kate's body was undergoing a major change.

Suddenly Kate's eyes opened wide and stared at her. Linda shrieked and snatched away her hand, then got a hold of herself and, leaning forward, she touched Kate's face.

For a second they stared at each other.

"Can you hear me?" Linda asked.

"Um," Kate murmured and Linda screamed again.

Jacob awoke with a jolt and sprang out of his chair. In the gloom he could see Linda bent over Kate's still figure and his heart sank.

"What the fuck's happened now?" he cried and lurched towards the bed.

He looked down at Kate and at first it didn't register. He kept staring then realised what was different; she was staring back at him.

"Shit!" he exclaimed and rang the bell for the nurse.

The hospital corridor buzzed with activity, and eventually the commotion woke Jermain who was sleeping in the family room. He opened the door and looked out into the hallway, and was aghast to see people careening in and out of Kate's room. He crossed the hallway and pushed past the doctors who were gathered by her bed. When he reached her side, he had fully prepared himself to find her dead, or at least for the doctors to have the crash cart in again, trying frantically to resuscitate her. So, when he saw her lying back against the pillow, her eyes open and looking around the room, he almost fainted.

"Kate! Oh God! *Kate*!" he yelled, falling to his knees beside her bed.

She clutched his hand, and whispered. He didn't catch her words, just threw his arms around her neck and held her as tightly as he could.

Chapter Thirteen

Tyler

It wasn't hard to track down Tyler Roth. Joe's mother, when he called her, confirmed he was still living in Brixton, and she had bumped into him a few times over the years around town.

"He always asks after you, Joe," she said, and Joe carried these words with him to England in the hope that Tyler would not shut the door in his face.

When he landed at Heathrow, he wished he had dressed more appropriately. It was autumn, and he felt far away from Cannes and the hot weather. His first port of call was to stop by the office in Camden, to see how everything was. He had left Zaire in a hurry and, although the Pygmies were no longer at risk of losing their home, he still felt guilty about leaving them so soon.

Steve Chapman greeted him at the door.

"Hey, man, you want to tell me what's been going on in *your* life?" Steve asked, pulling him into the office.

"You know, same old," replied Joe. He helped himself to a coffee.

"Yeah, right!" Steve scoffed, and threw down a pile of national newspapers.

Joe picked them up and glanced through them. The front page started with Kate's arrest, her dramatic escape and her re-capture. Joe swore as he saw he and Bruce had been named.

"Will there be any comeback on the company from this?" he asked.

"Nah, not since she was found not guilty," said Steve. "But what about all this?" He picked up another bundle of papers and showed them to Joe.

One of them portrayed a picture of Kate, lying on the ground outside the police station. Ester, having been shot by the police, lay a few feet away. Joe grimaced as he spotted himself crouched beside Kate.

"For Christ's sake," he muttered and, scooping them up, threw them all into Steve's trashcan.

"So...how is she?" asked Steve tentatively.

Joe shrugged. "Same. Listen, I need a couple of weeks off, but I want to know what my next assignment is."

Sensing that Joe did not want to talk about the girl or what had happened in France, Steve nodded and went over to the filing cabinet.

"Aboriginal settlement in Australia, town called Mackay. It's in Queensland, located on the coast of the Great Barrier Reef. The Aborigines are fine in themselves, they've just been granted around four hundred kilometres of land by the Government, but they need a mediator. The local farmers and citizens are not happy that their land apparently doesn't belong to them anymore. There's a lot of friction. The Australians are not happy about the Land Rights Act that was brought in. You need to speak with them."

Joe listened carefully and looked through the information Steve gave him. "Just talking to them, huh?" he asked.

"And planning, you have the land plans. Fences need to be built, barriers and that, just to show whose land is whose," said Steve. "When do you want to go?"

Joe was tempted to say, 'Today', but that would be too easy. He had come to London for a purpose, to see Tyler again after more than ten years, to get his forgiveness and repel the demons that haunted him.

"Give me a week, okay?" he said and, taking the information Steve had given him, left the office and headed for the tube.

When he got to Brixton, he made his way off the tube and up into the street. Brixton had not changed much. The boys were still out in force in the streets, playing football and hanging around the shops. It was grimy, wet and grey, and he didn't know how his parents or Tyler could still live here. He watched the boys playing football, feeling a sadness that the majority of them would never leave this place or go on to better things.

Joe's mother had said she thought Tyler lived in Heath Tower, a depressing block of high-rise flats in the roughest area of town. Before he could change his mind, he started to walk in that direction.

Tyler lived on the ground floor. Logical, supposed Joe, considering he was in a wheelchair. He waited a while before pressing the buzzer.

Nobody replied.

When it was clear that there was nobody at home, he sat down on the steps and waited.

* * * *

Kate lay and listened to Jermain as he brought her up to date with everything that had happened since they had set her free.

"What about the girl, Ester?" she asked.

"They shot her, they had to. They didn't know how many bullets she had in that damn gun," he replied.

"What a wasted life. Surely she knew John Campbell had been arrested?"

"Hmm, turned out she had a real thing for him. She'd wanted him for years, and couldn't handle the fact he had murdered her best friend. It was easier for her to accept you had killed her. It all came out that she was pretty messed up, on a cocktail of drugs, out of her mind." Jermain glanced at his watch. "I'll let you rest now, okay, honey?"

She nodded, tilting her face towards his as he kissed her cheek.

When he left the room, she pressed the bell for the nurse.

"Is Linda still here?" she asked when she came in.

"I think so, let me see," replied the nurse, and went out into the hallway.

Moments later she returned with Linda.

"I thought you were asleep." Linda came over to the bed.

"I need to talk to you," said Kate. "I need answers, and Dad won't give them to me. He's afraid."

Linda understood. Joe's disappearance had not been mentioned, neither had the full extent of her injuries.

"I'll tell you whatever you need to know," said Linda, knowing it was what she would have wanted if she had been in Kate's position.

"Where's Joe?"

"Nobody knows. He took off a week before you woke up. Bruce said it's something to do with his past, something that happened to someone he cared about, but he won't say any more than that."

Kate nodded slowly and wondered how to phrase her next question. "What about…Thomas?" she asked, not meeting Linda's eyes.

"Ah, now, Thomas," Linda sat back and sighed. "That's a strange one. He was here the whole time, right up until the night your heart got in trouble. Andy paid him the solicitor's fee, but he never cashed the cheque, and he's not been seen since, either. What happened between you two, Kate?"

Kate pulled the sheet up under her chin. What *had* happened between them? Nothing, as far as she could remember, except a conversation that had taken place when she had been comatose, a conversation she recalled very well, but had played no part in.

"Nothing happened, Linda." She smiled sadly. "And it won't now, will it?"

Linda hugged her. "Go to sleep now, and you'll be out of here in no time."

Kate caught her hand as she stood up to leave.

"One more thing—the doctors have skirted round my questions—am I going to walk again?"

Linda sat back down. "They are almost one hundred percent certain you will not suffer further effects from the bullet wounds and, after physiotherapy and plenty of rest, there's no reason why you won't walk again."

"I *will* walk. You see. Better than I did before, even," she said eventually, lying back against the pillows.

Linda kissed her goodbye with a promise to call in the following day.

As Linda left, Kate thought about all she had said. So, both Thomas and Joe had done a disappearing act? Interesting. After all she had been through with Joe, she now realised how hurt he must have been. She had run to him in Africa, and he had thought it was because she couldn't be without him. Then he had found out she was simply on the run and looking for a place to hide. A tear trickled down her cheek and she wiped it angrily away.

And Thomas, nothing had happened with him, but she knew she had not imagined all that he had said to her. She frowned as she recalled his words. So Andy and Joe had not believed she was innocent. Andy, she didn't really care one way or the other, but Joe, well that was something else altogether.

* * * *

Joe had been sitting on the steps for twenty minutes when he spotted a young man in a wheelchair coming up the street towards him. He stood up and took a deep breath as Tyler reached the block of flats.

They looked at each other for a moment while Joe tried to think of what to say.

"Hi," he said eventually.

"Palmer?" said Tyler.

"How are you?" he said quietly, trying not to look at the ugly burn scar on Tyler's face.

"Okay. Christ, it's been years, come in." He wheeled past Joe and unlocked the front door. "You look like you could do with a drink."

Following Tyler into his flat, he stopped and looked around. It was worse than he had imagined, almost bare of any furniture, except for a coffee table in the centre of the small room.

"Not quite the Ritz, I know," said Tyler as he wheeled himself into the room and turned to face Joe. "It's been ten years, Joe, why are you here now?"

Joe sat on the floor and wondered where to start, eventually beginning with the crash, and the months of rehabilitation, the shame and depression at having caused the accident, then the short period of hope when he had met Emily, only to lose her as well.

"What happened to her?"

"She died," replied Joe. "She got blood poisoning in her leg."

"But it wasn't your fault, you didn't cause it, and when our shit went down you weren't driving," said Tyler.

"But I was snorting coke, on the dash board. I distracted you." Joe felt tears well up in his eyes and realised he had never known how deeply affected he still was.

"Yeah, and I was eating the shit, too. I chose to drive off my head on booze, drugs—all sorts of shit. Don't be a martyr, Joe. It's not your responsibility."

Joe swore he saw a look of distaste in Tyler's eyes as he turned to pour them both a drink of whiskey from one of the many bottles on the coffee table.

"But it's happened again, there's this girl you see." In a trembling voice he brought Tyler up to date on the last ten years.

Tyler listened silently and, when Joe was finished, he looked him dead in the eye.

"You need help, mate. I thought *I* had problems, but you really need to speak to someone. This isn't your fault. *I* was driving that car that night. Your girl got blood poisoning. *You* didn't pull the trigger on the bird in France."

Joe knew he was right. He nodded. It was something he was going to have to get over in his own time. He shouldn't let his psychological problems ruin his chance with Kate, if she was still alive that was, and he told Tyler this.

"There you go, mate, you know I'm right," replied Tyler, pouring them both another hefty glass of whiskey.

Joe looked at him properly for the first time, and was shocked at what he saw. Tyler, always an attractive lad, had changed. He was thin and gaunt, his eyes dull and his hands shook as he held his glass.

"How have *you* been, Tyler?" he asked.

"Oh, you know, not much changes. You sticking around for a while?"

"A week, maybe we can get together?"

Tyler gave a non-committing shrug, and excused himself as he wheeled his chair towards what Joe presumed was the bathroom.

When he had left the room, Joe got up and walked around. He couldn't understand it. With the disability allowance, Tyler should be well off. Instead he was living in what would pass for a squat, with no furniture and looking as if he hadn't eaten in a week. With a look behind him to make sure Tyler wasn't coming back, he went into the kitchen. It was as bare as the lounge, with just a refrigerator in one corner and a dirty sink, filled with plates and cups. He opened the fridge and looked at the contents.

There were none.

Shaking his head, he turned to go back to the lounge, and almost fell over Tyler, behind him in the chair.

"Hungry?" asked Tyler with a raised eyebrow.

"Uh, was going to make a cup of tea but you've got no milk," Joe replied, thinking on his feet and giving a nervous laugh. "You've got nothing, in fact."

Tyler tilted himself on the two back wheels of the chair and spun around to face the lounge.

"I eat out mostly," he said by way of explanation.

"So, listen, I have to go now, but can I come by tomorrow, maybe treat you to dinner?"

"I don't do dinner," snapped Tyler. He looked up and his features softened. "Come by, we'll sort something, yeah?"

Joe nodded and, with one last glance around, let himself out of the flat.

He walked down the road, hurrying now, wanting to find himself a hotel for the night.

It was time to call France to find out if Kate was still alive.

The opening night for Cannes Central was rearranged. The citizens of the local area had apparently experienced an enormous guilt trip about their slating of Kate over the murder of Janine and, since the shooting, Jermain had been inundated with calls and visits from their neighbours. Even better than that, the investors had been in touch, wanting to know if the hotel was still in business. Instead of Christmas Eve, the opening was rescheduled for the first weekend in February, time to let Kate recuperate, so she could be part of it.

Linda had manned the phones since she had left the hospital. She sat on the reception desk, trying to organise interviews for the catering staff, and calling back the people they had already hired, to see if they were still available.

She had not returned to England since handing in her notice at the newspaper. Instead Jermain had asked for her help sorting out the staff at the hotel and casino, and she had willingly obliged in exchange for free board.

The future seemed solid for her and Jacob. Even though everything had happened so fast, it simply felt right. The baby was the icing on the cake and she still felt as much for him as she had when they had first met. The past few months had been a tough test, but they had pulled through and the events had only cemented their love. They had not decided where they were going to live, or even looked at any properties in the area since before the trial. But, as long as she continued to help Jermain with the business, he had promised her she could stay at the hotel until they started taking bookings.

As she went through the endless resumés of prospective employees, she received a telephone call that she hadn't been expecting. It was from Thomas.

"I just wanted to find out how Kate was doing," he said.

"Thomas! She's okay. She took a turn for the worse when you left. She was in a coma for over a week." Linda paused. "Why did you leave so suddenly, Thomas?"

"I, uh…work, you see," he stuttered. "But she's all right now?"

"Yes, she's still in the hospital, but she's going to be just fine. The doctors say she will be able to walk. Where are you, anyway?"

"Um, England, just for a while. Needed a break."

"Kate is talking about going back to England, just until the opening. Maybe you could visit her?" she said eagerly.

"Oh, well…whereabouts will she be?" he asked cautiously.

"At Jermain's place, somewhere near Darlington. If you like, I'll find out the address and email it to you," she replied.

"Yes," he said after a while. "Mail me, but don't mention this conversation to her, Linda. I'm not sure if I should see her yet. This has messed me up a bit, so if I don't call, please understand."

Linda understood all too well. It pained her to hear Thomas talk like he had no chance. After all, Joe had gone, and it would be good for Kate to have someone with her again.

"I understand, Thomas. I'll see you," she said and hung up.

Jacob came in moments later. She smiled.

"How's my favourite pregnant girlfriend?" he asked and kissed her.

"You're *only* pregnant girlfriend, I hope. Hey, listen, guess who that was on the phone?"

He shrugged as he picked up the faxes reeling off the machine.

"Thomas," she said and folded her arms with a smug expression on her face. "I told you there was something between him and Kate. When are you going to listen to me?"

He laughed aloud. "I'd never have thought it, quiet, gentle Thomas getting it on with the wildcat Kate," he said, slapping Linda on the backside. "Get your glad rags on, sweetheart. I'm taking you to dinner."

* * * *

When Joe called the hotel, he got the answering machine. He hung up and deliberated on whom to try next. He didn't want to call Jermain directly. He fully expected to get a bollocking from him for running out on Kate, from Linda, too, for that matter. In the end he tried Bruce's mobile. At least the doctor had some understanding of his behaviour.

Bruce answered on the second ring, as though he was waiting for his call.

"Bruce, it's me."

"About bloody time! Where the hell are you?"

"London. How is she?"

There was a pause and, for a moment, Joe feared the worst.

"She's fine. She's pulled through, Joe. *Now* will you come back and see her?" said Bruce, his tone softer.

"Yes, but not yet. I caught up with an old friend and I think he needs my help. But I'll be back as soon as I can. I want to see her before I leave."

"Leave?" Bruce sounded confused. "Leave for where?"

"Australia, my next job. And I'm going to ask Kate to come with me."

There was a silence at Bruce's end of the phone. Then he spoke slowly, with the patience of an adult speaking to a small child.

"Joe, you need to be here *now*. Kate is starting physiotherapy. She needs all the support she can get. This is no time for you to be hooking up with old mates *or* emigrating to the other bloody side of the world."

"Trust me, Bruce. I know all that, but I have to finish up my business here." Joe paused and wondered how he could explain the importance of spending at least a few days with Tyler. "I once let someone down badly, and I have a chance to make up a little of that now—a chance to finally put to bed all the stuff that's haunted me. Give me a week."

"Okay, I'll take your word on that but, Joe, you might want to hurry. Kate is talking about spending some time at her home in Darlington. You may need to see her there," replied Bruce.

"Okay, I'll call during the week and you can tell me where she is. I know I need to sort things out with her."

"All right, then. Just don't mess it up for yourself, okay,

boy?" growled Bruce and hung up.

When Joe put the phone down, he realised he needed to move quickly. Something was going on with Tyler and he had a bad feeling about it.

He decided to find out what it was, and help in whatever way he could.

Bruce was in a dilemma. Should he tell Kate Joe had phoned? He didn't think so. It seemed she was under the impression that Joe had left her for good. Expectations were the last thing she needed. Chucking his mobile on his bed, he wandered downstairs. He fancied some company and, now that Kate was on the mend, the hotel was back to its old self, a fun place to be.

He rounded up Jermain and Andy and coerced them into a poker game. It was soon almost midnight and the three men showed no signs of going to bed.

Not long after Andy had scooped his third big win, Jacob and Linda came in.

"Bruce?" Linda stood in the doorway.

"Hey, Linda, fancy a game?" he called and raised his glass to her.

"I'd love nothing better than to take all your money, Bruce, but I think you're going to need every penny for your impending divorce," she replied.

"Huh?"

She walked up to his chair and flicked a piece of paper down in front of him. He looked at it and gave her a bemused look.

"It's a message—from your wife. I took the call today and left you this, and you didn't even read it! Which means you didn't call her back." Linda's tone was stern.

"Shit," muttered Bruce.

With the events of the past few weeks, he had totally forgotten about his wife, and keeping her up to date with his movements. No wonder Linda was talking about divorce!

He stood up rapidly and made his way out to reception.

"I'll call her now," he said, as he passed Linda and gave

her a dark look.

Jacob laughed and picked up Bruce's hand. "I'll keep the old man in the game," he said and poured himself a drink.

And so it continued, as most of the recent evenings had—Jermain and Andy, silently thanking the Lord they had no ties and nobody to keep them in line but themselves, Bruce, feeling guilty for forgetting he had a wife back in England, then feeling even more guilty that he didn't really feel that bad about forgetting her, and Jacob, pulling Linda onto his lap, laughing at the older men knowing, one day, it would be him being nagged by his wife, and a fond sneaky look at Linda confirmed that he couldn't wait for those days.

Then there was Kate. Alone in the narrow hospital bed, lights out, the nurses' station deserted as the night staff crept off for their naps.

Night-time was when she did her best thinking. When the last light went out on the ward, she would haul herself out of bed, over to the door of her private room, and close it softly, pulling the blinds down so nobody would see her.

This she now did, limping, always holding firmly onto the side of the bed, lest her weak back gave way, and she tumbled to the floor like she had one morning in physiotherapy. When she was safely shut away from the world, she hobbled over to the window, dragging one of the visitor's chairs over. With the curtains pulled back and the window wide open, she sat and pulled out the cigarettes she had begged Linda to buy her. She lit one up and leaned across the windowsill to stare at the stars. As she smoked, silent tears rolled down her cheeks as she tried to muddle through the confusing thoughts running constantly through her head.

Joe and Thomas. Thomas and Joe.

Both men had come so suddenly into her life, and had departed even faster.

To her family and friends she had acted blasé and unaffected by them, but to her heart she couldn't deny the truth.

Maybe they had made it easier for her, by leaving. That

way she didn't have to choose between them.

She flicked the cigarette out of the window and looked around her room. Her bags were packed, ready for her to leave in the morning. Her plan was to spend a few days at the hotel before returning to England. The doctors were far from happy about her going so soon, but she didn't pay any heed to them—she had to get away. The cottage back home was a perfect place for her to recuperate and get her head together. She planned to come back to Cannes in February in time for the opening. And also, back in England, she would be kept busy by the daily physiotherapy sessions arranged for her, too busy to think about what could have been. That suited her just fine.

Chapter Fourteen

Joe set out to visit Tyler early. He had said he would take him to dinner but, as he had tracked him down sooner than he had expected, he had nothing else to do, so he intended to take him out for the day.

It was starting to drizzle when he jumped off the tube at Brixton, and he hurried along the road with his hood pulled up.

Before he could ring Tyler's bell, the door opened and two men came out. Joe caught the door and let himself in. Tyler's door was ajar. He paused outside, looking back at the two men before letting himself in. He glanced around the lounge. It had been totally trashed, not that there had been much to wreck in the first place. The coffee table was overturned, books and videos swept off the shelves, and the chairs had been slashed, their stuffing spilling out over the floor.

"Tyler!" Joe called, stepping over the CDs that lay in a pile by his feet.

There was no reply. He must have gone out, and someone who knew him must have seen him go, and broken in. Only if it were someone who knew him, and knew this *area*, surely they would know there was nothing to take?

He lifted the coffee table and set it the right way up. Kneeling down, he scooped up a handful of books and put them to one side. Underneath the books he spotted a small, clear plastic bag filled with brown powder. He picked it up and peered at it.

Heroin.

So, this hadn't been an ordinary burglary, after all. Tyler had got himself a nice little habit he couldn't afford, and the dealers had paid him a little visit as a warning.

It all clicked into place. The lousy flat with no furniture, no food in the cupboards, Tyler's emaciated appearance.

Joe sat back on his heels, the package still in his hand, and thought about his find. Should he approach Tyler? He didn't have to. He had made his peace with him, and could just leave him to it. And judging by the state of things, Tyler was too far gone to help, anyway.

Glancing around the room once more, he spotted Tyler's wheelchair, lying on its side, half in the kitchen. He stood up slowly, the implications registering in his mind.

If Tyler's wheelchair was there, he could not have gone out. Joe bolted for the kitchen, clambering over the chair. It was empty. He spun around and opened the door nearest to him—a bedroom, almost as bare as the other rooms, except for a futon in the centre. On the futon, curled foetus-like, and bleeding heavily from cuts covering every part of his face, lay his friend.

"Tyler," Joe whispered, clutching at the doorframe for support.

Tyler looked at him through his left eye, the right one so bruised and swollen, it had closed.

"They…might come back…go." He struggled to speak through his cut and swollen lips.

Joe didn't consider leaving. The thought that those heavies might come back to finish the job didn't faze him at all. Tyler needed him now, for quite a few different reasons it seemed, and Joe wasn't going to let him down again.

"Don't speak," he said, kneeling beside him. "Let me help you."

Tyler closed his one good eye and nodded.

Joe set to work patching him up, carefully cleaning his cuts and dousing his bruises with witch hazel found in the bathroom. When he was done, he rooted around the kitchen for something to feed Tyler on, for he looked like he hadn't eaten in days. He came up with a packet of powdered soup, and looked around for a kettle. It seemed that Tyler didn't possess one of those, either, so he put a pan on the hob and, while it warmed, he returned to the bedroom to sit with Tyler.

"How can I help you? Do you owe money?" he asked quietly.

"Mmm, yeah I do, lots of it, mate. Too much for you to lend me," replied Tyler, looking away. "I wish they'd finished me. What have I got to live for? I'm a drug addict, Joe. H, coke, any shit I can lay my hands on. I take it, and when I can't afford it, I drink until I pass out. When I can't afford booze, I drink fucking meths, paint fucking thinner, *anything*." He looked up, and Joe saw tears falling down his face. "I'm a fucking mess. I haven't spoken to my family in years, I have no friends. I've not had a girl in years. What have I got to live for? *You* tell me, Joe?"

"But you don't have to live like this. What about rehab?"

Tyler gave a harsh laugh. "Been there, done that, so many times I've lost count. Now nowhere will take me unless I go private, and I can't afford that. Even if I did have money to book myself in somewhere, do you really think I'd spend it on getting clean?"

Joe ran his hands through his hair. "Let me think about this," he muttered, and got up to check on the soup. He looked into the pan and frowned. It wasn't even warm. He raised his eyes skywards and went back into the bedroom.

"Tyler, do you even have any electricity?"

Tyler shook his head silently.

"Oh, God." He thought for a moment. "Okay, we're getting out of here."

"Where?"

"My hotel for tonight, we'll have to play it by ear after that."

What was he was getting into here? He was supposed to be leaving for Australia in under a week, and he had Kate to see before he left.

Kate.

His mind whirred. She was coming to England soon. Until then, her home would be empty.

"Listen." He knelt down beside the bed. "Remember that girl I told you about? She has a home here that's empty. Would you stay there with me? We could get you better, away from this shit hole, and you could think about what you want to do."

"And you'd help me? You'd stay with me?" He clutched Joe's hand.

Joe nodded and smiled.

"Yeah, I would, but you gotta know it won't be easy—for you, I mean. You won't have access to anything, no drugs, not even drink. And if you relapse and try any shit on me, then I'll bring you back here and that'll be the end of it."

Tyler grinned back. Tears sprung to Joe's eyes as he caught a glimpse of the boy he had once known.

"Let's do it!"

He nodded and started packing Tyler's clothes. Half of him wondered what the hell he was playing at. He had run out on Kate when she needed him most and now, here he was, planning to take over her home to live there with an addict. But if he knew Kate as well as he thought, he knew she would give him her blessing. After all, he was only doing for Tyler what Jacob had done for her. He planned to call her as soon as they got back to the hotel. And this time he would explain everything—why he had ran out on her, exactly how much she meant to him, and he would ask her for a chance to make it up.

Kate had returned to the hotel and was having a quiet drink with Linda when the phone rang. Linda got up to answer it.

Kate grabbed her crutches and walked over to the window. The view was one of the things she had missed during her stay in the hospital, and she knew she would miss it while she was in England, as well.

Linda hurried back into the room.

Kate turned away from the window. "Who was it?" she asked.

"Bloody hell, it's Joe, and he's still on the phone. He wants to talk to you," said Linda a look of excitement on her face.

She froze. She hadn't expected to hear from Joe ever again. Even Bruce hadn't heard from him lately.

"Well, talk to him!" Linda hissed, nudging her in the direction of the reception area.

"I don't know what to say. What does he want?" she asked as Linda propelled her toward the door.

"I don't know. Find out!"

Kate looked at the receiver on the front desk before gingerly picking it up.

"Joe?"

"Kate!" Just him saying her name made her anger fade a little.

"How are you, Joe? And *where* are you?" she asked, trying to stay cool.

"England, London in fact. I need to explain why I went so quickly."

"There's no need. You don't have to explain anything."

"But I do, and I want to. You see, there's this friend of mine, and part of the reason I'm here is because he's in trouble, and I needed to help him." Joe's words came out in a rush.

"Was he in a coma?" she asked sharply.

"What? No, why?"

"Well, *I* was, Joe. I needed you!" she burst out, mentally cursing herself for losing her cool. "Look, it doesn't matter now. What do you want? Why did you ring me?"

Joe was silent for a moment. Then, "I want to see you, when you come to England. Maybe I could come to your house?" he said eventually.

It was Kate's turn to be silent as she pondered his question. She wanted to see him again, she had unanswered questions and, if she were truthful, it was so good to hear from him. She also knew that, although he had not lived up to her expectations by running off when her health was at its most critical, she had not behaved very well towards him either, when she lied to him about coming to Africa.

"What would you say if I asked if I could spend a few nights there, before you arrived?" he said. "You see my friend—"

"Is in trouble, I know, you said." Kate sighed and wondered if a place to doss down was all he wanted, but she gave him the benefit of the doubt. "Is he in trouble with the police? Because if that's it, then no way."

"No, he's...sick," Joe finished lamely.

"Okay, you go to my house, take your sick friend and I'll

see you when I get there. The Post Office have the key. I'll call them and tell them you're going to collect it."

"I really appreciate this, Kate. I know I've no right, but this means a lot. And when you arrive, I'm going to explain everything to you."

"I'll see you, Joe." Kate replaced the receiver, and jumped as Linda put her arm around her.

"Well?" asked her friend.

She frowned and sat down, one hand still on the telephone.

"He wants to borrow the house. He has a sick friend he wants to take there."

"You what?" Linda dragged up a chair and sat opposite her. "What the hell's he playing at?"

"I don't know. He said he'll explain everything when I get there." Kate smiled suddenly. "I'm not going to worry about it, and I'm not in a hurry to leave, anyway. I'll have my last four physiotherapy sessions here, and then go back to England."

Jacob's arrival distracted Linda. Kate leaned back in her chair and replayed the telephone conversation in her head. Why had she said yes to Joe's requests? Because ever since she had met him, they had never really been able to give their relationship a chance? Because she wanted to find out if they could really have something together? Or maybe if she was once more with Joe, it might put Thomas King out of her mind, once and for all?

All of the above were good enough reasons to meet with Joe when she returned home.

* * * *

Tyler sat alone in Joe's hotel room while Joe went out to get some food. He wheeled himself around the room, smirking at the mini bar Joe had thoughtfully emptied, wondering if he would have had the strength not to touch the drink if Joe had left it there.

He thought the answer was probably 'no' and hated himself for being so weak.

On the taxi ride over, Joe had asked him when he had gotten back into drugs, and Tyler had answered shamefully that he had never stopped.

"Since the accident? All those years?" Joe was incredulous.

And thinking back, it was so many wasted years, never working, no friendships or relationships. His life had revolved around drugs. A shot of whiskey in his orange juice to get him started in the morning, along with a snort of cocaine. Shooting up around eleven o'clock, lying in a stupor until it wore off. The evening spent smoking fat joints, and finishing off the whiskey.

Just thinking about it made him break into a cold sweat, and he was disgusted to find he wanted it. Even now, when a hand had been held out to help him, he still craved the substances his body had become accustomed to.

As he levered himself onto the bed, thin arms wrapped around his body, he knew he wouldn't be able to last without the drugs.

The thought filled him with dread.

When Joe got back to the hotel, armed with food from the corner store, he was aghast to find Tyler huddled on the bed, shaking and sweating.

He dropped the bags and ran over to the bed.

"Jesus, Joe, this is going to *kill* me!" shrieked Tyler. "You gotta help me, man!"

He didn't know what to do. Oh, sure, he knew all about going cold turkey. He had read enough about it and seen enough movies in his time. 'Trainspotting' flicked through his mind, and he shuddered.

"What can I do?" he asked desperately, as he tried to cover him with a blanket.

Tyler writhed around on the bed, groaning. The blanket fell to the floor.

He moved away, and sat heavily in the chair in the corner of the room as Tyler ranted and raved. He was sure if Tyler had the use of his legs, he would be on his feet pummelling the shit out of Joe.

As his friend sobbed on the bed, he put his head in his hands. He had never felt more utterly useless in his life.

It was morning before Tyler became coherent again, and Joe naively thought the worst was over.

"Was I bad?" asked Tyler in a small voice as Joe helped him to the bathroom.

"You were burning up. It wasn't too good."

"I'm sorry, it will get better." But as he clutched onto Joe's arm he was still shaking.

It didn't get better. Joe tried to get him motivated into sorting out the trip to Appleby, but he just sat listlessly in his chair by the window. Eventually, Joe gave up and went to the train station to sort out tickets.

He took out his wallet to pay for them. No cash. Frowning, trying to remember where he had left the money, he passed over his credit card. As he signed for the card it came to him in a flash.

Tyler.

Tyler had taken his money, and he knew, for sure, what he was going to spend it on.

Stuffing the tickets and his card back in his pockets, he ran out of the station.

Back at the hotel, his room was inevitably empty. No Tyler, no wheelchair, and no money.

Using only his instincts as a guide, he turned and left the hotel, and headed over to Brixton.

Tyler's flat was empty, but something told him Tyler would return. So he sat himself down on the floor, and settled in for a long wait.

* * * *

Bruce was leaving. He had spoken with his wife on the telephone and listened to her rant and rave about his absence. He hugged Linda as she stood with Jacob and Jermain by the door.

"You come back soon," Linda said. "And bring Mrs L as

well, she'll be very welcome."

"I will." He shook Jacob's hand.

Jermain hugged him as he turned to leave. "Thank you for all your help with Kate, looking after her in Africa as well. And make sure you do return."

Andy, waiting in the car to take Bruce to the airport, honked his horn. Bruce picked up his case and waved goodbye to the little group that stood in the doorway.

"So, how are you going to make it up to the missus?" asked Andy as they headed for the airport.

"I might suggest a holiday," said Bruce. "But we will definitely avoid Cannes and Zaire!"

"Are you going to see Joe when you get back to England?"

"Yes, I thought I'd head straight over to his hotel, catch him before he leaves for Darlington, and find out what the hell he's got himself into this time."

Kate had told him about their conversation and he was intrigued as to who the friend was that Joe had to help, and why he had to take him to Kate's cottage in Appleby.

Well, he would find out soon enough. Brixton was only a tube ride away from Heathrow, and he had the name of the hotel where Joe was staying.

* * * *

Tyler was halfway across London. With Joe's money, he had found what he needed, and his new friend had been so impressed with the stash of cash, he had invited Tyler back to his house for a party. The dealer, Rod, had lately lost a lot of his regular custom and was happy to stumble upon Tyler who had money to burn.

So back to Rod's house they went. Taking the underground, they travelled from North Brixton to Uxbridge. Rod owned a small terraced house in the suburbs. He let Tyler in.

The party started. Rod had hard core goods that made Tyler drool in delight. He happily handed over Joe's cash in exchange for a hearty portion of cocaine and a fat package of heroin. He had been starved of his drugs for two days, and he worked on rectifying that in a frenzy. As the cocaine kicked in, he told Rod all about his good friend, Joe, who was trying to help him, and about the cottage he was taking him to, and the hotel he had put him up in.

"But you can't kick it, huh, mate?" Rod asked as he helped himself to two fat lines laid out on the table.

"Don't want to," mumbled Tyler as he started to burn the H on a spoon.

Rod didn't reply. Instead he watched with a worried look on his face as Tyler proceeded to eat away at the supplies he had purchased only moments earlier.

"Hey man, what hotel were you in with your mate?" he asked suddenly, and when Tyler told him he made a mental note of it.

If this guy was going to get in trouble in his house, he certainly didn't want to be held accountable for a corpse in his lounge.

Over the next few hours, Rod grew more and more alarmed as Tyler slipped further away from him. His stash was gone, and what Tyler had put away should have killed him. Earlier, he had tried to get Tyler to slow down by offering him some food. Tyler had knocked the plate away and Rod looked on in fright. Although he was a dealer, he didn't normally touch much of the stuff himself. *Don't shit on your own doorstep* was his motto and, come to think of it, he didn't usually invite strangers in his house to test the wine, so to speak. But greed had overcome Rod on this occasion, and he was paying for it now.

Reaching for his mobile, he got the number of the hotel and waited to be connected to the room Tyler had been staying in. There was no reply, and Rod quite rightly presumed that this friend of Tyler's was out searching the streets for him right now.

Not knowing what else he could do, he left Tyler on the couch and went to bed.

Eventually, Joe fell into a restless sleep. He cursed when he woke up and his back screamed at him for sleeping on the floor. Groaning, he got to his feet. He remembered where he was and woke up fully as he called out for Tyler. It was obvious he hadn't come home so, with a final look around the flat, he returned to the hotel.

As he trudged along the road, eyes flicking from left to right, checking out all the homeless bodies that lined the streets, in the hope that one of them would be Tyler, Joe had never felt so angry at himself. He knew first-hand about addiction and felt like he should have known better. He didn't ride the underground. Instead he walked the seven miles or so back to the hotel, with not one sighting of Tyler. He let himself into the hotel room, barely acknowledging the cheery receptionist who hailed him 'good morning'. As he looked around the room, a huge sense of disappointment came over him. He realised he had half expected Tyler to be waiting for him.

But he wasn't.

Throwing the keys on the bed, he picked up the phone. As he dialled the receptionist to see if there were any messages for him, there was a knock at the door. He slammed the phone back into its cradle and leapt over the bed. Throwing the door open, he came face to face with the last person he had expected to see.

"Bruce!" Joe was so overwhelmed with a bizarre mixture of relief that someone else was here to help him, and frustration that it wasn't Tyler, that he slumped back onto the bed.

"Joe, what's happened? Are you okay?" Bruce closed the door behind him.

"Far from okay," said Joe, and told him the whole sorry story.

"So you came all this way to visit Tyler, to try to make amends for what happened all those years ago, and you find out he never blamed you at all? He has much more serious issues, and now he's missing? With your money?" Bruce scratched his head.

"Yeah."

"Christ."

"How's Kate?" asked Joe as he put the kettle on.

"Good, walking good as new." Bruce paused and looked at Joe. "You are going to see her while you're here, aren't you?"

"I fully intended to be at her cottage by now," said Joe ruefully.

"Well, I know you're a sucker for someone in need, but don't mess this up, Joe. She's a good girl, and you know it," replied Bruce sternly.

Joe smiled to himself as he thought of Kate. Yes, she was a good girl, and he would be a fool to let her slip away from him. Once Tyler had been tracked down, she was going to be the very next item on his list.

As Joe handed Bruce a cup of tea, the phone rang. He picked it up.

"Hello?"

"Hey, brother, have you got a friend on wheels?" Joe didn't recognise the voice at the end of the line, but he knew immediately the caller was talking about Tyler.

"Tyler? A guy in a wheelchair?" Joe put his tea down and listened intently.

"Yeah, man, you want to come and get him? And I mean, like, now. This dude is in my house and he has not moved off my couch since last night. And I'll be fucked if I can move him." The man sounded scared, despite his hard words.

A shiver ran through Joe. "Is he okay?" he asked.

"Would I be calling you if we was having a party?" There was a pause and, in the background, Joe heard vomiting, along with a howl of disgust from the man on the line. "Shit man, you get here now and move this fucker out of my pad. Get me?"

"Yes, yes, where are you?" Joe fought rising panic and, as the caller reeled off the address, was already pulling on his jacket.

Bruce was standing by the door when he hung up the

phone.

"Trouble?" he asked.

"Yeah, big trouble." He opened the door and motioned Bruce out of the room.

When they arrived, a man, presumably the one who had made the call, was waiting by the open front door.

"Come on, in here." He ushered them in and, with a furtive glance around, closed the door. "I'd never have let him in if I'd known what sort of guy he was."

Entering into the lounge, Joe's heart sank as he spotted Tyler on the couch. Bruce rushed over and leant over his motionless form.

"Is he okay?" Joe asked. Bruce picked up a limp wrist, then put it down by his side and looked up at the stranger.

"How long has he been like this?" he asked.

The man shrugged as he nervously bit his fingernails.

"Bruce?" Joe moved closer.

Bruce switched his gaze to Joe and shook his head. "He's dead," he said. "I'm so sorry."

Joe stopped in his tracks. His jaw fell open. "No," he whispered. "Please, no…" He sat down heavily on the couch and stared at his dead friend. How had this happened? Why now, when he had finally come back into Tyler's life, did he have to die? He picked up the cold hand and held it. "I'm so sorry, Tyler," he whispered

Bruce took out his mobile phone, looking away as Joe's tears began to fall.

The police came. Joe watched as they took Tyler's body out into the ambulance, covered by a sheet. He told them everything he knew about his friend's addiction and, several hours later, when they turned their questions to the man who owned the house, he and Bruce left .

Joe felt numb as Bruce led him away from the house.

"What now, Joe?" asked Bruce as they walked in the direction of the hotel.

He shrugged and kicked at a stone in his path.

"Back to work, I guess." He stopped and turned to face the doctor. "But first I'm going to see Kate, and I'm going to ask her to come to Australia with me."

"Do you think she will?"

"It's worth a try. Life's too short, you saw that in there." Joe gestured back to the house. "That was a wasted life, and I don't intend to end up wasting mine."

"Need a drink?" asked Bruce pointing to a pub over the road.

Joe realised he was shaking and nodded gratefully. A drink was exactly what he needed.

Chapter Fifteen

Appleby

The incessant singing of a lark raised Kate from her slumber. She sat up and looked around her. For a moment she thought she was back in Cannes, and then the chill hit her, and she wrapped her fleece more tightly around herself.

Appleby.

Well, she was a little way from the Appleby home today, her second day back in England. This morning she had ventured out and headed south, into the heart of the Pennines. She had taken a taxi to Richmond, and packed a lunch and a litre bottle of water, along with a flask of hot tea. She was glad of her supplies when she arrived at the entrance to the moors, and read the signpost. It warned of the dangers, and showed numbers, running into hundreds, of how many people had got lost and died out there. It was a frightening thought but, to Kate, who had been born and raised on instinct and adrenalin, it was just what she needed.

She paid her cab fare and, taking a stick in each hand, she limped onwards. After an hour's walk she stumbled upon a flowing river and, although it was only January, it was one of those days where the air was pleasantly crisp and the sky was blue and cloudless with a hint of the promise of Spring. The stream was home to a series of flat red rocks, large enough to hold about three people comfortably. Manoeuvring her crutches and balancing her pack on her back, Kate made her way to a rock in the middle of the stream, pulled her hat on and lay back to stare at the sky.

Looking at her watch a while later, she realised she had been asleep for almost three hours. It was half past three. With a jolt, she realised it wasn't as bright as it had been. In fact dusk was almost upon her.

Cursing out loud, she got to her feet and made her way back to the riverbank. She had an hour's walk to get back to the entrance. By then it would be dark. The warning on the signpost spurred her to stumble along faster, and she shuddered as she remembered the horror stories that Jermain had told her when they lived there.

Men and women experienced in trekking or orienteering rarely remained on the moors after dark, for, even with their compasses and maps, everything looked the same, with barely any landmarks. The moors stretched for miles in every direction, and Kate knew that if she didn't find the entrance, she would need to spend the night there. Although the day had been bright and sunny, the temperature would fall below freezing, and hypothermia would set in.

With this thought spurring her on, Kate moved quickly over the moor in, what she hoped, was the right direction. A mist was beginning to descend. She broke into a jog, wincing at the pain in her back from the wounds that were still healing.

An hour later, just as she was starting to panic, she stumbled across a road. It was not where she had come onto the moor, but the traffic was steady and she felt a wave of relief as she realised she was back in civilisation. She started to walk along the road, holding out a stick every time a car passed and, eventually, a white Ford Escort stopped and the lady inside wound down the passenger side window.

"Where you headed?" she asked.

"Appleby," said Kate. "Or anywhere near there if that's the direction you're headed."

The lady, a blonde in her late twenties, Kate guessed, leaned over and opened the door.

"You're in luck. I'm going to Penrith, going right through Appleby." As Kate bundled the crutches on the back seat, she asked, "So what are you doing all the way out here?"

As she sat in the car, Kate felt herself crumble. Painfully embarrassed as the British so often are at showing emotion in front of strangers, she covered her mouth and shook her head.

"Sorry," she squeaked as she caught sight of the woman's alarmed face.

"Shit, that's okay. Here." The lady reached into the glove box and handed her a tissue.

She took it and mopped at her eyes.

"Better?"

"Much." She sighed and stuck out her hand. "I'm Kate, by the way."

"Carol."

As they pulled off the side of the road into the flow of traffic, Kate began to apologise once again.

"Hey, none of my business, girl, but if you want to get it off your chest I've got a good ear."

Kate sighed again and started her story, leaving nothing out. It felt good to get it all off her chest. Sometimes speaking with a stranger was easier.

Maybe that's why they invented therapy, she thought with a smile.

"And I was lost on the moors. It was the last straw. I was walking for hours." Kate drew a shaky breath. "I thought that was it."

"Wow, you've really been through it, huh?" At the sign for the Appleby turning, Carol pulled off the main road. "So, this Joe is coming to see you?"

"Yes, and I really feel so much for him, but then there's Thomas…" Kate rubbed her temples as she felt a headache begin to grow.

"You'll see this Thomas again and, when you do, you'll know the right decision to make," said Carol.

"I hope so. My turn-off is just here." Kate pointed to the way down to the cottage and Carol swung off the road.

As they pulled up at the cottage, she saw a figure sitting on the porch. Her heart lurched.

"Is that Joe?" Carol stopped the car and peered through the windscreen.

Kate turned to face her and shook her head. "It's Thomas," she whispered with growing excitement.

"Oh boy!" Carol patted her on the shoulder. "Remember, just go with your heart, yeah?"

She nodded and impulsively hugged the lady who had shown her such kindness.

"Thank you. For everything." She opened the door.

As Carol drove away, Kate stood in the driveway and

watched Thomas stand up and walk towards her. He stopped just in front of her. She could tell he was struggling to find the words he wanted to say.

"Hi," she said. "Are you coming in?"

He nodded and followed her to the door.

She settled him in the kitchen and put the kettle on. There was silence between them as she made the tea. When she bought the tray to the table, she sat down opposite him. For a long while they sat enclosed in the uncomfortable silence until eventually Kate spoke.

"Why did you leave the hospital?"

"I didn't really think I had a right to be there," he said.

"You said some things to me…when I was in the coma."

He looked down at the table and blushed furiously. "You heard me?"

She took a deep breath, reached across the table and took his hand. "I heard it all. I know everything, Thomas. I know some of the others, Joe included, didn't entirely believe I was innocent. I know you tried to take the bullet for me." Kate felt a lump in her throat and her voice thickened with tears. "I can't tell you how that made me feel." As a tear fell, Thomas dropped her hand and came round the table to kneel in front of her.

"I'd have died for you. And if you had been sent down, I'd never have stopped working to get you free. I'd give up anything for you."

It was the first time he had told her face to face how he felt. She felt a surge that travelled the length of her body as she realised she felt something for him, too.

"So, what now?" he asked. "Where do we go from here?"

"I'm not sure." She smiled and took his hand. "Stay with me?"

"Yes," he replied and resumed his place at the table.

Joe turned off the motorway. He was only a few miles from Kate's cottage. Excited about seeing her again, he wanted to sit down with her, and tell her everything that had made him behave the way he had.

After checking the map to make sure he hadn't gone the wrong way, he noticed a small driveway leading off the main road and pulled sharply to the left. As he approached the cottage he saw a light. He stopped the car and leapt out.

He stood at the front door for ages before summoning the courage to knock. Nobody answered, so he made his way around the side of the building to the kitchen door. He tried the handle and, when it opened, let himself in.

"Kate?" he called and listened for a sign of life.

Receiving no reply, he moved through the kitchen and into the hall. He could hear the faint sound of a television and walked towards it. The sight he stumbled upon in the living room was the last thing he had expected—Kate and Thomas, her solicitor, asleep on the couch. Kate's head rested on his chest and Thomas had his arms around her in a way that could only spell one thing.

He dropped his bag, staring dumbly at them. As it fell to the floor, it startled them out of their slumber.

"Joe!" Kate sat up. Thomas took his arms from around her as Joe backed out of the doorway.

"No, Joe, wait!" Kate stumbled to her feet.

When she reached the kitchen, he was standing with his back to her, one hand on the door handle.

"Don't go," she pleaded as she came around the table towards him.

He turned back to her. She flinched at the wounded look in his eyes.

"I wasn't aware, I mean, you two…" he muttered.

Kate closed the kitchen door and pulled him back to the table.

"You don't understand," she said. "Thomas only got here this evening. He wanted to see how I was."

"But we both know how he feels about you." Joe sat down, his head in his hands. "I screwed up. I'm sorry."

"I know you had your reasons." Kate sat up straight as a thought hit her. "Where's your friend?"

"Dead," said Joe with a hard edge to his voice.

"Dead?" Kate felt her heart sink as Joe struggled to contain his emotions. "Tell me everything."

"What about him?" Joe motioned to the lounge and Kate hung her head.

Carol had told her that, when she saw both of them, it would all become clear whom she wanted to be with. How could it be she wanted them both?

"Leave Thomas where he is for the time being. I need to know what happened with you, Joe," she said.

Joe told her the story about Emily and Tyler, and Tyler's death.

"So, do you understand now? Why I left? I bring such bad things to people I love, and I thought if I went away you might get better."

"I do understand," she said quietly. "After my mother died, I did the same."

Talk of her mother had been strictly off limits in the past, and he leaned forward to show that he was listening. "What happened?"

Shrugging, she looked away from him. She never talked about that night, she couldn't bring herself to think about it.

"It was a robbery gone wrong. When we got back to the boat where we lived she was on the floor, her throat had been…" She tailed off as the vision came flooding back. She cleared her throat and started again. "She was murdered. Jermain and I came back to England, to this cottage. We drifted apart. I went off to school and never came back."

"What changed you?" he asked. His question seemed to have an urgent tone to it, as though he could learn from her answer.

"Australia. I went to Europe, Greece, even back to India. But it was Australia and the people that really helped me back home to Jermain."

"And us?" he asked. "What about us?"

She took a deep breath, knowing the rest of her life depended on what she said now. The time had come to make her choice. She felt scared, unprepared to feel so strongly for both these men. But there was no backing out now.

"You need to make up your mind, Kate," Joe said. "Me or him?"

The door swung open and Thomas stood in the doorway. From his stance it was clear he had heard everything. He threw a glance at Joe and focused his intent gaze on Kate.

She backed away into the corner of the kitchen, flitting her gaze between Joe and Thomas.

"He's right, Kate. We both need to know where we stand."

She stood up and looked carefully at both of them. In a trembling voice, she said the name of the man she had chosen.

Chapter Sixteen

The Wedding

Kate sat and stared into the mirror. She felt numb, and slightly sick. She tried to tell herself it was just nerves but, deep down, she knew better.

The door opened. Linda came in, dressed in a red dress and massively pregnant.

"How're you feeling?" she asked as she passed Kate a glass of champagne.

"Sick," answered Kate and downed the champagne.

"No regrets?" Linda poured another glass.

She shook her head and smiled. "No regrets."

"Okay! So get up and let me see you."

She stood up and twirled around.

Her friend sniffed as she looked her up and down. "You look stunning," she said.

Kate agreed as she looked at her reflection in the mirror, at the Dior floor length white wedding dress, the bodice beaded with tiny pearls, and a floating diamond necklace Jermain had given her the night before, that had belonged to her mother.

"Ready to go?" Linda handed Kate her bouquet and opened the door.

"Is *he* here?" She paused in the doorway.

Linda didn't need to ask who *he* was.

"No, he's not," she said and smiled sadly.

She nodded and held the door open.

The wedding was at the Cathedral in Cannes. Outside Cannes Central a white Mercedes awaited Kate. Jermain stood beside it, looking resplendent in his black suit.

"You look a million dollars," he said as he held the car door open for her.

She smiled and clutched his hand tightly as she climbed in.

"Feeling okay?" he asked casually as they started the short

car journey to the cathedral.

"Fine." She looked out of the window and smiled at the people who had come to wave her off.

They rode the rest of the journey in silence. As they pulled up outside the church, Jermain caught her hand.

"It's not too late," he said. "Just so you know, you don't have to worry about anything but how you feel."

"Dad, I'm fine. I'm doing the right thing!" she exclaimed and hugged him. "Now get out and walk me down that aisle!"

He nodded, clearly satisfied she was happy, and ran round to her side of the car to help her out.

Once more in silence, they walked to the entrance. Jermain gave the signal. As the music started, he held out his arm. Kate linked hers in his and they walked down the aisle.

Kate glanced at the faces in the crowd, and smiled at Linda and Jacob who grinned back. As they reached the altar, she took a deep breath and turned to her right. As Thomas turned to face her, beaming in delight, she knew, without a doubt, that she had made the wrong choice.

Too late now! The voice whispered in her head with a certain amount of glee. *This is what you get for always rushing in.*

Somehow Kate stumbled through the ceremony, and when the vicar pronounced them husband and wife, the congregation presumed she was crying tears of joy.

The reception was to be held at the hotel. As Thomas and Kate made their way back there in the car, he clutched her hand tightly.

"Do you know how happy you've made me?" he asked.

She bit her lip and nodded. It was so unfair. Thomas was lovely, and over the past three months she had buried the feeling he was not the one for her so deeply inside she had almost convinced herself on a few occasions that she was wrong. As they swept through the town centre, Kate leaned her head against the window and thought back to the fateful night when she had made the decision that had changed her life.

"Thomas," she said in a small voice.

"What?" Joe leaned forward.

She couldn't look at him. Instead, she hung her head and repeated Thomas's name.

For a long moment nobody spoke. She heard the sound of a door banging and, when she looked up, Joe had gone. Thomas moved in front of her and, suddenly, she realised what Carol had meant earlier. With a sense of panic, she realised she didn't feel relief, or an immense feeling of love for Thomas, just regret and remorse that Joe had left. For a second she actually moved to run out after him, but Thomas had caught hold of her hand and was holding her so tightly she couldn't move anywhere.

Later that night, Kate moved on to the brandy and she and Thomas sat in the lounge by the open fire. The alcohol diminished her panic somewhat and, as she got drunker, Thomas did become more appealing. From that night, as plans were made and the more people they told, Kate buried her true feelings from everyone, including herself.

But now the panic was back with a vengeance. She was married! Married to a man she held in the highest regard, and loved in some way, but wasn't in love with. And for someone as passionate as Kate, that was the worst thing of all.

But it was too late for regrets.

When Thomas and Kate entered the reception to the cheers of the crowd, the first person she saw was Bruce. She wasn't prepared for him, and her heart leapt between wanting to hide from him and wanting to pump him for information about Joe. Eventually, she was able to disentangle herself from Thomas and make her way over to Bruce. He smiled and opened his arms. She smiled in relief and hugged him fiercely.

"You look wonderful," he said. "Thomas is a lucky man."

Tears sprung to her eyes and she hastily wiped them away. "How's Joe?" she demanded.

"Good. He sends his regards." Bruce shifted around in his seat.

Kate knew he was lying. She swore under her breath as she felt the tears rising again. "I'm so sorry," she said softly, looking at the ground.

"This was your choice, Kate, and, as much as I love Joe, it doesn't change the fact that you're my friend, too. I wish you all the best."

"Will you be seeing Joe?" she asked.

"Soon I hope. He's back in England later this month. He's in Australia, you know."

Kate was startled. "I didn't know! What about Zaire?"

"His work was finished there. He's in Australia with the Aborigines," said Bruce.

Kate's heart almost tore in two. Joe was in Australia, her favourite land, with her favourite people.

"He was going to ask you to go with him," continued Bruce. "I said it was stupid. You have your life here, anyway."

She gasped and clapped a hand over her mouth. She felt positively sick with this latest revelation. "I have to go," she said and, spinning around, she dashed out of the room, leaving Bruce staring after her.

As Linda stood chatting to Jermain, she spotted Kate across the room, talking to Bruce. After a brief exchange, she watched her run out of the room. Making her excuses to Jermain, she hurried out after her.

Coming through to the lobby, she spotted her leaning on the reception desk, breathing heavily.

"Kate?"

Kate stood up straight and turned around. Linda was aghast to see tears rolling down her face.

"Jesus, Kate, what's wrong?" She hurried over.

Kate shook her head. "Oh, Linda," she cried, wrapping her arms around her.

Casting a glance over her shoulder, she pulled her around the desk into the back room.

"I made a mistake, Linda. I don't know what to do," Kate whispered.

"Do you mean Thomas?" She sat her friend down and reached into the desk for the emergency whiskey Jermain always kept there.

"Yes, Thomas, poor Thomas," Kate sobbed and, with a shaking hand, took the glass. "I thought I could make it work, I really did. But I don't love him. I love Joe! I want Joe!"

"But why marry Thomas? It doesn't make sense."

"Oh, I felt like I owed him. That's such a stupid reason. Don't look at me like that, I *know*, but I mistook gratitude for love! And when he said Joe didn't believe I was innocent, it just pushed me closer to Thomas."

Linda looked alarmed as Kate began to wail. She kicked the door shut.

"So tell him. You cannot live the rest of your life with a man you don't love. It doesn't matter that it's your wedding night. You think it'll be easier to leave him in a month? Or a year?"

"I know you're right. I need to tell him." Just saying the words seemed to make Kate feel some sort of pressure release. "We're staying here tonight. I'll tell him. I have to."

Linda topped up the glass and noted with some relief that Kate had calmed down.

After a while Kate wiped her face and stood up. "Let's go," she muttered and headed for the door.

Linda pulled her into a hug and held her tight. "You'll be fine," she whispered.

"Dad?" Kate tugged at Jermain's arm, and he turned to her in surprise.

"Hello, I thought you were with Thomas," he said and passed her a glass of champagne.

"I was looking for him. Do you know where he is?" she asked as she downed the champagne in one go.

"In your suite, I think. Possibly trying desperately to sober up. He wasn't looking too good when I saw him." Jermain laughed and hugged her. "Go find him, and make him some coffee, for God's sake."

She nodded and edged out of the room, towards the lift. As she pressed the button, she felt sick all over again and wished she had brought up a bottle of drink to steady her nerves.

They had been given the penthouse suite as a wedding present from the three partners, and Kate had not been in it until now. When she opened the door, tears sprung to her eyes at how beautifully decorated it was, with balloons, streamers and rose petals covering the king sized four-poster bed. For a moment, she stood and stared until she heard a retching sound from the bathroom.

"Thomas?" she called out. "Are you okay?"

She ventured no further and, hearing the toilet flush, sat on the bed and waited.

When Thomas came out of the bathroom, she gasped. He looked ill, pale and clammy with bloodshot eyes.

"Jesus, how much have you had to drink?" she exclaimed as he sat heavily beside her.

"Not enough, not by a long, fucking shot," he said morosely. She raised her eyebrows. Bad language was most unlike Thomas. He must be feeling bad.

"I need to speak to you…" she started.

"I have to talk to you, too. There's something I've been hiding. I can't keep it from you anymore." He ran his hands through his hair.

Kate looked on in horror as a tear escaped and ran down the side of his face.

"Thomas?" She was scared now. Could he have already heard she was leaving him?

He rubbed his eyes and shook his head. "I'm not well," he said. As she opened her mouth to question him further, he said the dreaded words, "I've got cancer."

The words hung in the air. Something halfway between a sob and a hysterical giggle bubbled up within her.

"But…what? How…?" She trailed off, not sure what to say. This was the absolute last thing she expected. She couldn't even form a straight sentence, so deep was the shock.

"It's inoperable, Kate. That means—"

"I know what inoperable means!" she snarled, horrified at the anger she felt.

For a long time they sat in silence, before Kate spoke. "I'll look after you," she said quietly.

He looked up. She knew then she couldn't leave him. It would be callous and cruel, something she would feel guilty about for the rest of her life.

"You don't have to. I understand if you want to leave. I

have people around me. I can have a nurse."

For one terrible moment she considered it. It would be easy to pick up her things and go to Australia to find Joe.

"No. I'll stay," she said eventually. "But I need to know everything—what to expect, symptoms—everything."

"All right. But I'm shattered. Do you mind if I go to bed?"

She picked up his hand and kissed it. "That's fine. I'll go and see everyone off and join you soon."

He nodded and lay back on the bed. Walking towards the door, she let out a deep breath and looked back at him. With a heavy heart, she realised that Joe and herself would now never be.

Later, as Thomas slept soundly, Kate sat on the windowsill, staring out upon the beautiful sight of Cannes. The phone rang shrilly, startling her, and making Thomas stir. Grabbing the phone and a pack of cigarettes, she rushed into the bathroom.

"Hello?" she answered breathlessly.

"You're still there!" Linda said on the other end of the line.

She took a deep breath. "We're fine. I'm staying here."

There was a moment's silence before Linda answered.

"But you were leaving…Kate, is he holding you against your will?"

Yes, but not in the way you're thinking.

"Honest, Linda, it's all okay. We're going to England tomorrow as planned. I'll send you a postcard," replied Kate and hung up.

Kate opened the pack of cigarettes and, with a shaking hand, lit it in the darkness of the bathroom. It was beginning. The lie that was now her life had started and there was no backing out.

Chapter Seventeen

The Lost Years

The bell rang with such persistence that Kate nearly threw the kettle across the room.

"I'm coming!" she shrieked and immediately felt awful for yelling.

Working quickly, she filled the mugs, spilling water on her hand but not stopping to run it under the cold-water tap. She hurried into the lounge and knelt down beside Thomas.

"Who the fuck are you?" He turned and regarded her with cold eyes. "Get my wife!"

When Thomas had begun not to recognise her, Kate would leave the room and weep quietly. Now she was used to it and she dealt with his episodes in an efficient and brisk manner.

"It's me, Thomas," she said.

For a moment his features softened and recognition fleeted across his face. "Of course. Sorry," he mumbled.

But, as Kate held his head while he sipped the hot, sweet tea, she knew, in an hour she would once again become a stranger to him.

"Kate, I needed the toilet," he muttered and turned his face away.

Kate patted his hand as she stood up. "I'll fetch you some clean pyjamas," she said. "Be right back."

Pausing, as she reached for clean clothes hanging on the radiator, she reflected on how much her life had changed in the last four years.

She was twenty-nine, thirty in a few weeks' time, and hadn't been back to Cannes since her wedding. Jermain, Jacob and Linda were almost strangers, lost in her memory, and she knew she had hurt them badly by cutting them out of her life. But they had no idea that Thomas was dying, and she didn't intend to tell them. She couldn't bear the sympathy.

She and Thomas had become virtual recluses in the

farmhouse in Appleby, and that was fine. With Thomas, she didn't have to pretend. He slept mostly, anyway, and Kate tried not to think of how much longer he had left. The doctor came in every other day and fed him morphine through a tube. Every visit, he tried to persuade her to let Thomas go into a hospice, but she refused. She had promised to take care of him herself, and she had, and would, until God took him. It had been hard, though. Even though she had known what to expect, nobody had told her about the nasty stuff. Thomas couldn't hold his bladder or bowels now. He barely recognised her, and regularly became violent. As soon as it passed, he became contrite and childlike, and Kate took it all. After all, if it hadn't been for Thomas, she might still be festering in a French prison cell. She owed him, and she was paying for it.

"Kate!" Thomas yelped from the lounge. She picked up the pyjamas and jogged through.

"Here we are," she said. "Let's get these on and you can get some rest, okay?"

He nodded. Methodically and autonomously, she changed him, all the while keeping up inane chatter.

"Thank you," he said and lay back down.

She nodded and, with a small smile, left the room again.

In the kitchen, she realised the cupboards were bare and wondered how she had not noticed before that stock was running low.

"Shit," she swore. "I'll have to go into the village."

She hurried into Thomas and explained that she had to go to the shop. He nodded, and she pulled a coat around her shoulders and dashed out of the door. She hated leaving Thomas alone, but if she didn't go then she would have to wait until the doctor came the following afternoon. He had been really good, the closest thing she had to a confidante and it was comforting to have someone to talk to occasionally.

Pulling up at the Tesco Metro store, she grabbed a trolley. Appleby was not a large town, and the shop was quiet. It was so empty she couldn't help notice a man who seemed to be tailing her. Self-consciously she put her head down, letting her long hair fall over her face. They were almost at the end aisle when she heard him step up to her. She spun around, ready to snap.

"Look…" she started and then stopped.

The man stepped closer and studied her face. "It is, isn't it? It's Kate!"

She felt the blood drain from her face and, for a moment, almost smiled. "Bruce?" she whispered.

"Yes!" He laughed. "Good God, Kate, it's been bloody years!"

"Four years," she agreed, gripping the handle of the trolley.

Seeing him brought it all back, everything she didn't want to remember—Jermain, beautiful Cannes and her casino, Linda, Jacob and Joe. Most of all Joe.

"But how are you?" he was asking. "And Thomas?"

"Thomas is fine," she whispered. With dismay, she heard her voice crack. "We're both fine."

His face changed. "Kate, I've been to Cannes a lot, twice a year, in fact. I know you don't speak to your father anymore. What happened?"

Before she could come up with a reply, she felt her eyes rolling back in her head. The last thing she remembered was the floor rushing up to meet her before Bruce's arms caught her as everything turned black.

She opened her eyes and immediately remembered. Bruce.

She was in a car, not her car.

Bruce slammed the boot shut and climbed into the driving seat.

"I put your shopping in the back. You're not fit to drive, Kate." He turned to face her. "Are you going to tell me what's wrong? Are you ill?"

"No," she said. "I'm all right."

He studied her for a moment. "Well, I'm driving you home. We can worry about your car later."

Kate was too exhausted to argue.

During the silent ride home, Kate desperately wanted to

ask about her family and friends, and what Bruce was doing there, but it seemed as if all of her energy had been drained from her body.

She directed him where necessary and, before long, they pulled up at the farmhouse.

"Thanks, Bruce," she said and got out of the car.

"Is that it?" he said.

She stared blankly at him. "Oh!" She shook her head and rummaged in her bag. "I'm sorry, how much was my shopping?"

He gripped her arm with such strength that she gasped. "I don't want your bloody money! I want to know what happened to you. Look at you! You look fifty years old, Kate. You've let go of everyone who cares about you, and you're going around fainting in supermarkets, clearly from exhaustion!"

Tears filled her eyes. She shrugged silently.

Taking her bags from the boot, he sighed. She shut the boot and followed him to the door.

She knew she was expected to invite him in, and tried to think of an excuse when he put the bags down.

"I'm staying at the bed and breakfast on the High Street, if you need me. Or want to see me." He turned back towards the car.

With a sigh of relief, Kate pushed open the door and hauled the bags in. She dropped the shopping by her feet, shocked. The room looked like a bombsite.

"Thomas!" she called and ran through to the lounge. He was at the bottom of the stairs, lying curled in a ball. She screamed and ran back to the door.

Bruce was just starting the engine.

"Bruce!" Kate screamed.

He leapt out and followed her back in, to find her crouched over Thomas's inert body.

Carefully turning Thomas over, he gasped. He was skin and bone, couldn't weigh more than nine stone. Carefully he lifted him and carried him into the lounge as Kate held the door open. Gently he placed Thomas on the couch and, standing up, he turned to face her.

"Go through to the kitchen, Bruce. I'll be there in a minute."

Bruce knew there was something seriously wrong. Maybe Thomas was an alcoholic. It would account for him being in his pyjamas in the middle of the day, and for the weight loss too.

As he waited in the kitchen, he started to tidy up the mess that Thomas had obviously created. He remembered the shopping and had almost finished putting it away when Kate came through and slumped down at the kitchen table.

He poured her tea and silently put a mug in front of her.

"I don't want my father to know about this," she said eventually as she sipped at the tea.

Bruce joined her at the table. "Alcoholism is a dangerous disease, and I understand that you want to help him, but you shouldn't be doing this on your own."

She looked up sharply, and surprised him by throwing back her head and laughing. "Alcoholism! Oh, Bruce, is that what you think? You're supposed to be a doctor."

Bruce was flustered, and embarrassed for presuming that Thomas was an alcoholic. "Well, there's obviously something wrong," he said.

"He has cancer." Kate stared into her mug. "He's riddled with it. He's not got long left."

"Oh, Kate!" Everything made sense now. He knew Kate's pride would have stopped her asking her friends for help and he rightly guessed that she wouldn't have been able to stand the sympathy that came with the terrible illness.

"How long has he been ill?" Bruce asked.

Kate stood up and tipped her tea into the sink and reached for the whiskey bottle she kept at the back of the cupboard.

"I'm more of an alcoholic than him," she said somewhat bitterly as she waved the bottle at Bruce. "My only friend, right?"

He remained silent. Eventually, she came back to the

table and sat down.

"He's been ill for just over four years. He told me on our wedding night," she said as she poured a glass and raised the bottle at Bruce.

He nodded. After this revelation he certainly needed something stronger than tea.

"Do you want to know the funny thing, Bruce? What makes it so damned ironic?" she said as she came back to the table. "I was going to leave him that night. Before he told me, I realised I'd made the wrong decision in marrying him. I was going to pack my things and try to find Joe in Australia." Her voice broke as she uttered Joe's name.

Bruce shook his head. "I had no idea. None of us did. We thought you had settled here and didn't need anyone else except Thomas."

"I've been so lonely." Kate's voice was bleak, but she didn't cry. Her tears had been drained over the last few years. "I missed everyone, my dad and Linda. I wanted to be back in Cannes and I couldn't. And, it sounds awful, but when he said it was terminal, I didn't expect him to last this long. If I'd known that, four years later…"

Bruce came around the table and took her in his arms. His action reminded her of a night a long time ago, when Thomas had done the same to her. That same night, she had made the wrong choice in picking the man she didn't love.

"I'm here now, Kate. I'm not going anywhere, and I'll help you."

As Bruce spoke, she felt an enormous relief that she finally had a friend with her.

Later that evening, Kate felt close to normality as the day drew to a close. Bruce had spoken to Thomas's doctor and obtained his medical notes. He was now able to administer Thomas's pain relief. He had spoken to Thomas and, to Kate's delight, he had remembered Bruce. Together they explained that Bruce would be staying for a while, and the three of them had enjoyed quite a pleasant evening. Thomas was coherent and had even eaten some of the sausage casserole Kate had made. Now Thomas was sleeping. Kate and Bruce returned to the kitchen to talk some more.

"Tell me about Dad, and Linda and Jacob. How's the baby?" she asked as she retrieved the whiskey bottle once more and a clean ashtray.

"Not such a baby," said Bruce. "Michael's four now, Linda's doing freelance stuff around Cannes, and they have a place near the hotel. You'd love their home. You should see them, you know."

"I want to. Maybe when it's all over, I can go back," she replied. "What about you though? Why are you here?"

"I've retired. Mona, my wife, couldn't cope with me being around all the time, so we're having a bit of a break." Bruce laughed. "Sounds silly doesn't it, a couple in their sixties, having a break?"

"I'm sorry, Bruce. Really. But why come to Appleby?"

He looked sheepish. "I promised your Dad I would look in on you before I go to Australia, to see Joe, with a stop-off in Cannes."

A look of panic crossed her face. "Don't tell them, please, not about Thomas."

"I won't." Bruce finished his glass of whiskey. "But you have to."

"Oh no, they'd want to come here. I couldn't bear it. Look at me!" She pulled at the sweatshirt she was wearing. "You were right earlier, I look fifty years old! I don't want anyone to see me like this. I don't want them seeing Thomas like this."

"But I'm here. I've seen and it's not so bad, is it?" he said. "Why don't you ring them at least? Start with Linda, if you can't speak to Jermain yet. They won't see you over the phone, will they?"

She would dearly love to speak with Linda again. She must be hurt. They all must have been at the way she had shut them out.

"Okay," she whispered. "Shall I ring now?"

Bruce worked out the time difference. "It's only afternoon there. Why not? I'll leave you alone."

With that, he filled his glass and moved quietly out of the room.

For a while, Kate looked at the phone on the table. She was just about to pick it up and dial when Bruce came back in.

"The number!" he said and put a piece of paper in front of her. "You won't get far without her telephone number." And he left again.

With a jolt of shock, Kate realised she had been about to call the hotel. How about that, she mused. If Bruce hadn't have come back, she would have been speaking to Jermain now.

Slowly, she dialled the number Bruce had written down, and held the phone to her ear. It started to ring. She held her breath.

"Hello?" It was a man, Jacob. His voice was sharp and it brought her back to earth.

"Jacob?" She spoke quickly before he could hang up. "Can I speak to Linda?"

There was a pause. "Is that Kate?"

"Um, yes, it is."

"Well, God! You've left it long enough!" he roared. The delight that she heard in his voice made her smile.

"I'm sorry. I'm going to explain it all to Linda. Is she around?" she asked tentatively.

"Hell, yeah! Hold on! I ain't telling her it's you, this'll be the surprise of her life!" She heard the phone being put down on the side. "Linda! Phone!" she heard him yell, and then the sound of the phone being picked up again.

"Hello?" Linda came on the line. At the sound of her voice, Kate felt tears rising and, for a second, she couldn't speak.

"Linda?" Kate said softly.

There was a long silence. She panicked as the thought that Linda might hang up crossed her mind.

"Kate?" Linda's voice was filled with wonderment. "Holy God, is it really you?"

"Yes!" Kate half laughed, half sobbed.

"Oh, mate, it's been so long. Why didn't you keep in touch? Why won't you return our calls? Your dad, he doesn't understand, neither do I. What did we do, that you left us all like that?" Linda's voice was filled with hurt and Kate burst into tears at the thought of all the pain she had caused.

"I'm so sorry. It's been so hard for me, Linda, I've missed you so much."

"But why? Do you know the last time I spoke to you was at your wedding? You were leaving Thomas, then the next thing I knew, you two had moved to England and cut out all the people that care for you!"

"Oh, Linda. It's Thomas. He's very ill. He's got cancer." There, she'd said it. Set the wheels in motion of getting back her loved ones.

"Cancer? Oh, Jeez. Oh, no," Linda stuttered. "What sort of cancer? How long has he been ill? Is he having treatment?"

"Nope, it's too far gone. Linda, do you remember my wedding night when I went upstairs to tell Thomas I was leaving him? Well, he beat me to it with news that he was dying. How could I leave him then? Everyone would have hated me. *I* would have hated me," said Kate.

"Baby, I'm so sorry. How long…?" Linda whispered.

"Not long," said Kate flatly. "He doesn't know much now. Sometimes he doesn't recognise me. He's angry, too."

"Should I come over? I can help you."

"No, well, Bruce is here, you see. He's made me see sense and he's helping me out until…well, you know." God, it was depressing talking about her husband's impending death.

"Will you let us see you when it's over? Please?"

"Yes, I want to see you all. But I'm not sure whether to talk to Dad yet. Have I hurt him bad?"

"If you tell him, he'll understand. You're hurting him more by not saying anything. Please speak to him," Linda begged.

"I will, but not tonight. Don't mention it, okay?"

"I won't. Promise you'll phone again."

"I promise," said Kate.

"Bye, oh, and we missed you."

She smiled and clutched the phone tightly as tears threatened again. "I missed you too."

As she put the phone down, Bruce came back in.

"I really owe you one, Bruce," she said. "For coming here, making me see sense. God, it was good to talk to her."

Bruce hugged her. "I'm glad you're feeling a bit better about this whole sorry situation. And I'm not going anywhere."

Miles away in Cannes, Linda hung up the phone and burst into tears. Little Michael, standing at her feet, looked confused. She sat down on the floor and hugged him to her.

Jacob came out into the hall and dropped to his knees beside her.

"Linda? What's wrong?" he asked.

She put her hand over her mouth and shook her head. Gently he helped her to her feet and led her into the kitchen.

"Mikey, go play in the garden for a while, okay?" he said as he pulled a chair out for her.

Michael nodded and, with a worried glance at his mother, made his way out into the garden.

As Jacob sat down with Linda, she broke the news of why Kate had stayed away for so long.

"Cancer? Oh, Christ, that's bad." Jacob shook his head. "Poor old Thomas."

"You want to hear the worst thing?" asked Linda. "Four years ago, on her wedding night, that was the night he told her about it. And that was also the night she was going to leave him."

"What?" Jacob was aghast. "She'd had enough, and she hadn't even been married a day?"

"Oh, Jacob, it wasn't that simple. It was to do with Joe. She felt she owed Thomas, so that's why she chose him." She gave him a little smile. "I'm sure glad we never had to go through all that."

Jacob nodded in agreement. To everyone's surprise, he and Linda had lasted. Michael had only added to their joy.

"Has she called Jermain?" he asked.

"No. She will, though." She stood up and kissed him. "And she'll visit soon. Until then, we have to stay in contact and be ready for when she needs us."

When Kate awoke the next morning the familiar feeling of dread and loneliness washed over her. And then she remembered. Bruce was there, and she had spoken to Linda. Thomas had had a good night, too, unless Bruce had heard him and had tended to him.

She got out of bed and slung her dressing gown on. On her way downstairs, she smelled bacon and grinned to herself. Life *was* looking up!

Entering the kitchen, she paused in surprise at the sight that met her eyes. Bruce stood at the cooker, happily frying the bacon, and Thomas sat at the kitchen table. By the sounds of it they were talking.

"Thomas?" She walked over to him.

He looked up at her and smiled. "Hello, we thought we would have to wake you," he said.

She studied him carefully. He had a glow about him that had been missing for months. She couldn't remember the last time she had seen him like this. Normally he was either in bed or lying on the sofa.

"Did you sleep well?" she asked him.

"Like a log," he replied. "Bruce and I have been catching up."

She looked at Bruce.

He lifted the frying pan. "This is almost done. Sit down."

She pulled out a chair next to Thomas and sat down. "You didn't have to go to all this bother," she said. "But I'm glad you did." She watched Thomas out of one eye as Bruce served up the breakfast.

"Where's yours?" she asked as he put two plates down.

"I've had mine. Just thought I'd pop out for a walk. Is that okay?" he asked as he slipped his jacket on.

She understood. While Thomas was like this she should take advantage of it.

"Take your time," she said and the door closed after him.

"I want to thank you for looking after me," Thomas said. "I don't know what's so different about today. I feel…not better, clearer maybe?" He shrugged. "I don't know, but I know it wasn't easy for you. I know it's been so long as well. But I always loved you, Kate." He stopped as though the words had been an effort and she put her hand on his.

"I wouldn't have had it any other way. I said I'd take care of you, and I have, and I will. You're not going anywhere, Thomas."

"Oh, well, we know that's not true." He smiled weakly and she felt an anger at the unfairness of it all. "But, in case I don't get to say it again, I know what you've done for me. I know I wasn't the right person for you. Maybe that's why God is taking me, we don't know."

"Don't say that!" she cried.

"Shhh, we've no need to pretend. Let me talk, please."

She nodded and pushed her plate away as Thomas began to speak. "I would have liked children. Too late now but not for you, my love. You're young, not even thirty yet…" He looked at her for confirmation.

She nodded. Time had, after all, escaped him.

"You can have a new life when I'm gone, and I want you to know it's okay with me. You deserve someone special, Kate. You could have had someone special, but you chose me. I've no idea why, but you did, and for that I'm grateful. But, Kate, when I'm gone, promise me you'll go on. Bruce has already promised to look after you. But you need to look after yourself, too."

"Oh, I will." She wiped a tear away and hugged him. "I'll live life for both of us. But, please, no more talk of this today. Since you're feeling brighter, why don't we spend the day together? Would you feel up for going out in your chair?"

His face brightened and he nodded. "I'd like that."

And so they spent the day outside, Thomas wrapped up, even though it was August. They toured the grounds of the old farmhouse. It was a good day, and one Kate would remember for the rest of her life.

They spent a lazy evening in the lounge. They turned the television off and switched on the soul music Thomas loved so. The open fire roared and the three of them sat and talked until Thomas dropped off to sleep.

Not wanting to leave the warmth of the room or the company of the two men whom she loved in very different ways, Kate allowed herself to close her eyes and fall asleep on the couch.

The chill woke her and she sat up, noticing the fire had gone out. Struggling out from under the rug Bruce must have placed over her, she walked over to where Thomas lay peacefully sleeping on the other couch.

For a moment, she watched him with a small smile playing around the corners of her mouth. Then she froze as she realised something was wrong.

He wasn't breathing.

She opened her mouth to scream, then got a hold of herself. Calmly, she placed a kiss on his cold forehead and turned around to wake Bruce.

He struggled to open his eyes. "Kate?" he mumbled as he sat up. "Is everything okay?"

She took a deep breath and sat back down next to Thomas. Taking his hand, she looked up at Bruce. "He's gone."

On the other side of the world, Joe was in a town called Mackay, sitting high up on a cliff, watching the sun set over the Great Barrier Reef. It was truly a beautiful sight and one he came to watch almost every evening.

He had stayed in Australia for the last four years, only returning to Britain three times for the charity run he organised and took part in every year. It was coming up again soon, and he was preparing to fly home again, to join his friends and colleagues from Survival. But he knew he would return to Australia, a place that suited him and, being at opposite ends of the world to Kate Bryant it was what he needed. For if he were closer, he was afraid he would find himself on her doorstep, begging her to take him back. There had been nobody else in the last four years. Kate had been it, the one, and after her and Emily, he knew he had had his lot.

He was not unhappy, though. The work he was doing with the Aborigines was immensely satisfying and he had made some good friends.

He watched as the great orange ball in the sky finally dipped beyond the horizon, and stood up. Making his way carefully down to the beach bar he frequented most evenings, he mused over his new life. Sometimes he missed England. He missed Bruce, although he sent him a postcard at least every couple of months. He wished Bruce would join him. Maybe, when he returned to England next month, he would look him up, see if he couldn't persuade him to come back with him.

As he entered the beach bar, somebody immediately pushed a pint into his hand, and he was surrounded by people greeting him. He was a popular man in these parts. Although his work wasn't confined to Mackay, he had made it his base and, over the last few years, he had become almost family to the people. It had all been very different when he had arrived. The Aborigines were suspicious of any white man, and the locals were already up in arms about the Aborigines getting their land rights.

Eventually, the Aborigines had understood Joe was there to help, to act as mediator in the middle of the power struggle. The locals listened to him, as well. Now, four years on, the farmers, teachers, policemen, businessmen and their families lived alongside the Aborigines. They mingled in the same bars, shared the same shops and ate at the same roadside diners. The most satisfying sight Joe now saw was the children of the locals playing with the Aborigine kids. A whole new generation were learning about the differences in their fellow human beings, without the ignorance that had spoiled the adults. Mackay and its surrounding area was now peaceful. And Joe stayed because of that peace.

As he took his beer to a quiet table on the veranda of the beach bar, he pulled a postcard out of his pocket and scribbled a note to Bruce, informing him of his pending arrival in England, and his hopes to meet up. The postcard finished, he leaned back and smiled to himself. He was looking forward to going back, but he knew it wouldn't be long before he returned to Mackay.

Back in Appleby, Kate stood at the door as they carried Thomas out on a stretcher. Bruce put his arm around her and led her to the couch.

"I'm okay, really," she said. "But he seemed to be so much better. I don't understand."

"It's a common thing. I've seen countless people who are terminally ill suddenly seem…revived, I guess. And people with Alzheimer's who haven't known their families for years suddenly talk to them normally. You know then they're on their way out. I like to think of it as a last chance, a last opportunity to tell their loved ones… I don't know, one last message, that they love them, whatever."

"It was a good day. It was a good end." She shook her head in wonder.

She felt so strange. Like a huge hole had opened up in her life. Time which she now had to fill. She was free. Nothing tied her to Appleby or England any longer. But she was scared, too. Scared of seeing Jermain, and watching him turn his back on her like she had done to him.

She told Bruce about her fears.

"I'm here, aren't I? I understood why you went away, so did Linda and Jacob. Jermain will welcome you with open arms."

"Again." She smiled ruefully. "Why am I always running away from him, when he's the one I love most of all?"

Without warning, the floodgates opened and Kate cried like she hadn't cried in years. As Bruce held her tightly, she shed tears for the lonely years she had spent there, for Jermain and her mother, for Thomas, and for Joe. Finally spent, she leaned back on the couch and closed her eyes.

"Better?" asked Bruce.

She looked up, cocking her head to one side. She *did* feel better. Her head was clear, and she felt like there was no time to waste. As soon as the funeral was over with, she would return to Cannes and meet Jermain. She would take up her rightful place as partner in the hotel, and start living again.

She told Bruce of her plans and he nodded, pleased to see a bit of the Kate of old.

"We'll need to contact his family. Where are they from?" he asked.

"He had none. Well, I mean, he did, but his parents died within three months of each other, just after we married. He didn't have any brothers or sisters, either." She clapped her hand to her mouth as she realised the terrible truth. "Shit, Bruce, there will only be you and me at his funeral. That's awful!"

"How about…? Let me think…" Bruce stood up and paced the room. "How do you think Thomas would feel about being buried in Cannes?"

Kate thought about it. It seemed to fit. It was where they had met, after all. And her family, who had liked and admired him, too, were there.

"Bloody good idea!" She hugged him and stood back, clasping his broad shoulders and regarding him seriously. "I don't know what I would have done without you. I might not have coped."

"Oh, you would have. You already were. I'm just glad I can be here now," Bruce replied modestly. "Are you going to call your father?"

Kate nodded with a sigh of resignation. She couldn't put it off any longer.

Bruce patted her on the shoulder. "I'll leave you be. Call if you need anything."

"Thank you, Bruce. I really mean that," she said as he left the room.

Kate lit a cigarette and, with shaking fingers, she dialled the number of the hotel. It rang and rang, and she cursed at the thought that nobody would answer. Did they not have a receptionist? As she was about to hang up, a breathless voice hailed a greeting and her heart leapt.

"Daddy," she whispered.

"Oh, Kate." He sounded so near she could almost see him standing behind the desk at Cannes Central. "Kate, where…? why…?"

"I'm so sorry, Dad. I've so much to tell you. I can explain why I stayed away. But I never stopped loving you. I missed you so much." She was babbling and, when her last words ended in a wail, she took a deep drag on the cigarette and tried to calm herself down.

When she spoke again, she started her story. Feeling ashamed, she told him how she had realised she wasn't in love with Thomas and had been on her way to tell him she was leaving him. But after he dropped the bombshell she had had to stay.

"For better or worse, right, Dad?" she said ruefully.

"Oh, sweetheart, I'm so sorry. But, Jesus Christ, I could have been there for you both," he said.

"I know. And I can't explain my actions. But then I saw Bruce, completely by chance. And he's helped so much. He made me see sense, see what I was doing to myself, shutting you all out of my life."

"Thank God for that man. I owe him big time. But you've made contact now, sweetheart, the hard part's done. Let me see you. I'll come over. It must be hard work with Thomas. I can look after him, give you a break," he pleaded.

"Oh, Dad." Kate swallowed past the lump in her throat. "Thomas died this morning."

There was a long silence. Kate feared they had been disconnected.

"Dad?"

"Oh, my love, I'm so sorry." Jermain was weeping and she knew it wasn't just for Thomas, but for her, too.

"Daddy? It's okay. He was so much better at the end. We spent such a nice day together yesterday, and he was so peaceful at the end." It was bizarre, she was comforting him!

"And the funeral? I'll be there, we all will," he said.

"I know, 'cause guess what? We're bringing him home, I mean to Cannes. I want to see you all so badly, and I know Thomas would have liked it too."

"Oh, thank God!" Jermain gave a half laugh and she smiled as she pictured him. "When are you coming?"

"Soon. I'll speak to Bruce and get everything sorted. Oh, Dad, I can't wait to see you, and I'm so sorry. I'll never go away again, I promise." She wiped the tears from her cheeks.

Chapter Eighteen

The Burial

Six days after Thomas's death, Kate and Bruce found themselves on a private jet on their way to Cannes. Kate was so nervous about seeing Jermain again, and the fact that Thomas's body lay in the coffin in the cargo bay wasn't doing too much for her nerves.

Everything had happened so fast. She had spoken at length with Jermain and they had come to the decision to sell the Appleby house. After living in it with Thomas for the last four years, she knew she would never want to live there again. Her exile was over. She was returning to her friends and family, and she couldn't wait.

"What will you do, Bruce?" She turned her attention to him as the stewardess brought them each another glass of wine.

"Hell, I have no idea. I quite like the idea of being a free agent. Of course, I'll come back to England with you after the funeral to help you with the house sale," he replied.

"You don't have to do that. Honest, I'll be fine," she said quickly.

She felt she had taken up too much of his time already.

"We'll see. After that, I may stay in Cannes for a while. Who knows, I might pay a visit to Joe in Australia." She saw him cast a glance at her. Joe was an unmentioned subject between them, except for the odd reference here and there.

"Hmm, you're a lucky man, Bruce. Your time is your own and you can go anywhere you please," she mused.

"Maybe…you'd come too. To see Joe, I mean." He looked out of the window.

"Oh, no, I couldn't. After treating him so badly, he'd never want to clap eyes on me again." She laughed but the pain was audible in her voice.

He patted her knee and leaned back in his chair. "All in good time."

As Bruce slept, Kate felt free to turn her thoughts to Joe. She had never stopped loving him. In all the years of her marriage she had thought of him every day. Sometimes, she was angry as she imagined him enjoying his carefree life in Australia, other times she was wistful and sad. How would he react if he saw her now? She hadn't felt comfortable enough to press Bruce for information about him, although she knew they were still in touch. Did Joe ever mention her? She downed the glass of wine and decided to start drinking less as a slight headache hovered over her eyes. Deciding sleep was the best remedy to clear her head, she reclined her chair and closed her eyes.

* * * *

Jermain had been pacing back and forth all morning as he eagerly awaited Kate's arrival. He had ordered the chefs to bring out the best dinner menus, and eventually Linda had to sit him down.

"You'll give yourself a heart attack," she said. "Now everything is sorted, the food, the drink, there's nothing more to do, so just stop getting agitated."

Jermain pulled her into a swift hug and thanked God she had stayed. What a comfort she had been in the years Kate had been away.

A short while later, having taken a seat by the window, Jermain suddenly leapt up.

"They're here!" he cried.

Andy, Jacob and Linda rushed over to the window and peered out. Sure enough, Bruce and Kate were walking up the long winding driveway towards the hotel.

As Linda and Andy rushed to the door to welcome them, Jermain remained at the window, transfixed by the sight of her.

"It's good to have her back, right?" said Jacob quietly.

Jermain started, as if in a trance and turned round to face him.

"God, yeah," he said, eyes shining. "It's good to have her home."

With a pat on the back, Jacob gestured towards the door. Jermain smiled and went to meet his daughter.

"It's not changed," said Kate as she walked with Bruce towards the hotel.

She had insisted the car drop them at the bottom of the driveway, so she could see the hotel in all its glory.

As they neared the entrance, she saw Linda first and squealed in delight. Andy stood behind her, and then Jermain appeared at the door. Dropping her case, she sprinted the rest of the way and hurled herself into his arms.

Dinner that night was an affair of mixed emotions. The group were happy to be together again after so long, but they could not forget the reason why they were finally reunited. They spoke at length about Thomas.

Talk soon turned to cheerier issues, and Kate was delighted to catch up with Michael, whom she had never even met.

Later, as they retired to the bar, she spent some time alone with Linda.

"So you and Jacob, you're still going strong, huh?" she said as they took a bottle of wine from behind the bar.

"I know, who would have thought that, five years ago, I came here for a week long assignment, and I'm still here! I love him though, him and Mikey. They're the best thing that ever happened to me," replied Linda.

"You're very lucky," said Kate as she turned away to look for the corkscrew.

"And you, what are you going to do?" Linda changed the subject.

"Oh, I'll stay here, I think. Of course, I have to go back after the funeral to sign all the stuff about the house sale. But I'll be back."

"Glad to hear you're sticking around. It's great we're all together again. Well, almost all."

Kate gave her a quizzical look. "Almost all of us?"

"Well, we're all here except Joe."

Hearing his name sent a pain through Kate's chest. She lowered her eyes.

"Joe's history," she said quietly.

"He doesn't have to be."

"Enough!" Kate snapped and, as Linda jumped, she lowered her voice. "No more talk of him."

Tactfully, Linda changed the subject and soon Jacob came over to join in.

Kate was only half listening to them. She wished people would stop talking about Joe. They might think she no longer cared, but the truth was, it hurt to talk about him. It was a physical pain even to hear his name.

She had been given many chances with Joe Palmer, and she had blown every single one of them. There was no going back. The past was the past, and she was looking towards the future.

Later, she pondered how strange it felt to be back in the bridal suite. A lot of action had happened in that room and, as Kate closed the door and looked around, there seemed to be ghosts in every corner. Was it really four years ago she had sat on that same bed with Thomas and listened as he had given her his own life sentence?

Well, she was four years older and four years wiser. She had been given a second chance and this time she was going to do things differently. She had responsibilities, a family and friends to care for and a hotel she would help to run. That was her future and she was looking forward to it.

A knock at the door startled her. She opened it cautiously to see Jermain, looking anxious.

"Hey, Dad, what's up?"

He stepped inside and closed the door. "I'm really sorry." He wrung his hands. "I didn't think until just a moment ago… about this room, I mean. The bridal suite!"

"Oh, Dad." She hugged him. "It's okay, honestly. Although I would prefer not to have this as my permanent room."

"Absolutely. Tomorrow you get one of your choice." He paused as he went to open the door and turned back. "It's good to have you home."

"It's good to *be* home, Dad."

* * * *

The morning of Thomas's funeral dawned fine and bright. Kate had surprised herself by sleeping well. When she awoke and looked out of the window, she felt refreshed. She dressed carefully in her black suit, and put on the diamond engagement and wedding rings Thomas had bought her. With a last glance in the mirror, she made her way downstairs.

Breakfast was a sombre affair. With the funeral service imminent, nobody seemed to have much of an appetite and they all picked quietly at the food. At ten o'clock the cars drew up and, together, they went outside.

Kate paused at the hearse that held Thomas's coffin. For a while she looked at it, trying to imagine Thomas in there.

"Okay?" Linda put an arm round her.

"Yeah. Seems strange to think of him in there."

"I can imagine. But at least he's not suffering anymore."

She nodded in agreement. "It's not really Thomas in there, anyway. I lost him a long time ago, but there were good times too," she said as she remembered his final perfect day

As is the custom in France, flowers and wreaths had been lined up along the front wall of the church. She crouched down, intently studying them.

"Are they all for Thomas?" asked Linda as she joined her.

"Yeah. See this one?" She pointed out a wreath of lilies and ferns. "It's from his old law firm." She stood up and turned to Linda. "Do you know, they fired him when he married me?"

"No!" Linda was clearly shocked. "I didn't know that."

"He gave up a lot for me."

"You gave up a lot for him."

The service was brief, attended, as Kate had expected, by just her, Jermain, Linda, Jacob, Andy and Bruce. After it had finished, they left the church and headed towards the graveyard.

"I'm sorry there were not many people," said Jermain as they walked together a little way behind the others.

"I had everyone I needed," replied Kate. "Just think, if Bruce hadn't found me I would have been doing this on my own."

Jermain stopped and looked into her eyes. "Promise me you'll never run away from me again. I couldn't take it."

She nodded dumbly, aware he was still hurting. "I don't know why I do," she said quietly and looked down at the ground. "It's my stupid pride."

"You keep your pride for strangers. Not for me, okay?" His tone was harsh and, seeing the tears well up in her eyes, he hugged her to him and they began to walk again.

"I'll be going back to finalise the house sale. Then I'll be back, I promise," she said.

"Let me come with you. It's my house, I should be sorting it," he said.

"No, if it's okay, I just want to wrap it all up, then I can come back here and start afresh."

"All right, if you feel you need to. When are you leaving?"

She stopped as they reached the gates of the cemetery. "Tonight. The sooner I go, the sooner I can come home again." She smiled. "Right?"

"Right."

* * * *

Joe was packed and ready to leave. He took one last glance around the beach hut that served as his home, and sat back down on the bed.

He called this place home, but it wasn't. No matter how much he loved Australia, it wasn't his home. But where was? Brixton? Certainly not. Zaire? Just a stopgap. The thought had been running through his mind a lot lately, and it troubled him somewhat. For if a man didn't have a home, what did he have?

Not having the time to dwell on such matters, Joe stood up and heaved his bag on his back and went out to the waiting taxi.

He was looking forward to seeing Bruce. Maybe he could help him out of the blackness that seemed to envelop him these days, although, since he had sent the postcard to Bruce, he hadn't had any contact. Oh, well, he would find him, he supposed.

* * * *

Kate waited for her plane to take off. It felt strange to be out on her own again, but she liked the feeling. For the first time since she had married Thomas, she felt alive and free. She smiled to herself and lay back in her seat. Life had started again, and about time, too.

It seemed she had barely closed her eyes when the announcement came over the tannoy that they were due to land. She sat up and peered out of the window. Through the patchy white clouds, she could make out fields of green. Clicking her seat belt in place, she tapped her feet impatiently. Her plan was to be in and out of England as quickly as she could. She didn't intend spending an extra second in the dreary country more than she had to.

Joe waited for the rush to end and, when nearly everyone had left, he stood up and stretched. Grabbing his hand luggage, he sauntered off the plane and waited in the queue for passport control.

He glanced out of the window at the rain, and hoped the weather would turn in time for the walk.

Kate waited like a tiger ready to pounce. As soon as the seat belt sign went off, she was out of the seat and jogging down the aisle. The plane door opened. She clattered down the metal steps and ran for the door. To her delight, there was no queue at passport control and, with a cursory glance at her passport, the guard waved her through.

Joe stood by the carousal and idly lit up a cigarette. There were big 'No Smoking' signs plastered to every wall in the hall, but nobody ever took any notice of them. He watched with some amusement as they crowd from his flight scrambled for the best place. Let them get their bags if they were in so much of a hurry. His time was his own.

Kate walked quickly through the corridors, glancing behind her every few seconds. She was well ahead of her fellow passengers, and wanted to get a good spot at the carousel so she could grab her bag and be out of there.

Bursting through the door that led to luggage collection, she looked around. The hall held three carousels, one with a large group of people, waiting for it to start up, the other two empty. She glanced at the screens and saw the first one was for luggage from Queensland, definitely not hers. The one at the far end said her bag would be on it once the plane was unloaded and, seeing people from her flight almost at the entrance, she jogged over to that one.

The two carousels started up at the same time and Joe glanced up from his book as the passengers surged forward. He heard the sound of the carousel starting at the far end of the hall and looked over. He swept his gaze over the few people gathered there, and was about to look back down at his book when his head snapped back. A lady waiting at the carousal looked familiar, *very* familiar. The book dropped from his hands.

Surely it couldn't be…

He took a couple of steps back and leapt up onto an empty seat to get a better view over the crowd.

It was! It was Kate, standing not thirty feet away from him. His heart leapt in excitement.

Flinging the cigarette away, he jumped off the seat and jogged across the hall towards her.

Kate was delighted when her bag was the third one to come tumbling out. She grabbed it as it trundled past her, and turned for the exit.

As Joe skirted around the crowd, the rest of Kate's fellow passengers surged forward, momentarily blocking his path. With a grunt, he wrestled his way through, and finally reached the far end of the hall. She was gone. He spun around, scanning the exits. Through the glass wall he saw a mane of blonde hair, hurrying towards the underground. He sprinted toward the exit, praying he would reach her before she got to the trains.

Kate skipped down the steps into the underground station. As she turned the corner, she saw the train coming. Breaking into a run, clutching her small case, she squeezed onto the already packed train.

Joe took the steps two at a time. Seeing the train in the station, he jumped the last three steps onto the platform. The doors were closing. He ran alongside it, searching through the windows. There she was, standing with her back to the window. The train pulled away. He banged hard on the glass.

She never turned around.

He watched until the train had disappeared and wandered back towards the luggage hall, his shoulders slumped.

Where was she going? Appleby maybe? And where was Thomas? Shaking his head, he moaned in anguish. Kate still had as big a hold on him as ever.

By the time Kate reached the farmhouse in Appleby it was almost dawn. She thanked the cab driver and, as he drove out of the gates, she turned toward the big house and took a deep breath. It had been a big decision to sell the place, after all it was her inheritance, but it seemed she had nothing but bad memories of it. Yes, the house was to be sold, and she and Jermain could resume their new life in Cannes.

She let herself in and dropped her bag in the hall.

Gingerly, she went into the lounge and stared at the armchair where Thomas had passed away. After wandering around the room, making mental notes of what needed to be packed away in storage, she slumped down in the chair. Leaning over, she poured a glass of whiskey from the decanter and looked at the framed photograph of her and Thomas on their wedding day, tilting the glass to it in a silent toast. She downed the drink, leaned back in the chair, and promptly fell asleep.

Joe awoke in the London hotel early. After a hasty breakfast, he retired to his room to make some calls. First on his list was Bruce, but he was disappointed to hear from Mrs Levinstein he was not at home, and, indeed, didn't live there anymore since they were "having a break".

Joe murmured his condolences and hung up. Where to try next? Bruce could be anywhere, such was his love for travel, and he really didn't know where to begin. After racking his brains, he gave up and reached for his jacket. Sauntering out of the hotel, he made his way to the Survival International headquarters to catch up with some old friends.

Steve Chapman was the first person he saw. His face lit up as Joe walked into the office.

"Joe!" He stood up and they shook hands. "Good to see you, mate. How're things down under?"

"Good, very good in fact," replied Joe as he took the chair that Steve offered.

"Glad to hear it. Ready for another assignment yet?"

He sighed. HQ had been trying to get him out of Australia for the past two and a half years.

"Tell me what you've got. See if anything takes my fancy."

Steve opened his desk drawer and pulled out a file, ten inches thick.

"There's certainly enough to choose from." Steve flicked through the papers. "More Aboriginal settlements like the ones you've been working on, an Indian tribe in South America, Africa…always Africa, or—this is a new one—peace talks in Thailand. Mediator between the Thai and the British and

American tourists?"

Joe leaned forward. "I'm a survival and wildlife expert, not a politician."

"Yeah, yeah, I hear you." Steve closed the file and sat back. "Why don't you tell me what *you* want to do?"

"I don't know." Joe shook his head. "Truth is, I just don't know anymore."

Steve, clearly sensing Joe clearly wasn't in the mood for work talk, changed tack. "Well, you've got the walk to concentrate on. Are you all set for tomorrow?"

Joe nodded and looked out of the window.

"So, what's been going on in your life while you've been away?" Steve raised his eyebrows suggestively. "Anyone special waiting for you back in Oz?"

"No."

"Whatever happened to that lady? The crazy loon who killed that girl?"

He glared. "Her name's Kate, and she's not a loon, and she didn't kill anyone. Remember?"

"Okay, okay. Well?"

"She got married," said Joe tonelessly.

"Oh." Steve chewed on the end of his pen and regarded him through narrowed eyes.

Joe stood up to leave. "See you tomorrow, Stevie."

Steve stood up and they shook hands again. "Yeah," he said, evidently relieved. "See you."

With some relief of his own, Joe left the office without seeing any of his other colleagues, and made his way across the road to a coffee bar. He took a window seat and ordered a mug of strong black coffee. When it came, he took it and, turning his back on the rest of the shop, he gazed out of the window.

Seeing Steve had made him face up to the fact he was a lost man. He didn't like the revelation. He didn't know why he felt so low.

Chapter Nineteen

The Long Walk

After signing away the deeds to the farmhouse, Kate was on a high. It was sold, lock, stock and barrel, which meant she could go home.

After the Estate Agents, she made her way to the local Post Office to advise them of her change of address.

"You want your mail?" The lady behind the counter asked, and pushed a pile of envelopes through.

Kate thanked her and wrote down the address of the hotel in Cannes. Taking her mail, she returned to the farmhouse.

While she waited for the kettle to boil, she flicked through the pile of envelopes and noted, with some amusement, that Bruce had had his mail redirected to Appleby. *He must have been planning to stay the course,* she thought with affection, and made a separate pile of mail to take back to him in Cannes.

She stopped as she came across a postcard. Even before she turned it over, she knew who the sender was.

"Joe," she whispered and stared at the picture on the front for what seemed like an eternity.

Eventually, she turned it over and read it.

Bruce,

Hope all is well with you. Just dropping you a line to let you know I'll be in Canterbury for the walk on the 12th September. Hope you can make it. It'll be good to catch up.

Joe

Kate read it through twice before putting it on the counter with shaking hands. It was a shock to touch something Joe had touched, read the words he had written. She snatched the card up again.

12th September, Joe was coming.

She picked up her diary and stared at that day's date.

11th September.

"Bloody hell," she whispered.

Joe would be in England. She could see him. She could go to Kent and actually *see* him.

Trembling with excitement, she abandoned the kettle and lit a cigarette. Could she really see him? Would he speak to her? Or was it best left in the past? There was only one person to ask.

"Linda," she muttered and reached for the phone.

Halfway through dialling the number, she hung up. Regardless of what Linda said, she would go, anyway.

Stubbing out the half-smoked cigarette, she ran upstairs to pack her bag.

The next day Kate pulled open the curtains and winced at the bright sunlight. She stared out for a moment over the moors. It was to be her last day there, and it was a relief to be leaving. She glanced at the bags that were already packed, and felt a thrill of excitement at the detour she had planned on her way to the airport.

What would it be like to see Joe again? she wondered as she took a last look out of the window.

Dashing down the stairs, she put the kettle on to boil and called the local Hertz dealership to rent a car to take her to Kent. When she hung up, she made a mug of tea, and rang the hotel in Cannes. Linda answered the telephone, her professional tone lapsing as she realised that it was Kate.

"Hey, you, guess where I'm going today?" asked Kate as she sipped the hot tea.

"Um, Cannes?" said Linda hopefully.

"*Before* I come home," she giggled.

"I give up."

"I'm going to Kent, Canterbury in fact."

"Why? What's in Kent?"

"Joe!" she shrieked, unable to keep her excitement in check.

"How do you know? Have you seen him? I thought you didn't want to see him!" Linda cried.

Kate explained about the postcard she had intercepted

and told her about the walk Joe did annually in aid of the charity.

"So I thought I'd go to Canterbury, where the walk finishes, and meet him at the end. You know I want to see *him*. Whether he'll feel the same is a different matter."

"Oh, this is fantastic! He'll be thrilled to see you," said Linda. "You must tell me everything. If you don't get back here tonight, phone me!"

With a promise that she would call, Kate hung up and hurriedly finished the tea. She was raring to go and, after a last check around the house, she locked up and made her way to the town centre.

"Who was it?" Jacob asked as he sat on the other side of the reception desk, patiently waiting to take Linda home.

"Kate." Linda stacked some papers up behind the desk and made sure she had left everything tidy for the receptionist who was coming on shift. "Guess who she's planning to see today?"

"Hmm, Joe?" asked Jacob as they walked out of the building.

"How'd you know?"

"By the excited squeals coming down the phone line. He won't have it, you know."

She stopped walking and turned to face him. "What do you mean?"

"She ditched him, and not for the first time. And not only ditched him but *married* someone else! A guy can only take so much rejection."

"Oh," Linda said worriedly. "But it wasn't a case of her ditching him, it was timing."

"Yeah, right." Jacob unlocked the car door and held it open for her. "But will *he* see it that way?"

On autopilot, Joe had coordinated the big event and, now that everything was in place, and everyone was ready to take part, it was his own time, a time of reflection.

Although he loved the walk, all of it, the build-up, the

actual event and the party afterwards, he hated the fact that, for all of the years he had been doing it, the one person he had originally started it for was not there.

Lost in thought, he sat near the start line and flipped Emily's St Christopher necklace from hand to hand. A shadow fell over him, and he looked up to see Emily's father standing next to him.

Smiling broadly, he stood up and the two men embraced.

"Another year," sighed Bernie.

Joe nodded and they sat back down.

"Still got that old thing?" Bernie's tone was one of amusement but Joe knew he was touched.

"It's always with me. So is she."

Bernie nodded, smiling to himself. "I'm glad you still do this. It means a lot for us to come here every year, to know that someone apart from her Mother and me didn't forget her."

Joe clapped the old man on the shoulder and stood up as the crowd began to gather at the start line.

"See you at the finish, boy," said Bernie, and Joe waved as he disappeared into the crowd.

The walk was much the same as always. After the first year, when he had won for Emily, Joe had never crossed the finish line first. He left that accolade to some other person who needed it, as he had needed it all those years ago.

As he wandered along, people fell in to step beside him and he passed the day chatting to people he only ever saw once a year. It made the time go faster, and gave him a chance to catch up with people that meant a lot to him, and to some who had moulded him into who he was. One of them was Jenny, a nurse who had been at the rehabilitation home at the same time as Joe and Emily.

"So where have you been?" she asked as she bounced along beside him.

"Australia recently, but I don't know if I'm going back." He gratefully accepted the bottle of water she handed him.

"Really? So what are your plans next?"

Joe sighed and turned to face her. "For the first time in

my life, I have no idea."

She nodded and elbowed him playfully.

"Sometimes that can be a good thing." She waved to one of her colleagues in the crowd and moved off towards him.

Joe caught her words as she moved away. "Maybe it's time to let things come to you for once!"

For the last part of the walk he put his head down and walked alone. From the cheers up ahead, he could hear some walkers had already crossed the finish line. Glancing up as he rounded the street corner, he could see he was nearly at the end.

Squinting against the bright sunshine, he spotted Bernie amongst the crowd and waved to him. As he turned back to face the finish line, he saw the usual crowd standing there. Jenny, having sped up towards the end, was one of them, along with the nurses who were always on hand to give out plasters for the inevitable blisters. He gave a thumbs-up to Steve who had travelled down from London, and then stopped in his tracks.

Kate.

Dressed casually in blue jeans and a black vest, she had never looked so beautiful. He was dumbfounded to see her there. Was she there for him? Or was it an incredible coincidence?

Kate started visibly. For a moment, they stood still. As their eyes locked, it was as if they were totally alone.

Joe got a hold of himself and started walking again. When he reached her, he stopped, wondering what he should say to her. What could you say to someone who had stopped your life the moment she had chosen another man?

"Hi, Joe," she said quietly and removed her shades. "I know it's weird me being here, but…I thought I'd stop by on my way home."

She was different somehow, softer maybe? And her eyes didn't flash with passion as he remembered. Instead they held an expression of…sadness perhaps?

Or longing? He barely dared to contemplate it.

"It's good to see you," he said. "Can you stay long?"

"Yeah, I'm not in a hurry. Maybe we can go get a drink somewhere?"

"Yeah, sure." Joe looked around him and caught sight of Steve watching them. "See that pub on the corner? Why don't you find us a seat and I'll be right over?"

"Okay. I'll get some drinks," she said.

He watched her as she crossed the road to the pub, then jumped into action and grabbed Steve. "I have to be somewhere. I'll catch up with you later, okay?"

"Er, sure."

Joe pulled him behind one of the St John Ambulance tents. "Give me your shirt!" he demanded as he pulled off his t-shirt.

"*What?*" Steve backed away in mock horror.

"Don't fuck around, this is important!" said Joe. "I have to see someone, and I've been walking in the bloody heat all day in this." He flung his shirt at him.

"Okay." Steve pulled off his shirt and handed it over. "I'm not gonna ask, but is this to do with that blonde?"

"Yeah, it is. And I'll fill you in later. Right now I have a cold drink waiting for me," Joe said and jogged off towards the pub.

He saw her as he crossed the road. She was in the beer garden. For a moment he stood still and watched her as she chose a table in the shade.

She glanced up and caught him staring. He nodded in her direction and jogged over.

"I got you a coke," she said.

"Perfect," he replied and took the seat opposite her. "Why are you here?"

She looked down and sighed. "I don't know where to begin."

"How about starting from the night you agreed to stay with Thomas?"

Her shoulders drooped.

"Sorry," he muttered.

"No, I deserved it. I deserved everything that happened to me. But you're right. I should start from then," she said.

"Does Thomas know you're here?" he asked.

"Oh!" she looked surprised. "Well, see, that's part of the story."

"Okay." He leaned back with a serious expression. "I'm listening."

"We got married, me and Thomas I mean. And on my wedding night I planned to tell him I was leaving him." She glanced up and, when his expression didn't change, she continued. "Bruce told me you were in Australia, and you had been going to ask me to go with you, and I realised I had made such a terrible mistake. Well, I'd actually realised before then, but that was when it hit me," she paused. "But Thomas had some news of his own. He had cancer, you see. So, I couldn't leave. Well, I suppose I could have, but I would have been the world's biggest bitch if I had."

"*Cancer*?" Joe shook his head. "I'm sorry." The words sounded hollow to his ears.

"So, I stayed with him. I moved to England, to the cottage and took care of him. I didn't speak to my dad, Linda or anyone back home. I couldn't bear to let them see what I had become. Anyway, by chance I bumped into Bruce. He was wonderful, helping out and everything. He made me see sense, with my dad and everyone. So I've sold up and I'm going back to Cannes. But then I saw your postcard, and I had to see you."

"And Thomas?" asked Joe.

"Thomas died. A couple of weeks ago."

"I don't know what to say. I thought you had forgotten about me."

Tears filled her eyes and she grabbed his hand. "I never did. I thought about you every day, and I fucking cursed myself for being such an idiot. I couldn't leave. I was stuck there, with a husband who didn't even know who I was half the time."

There was a long silence before Joe spoke again. "How are you, after the shooting?"

"Not bad. My back hurts when it's cold. Luckily it's mostly warm in Cannes. I've suffered here in England. I was lucky, though."

"I saw you, you know. A few days ago at the airport," he said.

"*What?*"

"At Heathrow. I'd just got off the plane from Queensland and you were waiting for your luggage. I ran after you but you'd gone," he said.

"I—I didn't see you..." She shook her head. "I even remember looking at the computer screen that held information about the flight from Queensland."

He grimaced. "So, what now? When do you go back to France?"

She shrugged. "Whenever, I've got an open ticket. What about you?"

"Me?" He shook his head. "Back to the office, I guess, see what's next in line."

"Would you...? Could I maybe see you?" She blushed and looked down. "If I stayed around."

A thousand thoughts ran through his head. This was what he had wanted for so long. For Kate to be back in his life, in his arms, was all he had desired.

For a long moment there was silence.

"I don't think it would be a good idea," he said finally, and to say those words nearly tore his heart in two.

"You...don't?" she whispered.

"Oh, Kate." He ran his hand through his hair in a gesture of frustration. "I want nothing more than to see you. I bloody see you every night in my dreams. But we're worlds apart. You live in France, I live in Australia. Even if I don't go back there, my work would never in a million years take me to France."

She gave a small smile and nodded in agreement. When she slipped her shades back on, he knew she was lost to him forever.

"I understand," she said. "But it was good to see you again, anyway."

Oh God, he had hurt her badly. He had rejected her and she was slipping away...

"Kate..."

She stood up and, leaning over the table, she kissed him

softly. Behind the shades, he couldn't read her expression.

"I have to go, there's a flight, if I hurry…" She tailed off and, for a moment, they stared at each other. "See you."

She was gone.

Joe sat at the table and put his head in his hands.

"Shit!" he swore and banged his fist down.

Hurrying away from the pub down the side road where she had parked her car, Kate wiped the tears from her face.

It was over. At least they had finished it. No going back. Closure.

Reaching the rental car, she threw her purse on the passenger seat and gunned the engine.

She was angry, angry at Thomas for being ill, angry at Joe for turning her down, but most of all she was angry with herself for coming here, and allowing her heart to be broken all over again.

"Never again," she muttered fiercely as she raced towards the motorway.

Chapter Twenty

The End

Maybe it's time to let things come to you for once.

Jenny's words ran through his head over and over again.

Kate had come, and he had turned her away for the sole purpose of his work. For the first time in his life he had the chance to settle down with someone he really loved, and he had thrown it away.

He went to the party after the walk, but his heart wasn't in it. Grabbing his coat, he made his way towards the door, but was stopped by Steve.

"My shirt, I presume I'll get it back?" he asked.

"Oh, uh, yeah. I'll drop it in the office," said Joe as he tried to pass him.

"Joe, are you okay? You seem a little out of it."

Joe paused and turned around. "Steve, if I wanted to come out of the field, what would you say?"

"I'd say we'd lose the best man we've got out there," replied Steve without hesitation.

"Thought so," said Joe and made to leave.

Steve stopped him by grabbing his arm. "But I'd rather have a happy employee than a miserable one. And if that means finding something else for you, then so be it."

Joe leaned back against the wall.

Steve was offering him a compromise, a way towards the future. The question was, did he really want to take it?

* * * *

"Kate!" Linda yelled as she came into the hotel.

Kate dropped her bags and threw her arms around her.

"Oh, it's good to be back. I'm not going anywhere for a while now." Kate looked around. "Where is everyone?"

"In here." Linda herded her into the bar where Jermain, Andy, Jacob and Bruce were waiting with a bottle of champagne.

They cheered when she came in and she hugged them all in turn.

"Hope you're hungry, we've laid on a right feast," said Bruce. "How was England?"

"Okay, but it's good to be home," she replied, avoiding Linda's questioning gaze.

After dinner, Linda pulled Kate to one side and asked her about Joe.

"He said *no.*" She looked away as her eyes filled with tears. "He said it was because of his work, but I think he was wary because of all that has happened in the past."

"I'm so sorry. I really thought things would work out."

She shrugged. "These things happen. I can't blame him. At least I tried."

Linda nodded.

Kate felt herself slipping back into the life she had left behind and liked the feeling of belonging again to a unit. By day she helped out around the hotel or lunched with Linda. Most nights Linda and Jacob would come over and, whilst Jacob kept an eye on the happenings in the casino, they would take in a film, or sit in the gardens with little Michael.

Kate had been home for three weeks when Jermain woke her early.

"I've got a surprise for you," he said. "Meet me in the lobby in an hour."

Intrigued, she threw on her jeans and, dragging a brush through her hair, went downstairs.

Jermain shepherded her to a waiting car.

"Where are we going?" she laughed as they sped towards the Marina.

"You'll see," he said.

Finally they arrived and Kate plied him with questions as he led her onto the jetty.

"Sssh, you'll spoil my surprise. Cover your eyes," he instructed.

"*What?*"

"Just do it!"

Giggling, she put her hands over her eyes as he led her carefully down the platform to the waters' edge.

"Okay," he said. "Open them."

She opened her eyes and clapped her hands to her mouth. "Oh, my God!"

"What do you think?" Jermain said.

Nestling gently against the edge of the jetty was the Sara-Kate, the boat where she had been raised and spent so many happy years.

She had obviously had some work done on her, with a fresh coat of paint, and not a spot of rust, after being left in the outhouse of their home in Appleby for so long.

"I don't know what to say." She threw her arms around him. "When did you do all this?"

"Quite recently. There's still some work to be done, but I thought we could do it together," he replied.

Totally overwhelmed by the sight before her, it was all she could do to nod her head. "Can I go on board?" she asked.

"Of course."

They spent the next half hour roaming the boat, Jermain showing her the work that had been done and Kate remembering all of the happy times she had spent there.

As they walked back to the car, she linked arms and grinned. "Now I'm starting to feel like I've come home."

* * * *

After four weeks in England, Joe was ready to leave. Purposefully, he had stayed longer than he had originally intended, to try and figure out what he really wanted. He had spent time with Steve, both in the office and out of it, and had discovered his colleague was actually quite a good guy. It was amazing that you could work alongside someone for so many years and not really know them at all.

He had also spent a lot of time with his parents, which he knew had pleased them enormously, and the three of them had enjoyed some good times getting to know each other again.

He had also spent some time on his own, wandering around London, enjoying the bustle of people more than he thought he would.

After a month, he knew what he had to do.

"Good luck, mate," said Steve as they stood outside the office.

"Thanks." Joe shook Steve's hand. "I'll speak to you soon, let you know how things are going."

Joe turned to his mother, who had come to see him off, and hugged her tightly.

"It's been good to have you around. Don't stay away so long," she said, trying not to cry.

He nodded, hugging her again before getting into the waiting taxi. As the cab pulled away, he turned and waved to the people who had helped him over the last month see what he needed to do.

How strange that, after ten years, he had found closeness with his family he had never had before. It all made sense to him now, that when he had been travelling the world, he hadn't been working towards a better future. It had all been an excuse to run away and hide from mistakes he had created at home. He didn't regret it, though. His work had been a huge part of his life for so long, and he was proud of everything he had achieved in all the countries he had visited. But he had come full circle. It was time to turn to new things in his life, and things that had yet to be achieved.

* * * *

The man sat on the harbour wall and watched her for well over an hour. He had been told where to find her and, now he was there, he wanted a little time to have her to himself, before he made his presence known. *She was obviously in an environment that suited her*, he thought, as he watched her on the boat. He tilted his face upwards as he followed her climbing up the mast to check the sail.

It was almost sunset. He stood up and started to walk.

Kate had been gradually aware of someone watching her for a while but, being used to looks from the villagers as she worked away on the boat, she had pressed on with it.

The next time she looked around, the figure on the harbour wall had vanished.

Finally, the boat was complete. She dropped the tools and stood back to admire the work that Jermain and herself had done on the Sara-Kate. She looked as good as new, and Kate was proud. It had taken another few weeks before the boat had been ready for life at sea again, although if the truth be told, she knew she could have finished sooner, but had wanted to take her time. Something had been pulling her back from completion, although what, she did not know.

Her gaze flickered out to sea and a small smile played around her mouth as she jumped back aboard. She couldn't wait to take the boat on her maiden voyage, and now was as good a time as any. As she checked the sail that was now in perfect condition, she spotted, out of the corner of her eye, one of the men who she presumed was from the boat yard, walking past.

Without turning around, she called out to him. "Untie her for me, will you, mate?"

"Sure," he replied. Something in his voice made her stop.

She spun around and grabbed the mast with both hands lest she fall down with shock. "It's you," she whispered.

Joe continued to untie the boat and, as he pushed her away from the jetty, he jumped aboard. "It's me," he confirmed and handed her the rope.

Wordlessly, she took it from him and electricity sparked as their fingers touched.

"I think I was waiting for you," she stuttered.

He turned his face into the wind and, as the sunlight bounced off his face and cast the boat into golden light, he took a deep breath and closed his eyes.

"I know. I've been waiting for me too."

He smiled at her and, for the first time, she noted in surprise there were no barriers there at all. Joe's face was open and receptive, and alive in a way she had not seen before. He seemed peaceful, a lot like how *she* felt, and when he reached out his hand, she took it, knowing this time, she really *had* come home.

About The Author

Jeanette's first novel, *Freedom First Peace Later*, was published in December 2010. Her short story; *Ellen's Journey*, won a silver award in the author vs. author short story competition 2008, supported by the National Literary Trust. The same story was also published in the December 2007 edition of the Jimston Journal, an online literary magazine and has been published in the Bluewood Christmas 2011 anthology.

Jeanette has also previously worked with The Front List, a website with the aim of allowing their community of writers to self-select promising work by providing detailed feedback in the form of a critique. On the back of an article that she wrote about her novel she was offered work in a freelance capacity for Spike Magazine, and is now a regular contributor.

Worlds Apart is Jeanette's second published novel. For more information and future projects, please visit *www.jeanettehewitt.com*

Lightning Source UK Ltd.
Milton Keynes UK
UKOW04f0638240116

266957UK00001B/5/P